BLOODSTONE

THE CURSE OF TIME BOOK 1

M.J. MALLON

To my lovely mum and dad thank you for your unfaltering belief in me, for my stimulating and extraordinary childhood and adolescent years, and your continued love and support through more recent times.

INSPIRATIONS

The Curse of Time series is inspired by the Corpus Christi Chronophage clock in Kings Parade, Cambridge and Juniper Artland's Crystal Grotto in Wilkieston, Scotland: The Light Pours Out of Me, by artist Anya Gallaccio.

Anya Gallaccio is a British artist born in 1963 who creates minimalist installations working with organic matter. Anya Gallaccio: The Light Pours Out Of Me – Jupiter Artland

Both creations were intended to be beautiful but unsettling. On first encountering the clock and the grotto, I was overcome with conflicting emotions. The chronophage's disturbing nature characterised by the grasshopper's pincer sharp teeth continues long after the grotto's initial strangeness.

These are incredible visions of creativity and well worth a visit. The above photo depicts the grasshopper of the chronophage gobbling time. **Photo courtesy of—Dr John C Taylor, OBE.**

The Corpus Christi Chronophage is a popular tourist attraction located on Kings Parade in Cambridge, UK, and is one of the most incredible creations I have ever seen. It was invented by the esteemed inventor, Dr John C Taylor, OBE, who I had the pleasure of meeting in September 2017. It was an extraordinarily inspiring moment, and one I will treasure forever.

Who would have thought I would have the opportunity to spend time with one of the greatest living inventors of our time? This intriguing gentleman is also a pilot, adventurer, photographer, architect and philanthropist. His striking invention, the Chronophage clock was one of Time's Best Inventions of 2008. Dr Taylor invested five years and £1 million in the Corpus Clock project, and a team of two hundred people, including engineers, sculptors, scientists, jewellers, and calligraphers were involved in its creation.

Also, I was thrilled to be invited to a Horology Hour online talk...on Midsummer's Day Jun 24, 2020, with Dr. Taylor. It was fascinating!

Find out more about Dr Taylor, OBE, here: http://www.johnctaylor.com/the-chronophage/

And on my blog here:

https://mjmallon.com/2017/09/17/poetry-inspired-by-the-dragon-chronopage-colleens-weekly-poetry-challenge-no-50-haiku-tanka-haibun-voice-watch/

PRAISE FOR BLOODSTONE—CURSE OF TIME BOOK 1

This delightful book will appeal to teens and young adults who love stories filled with magical crystals, dark family curses, and mysteries waiting to be solved around every corner. Each chapter leads you on a journey of discovery where Amelina earns the right to use three wizard stones to reset the balance of time and finally break the curse that holds her family captive. A captivating tale! Author Colleen Chesebro

This is a totally different genre for me, but this year I have been reading books by so many exciting new authors that I wanted to give this book a try. This novel would be great for teenagers, or young adults and it follows the magical story of teenager Amelina as she steps into a world of crystals, magic and wonderment. There are some likeable and not so likeable characters and both are really well written. The book weaves a story of the main character learning new skills and you see her personal growth throughout the story. Nothing is what is seems and you want to find out how Amelia will use her enchanted gifts and learn who she can trust. A book packed full of intrigue, believable characters and poetic verse. Author Lizzie Chantree

This is a brilliant book for young adults interested in magic, supernatural, paranormal, fantasy and myth. I found it highly readable and the author's imagination is phenomenal, as is the fluency of her language and the dazzling way she describes the curious events and characters in her story. I loved the idea of Esme, the girl trapped in the mirror. Author S C Skillman

An intricate fantasy novel with unique supernatural and magical elements which serves as a highly entertaining read. I had a great time reading this novel and exploring the magical world of Amelina full of magic crystals and enchanted mirrors. Author, Editor and Book Reviewer Heena Rathore P.

At its core, this is an emotional tale about a young girl figuring out her identity, learning who to trust, and discovering there is more to the world than the tangible things she's experienced in the first one-and-a-half decades of her life. Magic Mirrors? Mysterious appearances? Letters that cannot be destroyed? Puzzling trust? What's a girl to do when she's followed by two strange boys in the park, only to realize something darker is beginning to happen? Mallon explores the fears in a young girl who wants to break out of her life but doesn't know where to turn. She's unsure about trusting friends and family. Ryder, who saves the day, might actually not be the best thing for her... safety... sanity... security. Can she fight the feelings burgeoning around her? Author James Cudney

This magical young adult story is brimming with fresh imaginative ideas avoiding tropes often associated with fantasy. I was impressed with the unique vivid visual descriptions which brought both the settings and characters to life and the wonderful standard of writing throughout the story. A magical mystery unfolds for the main character Amelina, who makes discoveries during the plot, so we can enjoy seeing her grow in confidence and skill. The story involves complex content which was difficult to follow initially but becomes more understandable as the story develops. The introduction of the antagonist, Ryder, really helps us to root for Amelina. He is well written, and I enjoyed that he wasn't given the typical look of a baddie but rather slowly and disconcertingly reveals his darker side, inserting himself between Amelina and her friends. I can see this being the start of a fabulous young adult series and hope there are more books to come! Sarah Northwood Poet and Author

Amelina is written so well. There is a part of her that all of us will recognise and emphasise with. At that awkward age where nothing fits and at the same time you feel as if you can conquer the world.

Darkness creeps in slowly in the form of Ryder who at first seems the answer to all Amelina desires, or is he? Author Adele Marie Park

The overall world-building creates a wonderful, spiritual atmosphere. There's a bit of poetry at the start of every chapter, a nice touch which leads us into the action. The story bravely tackles issues of mental health and self-harm, but in such a sensitive way that it can only help improve understanding. Author Richard Dee

Amelina is a teenage girl whose world has been turned upside down by a curse within a world where magic is hidden and most don't seem to know of its existence. In fact, it seems she's a descendant of a line of magic-wielding enchanters who have a special relationship with crystals. But with this curse, her father is time-ravaged, a girl is trapped in her mirror, and her family is falling apart. There are a lot of unanswered questions come the end of the book, so be on the lookout for more in the series. There are mentions of delicate issues such as cutting and anorexia, both handled with care, and a séance, but I'd recommend this book for older teens and people who love magical stories that involve power within crystals, curses, and unexplainable happenings. Author Rachael Ritchey

This is a wonderful YA fantasy read. It's very different from others I've read and I say this in the most positive manner. One way or is unique is through the use of original short poetry at the beginning of each chapter providing a clue to the chapter content. It is very well done. I do love originality. The whole work has a magical feel about it which draws the reader in with a yearning to learn more about all of the characters and their plight. My favourite characters are, Esme... The girl trapped in the mirror, and Shadow, the black cat. These two characters alone were enough to keep me rooted. Meanwhile, on the serious side of things, there are so many issues going on in this work in addition to that of dealing with a dysfunctional family. One's familiarity will be tested and emotions may arise. That aside, when you add magic, a black cat, and a guitar and music into the mix... What is there not to love about this work? Author/Reviewer Kevin Cooper

Amelina is an indomitable heroine who will not rest until she solves the mystery and sets the world to rights. The device of magic crystals as a source of magic is novel and works well. There are loose ends that are clearly available to be addressed in future episodes of this series. As a precursor story that is relatively complete in itself, … as an introduction to the storyline and invitation to read on. MJ Mallon is not afraid to broach the risks that young girls on the cusp are subject to in these unruly times. Both physical violence and dangerous sexual attraction are broached in this tale. Poet Frank Prem.

Beautifully written and poetic fantasy novel that perfectly sustains mystery and drama throughout the pages. The characters are very vivid and the world is rich in detail and atmosphere. Marjorie is excellent at painting imaginative and believable scenes with words and magic. A fantastic debut! Looking forward to her next book. Author/Illustrator Alina Surnaite

PROLOGUE

Most people would call our existence strange, but this is more than that; this deserves a headline. We're not spectacular enough to feature on the national or international news, but we warranted a column in the local newspaper headed by seven not so lucky words: Missing Father Returns After Weird Aging Phenomenon. I'm glad that our short-lived fame died and the paparazzi, (what a joke,) got bored with us. Now we can get back to the day to day living if you can call it that.

We live in a typical suburb of Cambridge in an untypical house. It's no bungalow, the floors just go on and on, and so do the rumours about us. When I say we, I mean our strange extended family comprising mature, tantrum-prone Mum, Dad (alias: old man before his time), teenage me, the most stable of us all (I think), and self-harming Esme, who isn't my sister but might as well be. I could write a whole book devoted to her alone. Oh, and I forgot to mention our permanent house guest, Shadow, a black cat of indeterminate age and parentage who arrived one day and never left. The rest of the inhabitants of our household (except perhaps for me and Shadow, although his status is open to debate) are dysfunctional, weirded-out characters.

I have to cope with a lot (and that's an understatement), so I resort to painting, rock-and-roll, collecting crystals, and writing songs and poetry. I enjoy writing haiku, a Japanese form of poetry with three lines and some syllables to count. It soothes me. I write Tanka too; adding two longer lines at the end, which soothes me more. Each poetic puzzle I jot down serves as a clue for less afflicted folk to decipher what the hell I am talking about.

So, what am I talking about? The trouble is I don't know; I'm still muddling through. Although I expect it's a cry for help (a yell), combined with me dissecting the details about Mum's life, Dad's existence and his disappearance, Esme's imprisonment, and Shadow's ability to appear and reappear at a moment's notice. And that's saying nothing about living in a house that feels like a living being!

Yes, I joke to stay sane. That's a lot to process (sorry), and it's only a fraction, a haiku tidbit, so let's keep it simple but poetic and start with a view.

A view, I jest not; I saw this sky through my kitchen window today…

PUZZLE PIECE 1:
THE INVITATION

Opportunity,
An unexpected invite,
Such a mystery,
To explore and discover,
A hidden cottage of light.

I found it to be a mystifying situation. An unnatural stillness seemed to linger after many days of storms. Today, the sky reminded me of a painting. It appeared too perfect, too bright, too still, a picture landscape with no beginning or end. Instead, the vault of heaven spread out toward an endless grey forever, as if seeping around the edges of an untamed watercolour bleeding into the rest of the day. Even so, the sight filled my heart with promise, a ray of hope in an otherwise dull morning.

The quietness of my contemplation came to an abrupt end. I heard the sound of an envelope crashing through the mailbox. I jumped at the clatter. The letter landed on the floor as the sound of a thousand crystal chandeliers echoed throughout the house. I rushed to retrieve the envelope and turned it this way and that. I couldn't find an address label and wondered if the note had been hand-delivered. Who could this message be for?

I stood puzzling over this peculiar circumstance when out of nowhere my name: **Amelina Scott** appeared in bold writing. I watched wide-eyed as the final character of my surname was spelled out in a delicate font. I tore the dispatch open and inside I discovered a card printed on the finest paper with gilt edges and embossed calligraphy. There were few details, just an instruction to visit:

Crystal Cottage, River Walk, Cambridge, and the following added at the bottom as an afterthought: R.S.V.P—Not required. We promise to be welcoming when you arrive. When you're ready, you'll discover us.

I shook my head in disbelief. Nothing good ever happened to the Scotts, so this invitation might have looked magical, but surely it must have been nonsense. Weird messages from unknown sources counted as dubious junk mail, the way I looked at it.

I grabbed the envelope and attempted to rip it into pieces, but it wouldn't tear. With a mind of its own the envelope curled its edges in protest. I searched in a drawer until I found scissors and tried to cut the invite. That didn't work either. My hand ached, but the invitation endured intact as if mocking me.

Frustrated, I tried to cut the invitation again. A sputtered cursing sound filled the room even though I was alone. On my third attempt, I tore into the card with success. (I think it let me.) And once again, I perceived a noise, an angry murmur, and then nothing. Quiet descended in the room, so I threw the torn parts into the bin.

Finally satisfied that the annoying issue with the strange invite would no longer plague me, I brushed my hands together and picked an apple out of the bowl on the kitchen counter, polished it on my jumper and then took a bite. In no time my hunger had abated, and as I chucked the core towards the bin, I registered a chuckle. I stopped, my feet rooted to the ground as a feeling of certainty filled my soul. I knew what to expect. I have no idea how I did, but I could see the image in my mind, the invitation had

6

reformed. *The invitation was playing games with me!* I peered in the rubbish, and there I saw the envelope, connected in one perfect, unblemished piece.

'What the heck?'

I picked up the frustrating item. This time I took no chances. I cut it into tiny postage stamp-sized bits and left it on the counter. I didn't have to eat another morsel of fruit to observe what happened next. The invite laughed. It knitted itself in quick succession in front of my eyes. My heart hammered a staccato beat in my chest. Even though I lived with weirdness every day of my life, this strange envelope and its contents had begun to faze me.

Fazed or not, I decided I'd had enough, so I threw the wretched invite across the room. It responded by doing a merry jig in my lounge. It sang: 'You can't rip me up! I'm alive. Open up your laptop! Open up your laptop!'

I tried to squash the irritating envelope with my foot, but it kept dancing around me singing the same refrain over and over again. By now I could have throttled the envelope and its companion the invite in my urgency to get them both to shut up. I ran upstairs to my bedroom to retrieve my laptop. As I stumbled up the steps, I glanced over my shoulder. I couldn't believe it, but the card and the envelope pursued me, cartwheeling up the stairs.

I sat on the edge of my bed and warily opened my computer. As if the card and the envelope recognised my actions, they collapsed into a crushed silence on the floor. Remembering the specified address, I typed in an internet search looking for the name, *River Walk*, but before I could find the location, a bunch of strange hieroglyphics appeared on the screen, followed by a more detailed message:

You've been chosen to visit the Crystal Cottage. Please bring an open mind. Be Patient. The cottage will find you. Follow your dreams, R.S.V.P. Not Required. The Crystal Cottage, River Walk, University of Cambridge, City of Learned Magic and Gifted Spirits.

I scratched my head. What an extraordinary message. I didn't know what to make of it. The envelope answered by dancing another jig as if it already knew my answer. In a split second, the card folded itself into an assortment of shapes and pointed an origami finger at my bedroom door.

'Go! Go!' it yelled. 'You'll find magic and Krystallos light in the mighty cottage, thrilling power and answers aplenty!'

'You better not be teasing me, Mr Origami Finger—magic, thrilling power and Krystallos light sound exciting and fun!'

Bursting with curiosity, I hurriedly dressed. I had to discover more about this Crystal Cottage business. Shadow trailed after me, slinking toward the stairs, twitching his whiskers, knowing something had excited me. I patted his sleek black fur. He rubbed himself around my legs, purring with delight.

Slipping into the kitchen, I snatched an energy bar and placed it in my pocket. I rushed, throwing my coat and scarf on without a second thought. Out of the corner of my eye, I spied my camera hanging in the closet. I grabbed it as I slammed the door behind me, leaving my soulless home behind. With sure footsteps, I followed the pathway that led to the river, leaving Shadow alone.

As I walked and half ran down the path, my mother's words of advice flooded back to me, 'Don't walk along the river on your own —it's dangerous.' I knew it was an unlikely thing to say in such a quiet suburb of Cambridge, and yet it made me shiver. I chose to ignore the echo of my mother's shrill voice pounding in my thoughts, yammering nonsense. In fact, her bossy arguments made me even more determined to go. For months, I'd dreamed that I might escape. I welcomed this chance to find this mysterious Crystal Cottage. Nothing could stop me.

With each step forward, I sensed that the promise of the morning had been met; it couldn't have been a more delightful day. The sun shone, with a stunning brilliance. I guessed my escapade would prove to be one of those magical days that would inspire the darkest of spirits.

At first, my footsteps were marked with a heavy tread, but they became lighter the further I roamed away from my home. After a short while, I thought I heard footsteps behind me, but each time I looked around, I could see and hear nothing. My mother's words of warning drummed in my head, becoming louder and louder. I screwed my eyes tight, gritted my teeth, and continued forward.

The footfalls started again, coming closer and closer. Picking up my pace, I rushed ahead. By now my breath escaped in brief bursts of rising panic, catching in my rib cage. I knew I had to face it, to confront whatever dared to tail me. I swivelled and my body turned, but my vision refused to follow. Peering down at ground level I sought the source of the sound. There, twisting around my legs, I found the welcome sight of Shadow's gleaming green eyes.

I laughed a thankful giggle of relief, stroking Shadow's glistening fur. 'Shadow, you rascal, you're spooking me. I thought you'd stayed in. Go,' I said, pointing down the path toward home.

Shadow gave me a disapproving look but followed my advice and turned tail, emitting a short, sharp meow. I gazed at him guiltily. No wonder he didn't want to go home. I didn't blame him. I yearned to escape the confines of my home too.

I paused and smiled. The momentary interlude with my cat had reassured me for a moment. But those heavy footsteps kept playing on my imagination. My senses continued to work at a fever pitch, picking out every single rustle of grass, and each whisper in the breeze. I walked all the way down the narrow pathway to the river, listening and searching for the Crystal Cottage, but no sign of it transpired.

Mr Origami finger hadn't told me I'd have to wait, but the words of the message, 'be patient, the cottage will find you,' repeated in my thoughts. It was odd, but I sensed that the cottage preferred to remain hidden today, concealed from the maker of those strange footsteps. I sighed. I had no choice—I would have to be patient. I walked on, accompanied by my frustrated thoughts.

PUZZLE PIECE 2:

RIVER PATHWAY

The word forbidden,
Has a certain quality,
That draws me to it,
Like a long winding pathway,
With unexpected delights.

I continued to wander along the Fen Rivers Walkway where usually a few random dog walkers and over enthusiastic joggers crossed my way, but today I saw no one. My eyes sought out but were repelled by the fork in the route ahead. I glanced to the right and marvelled at the bright lights that seemed to tempt me to walk toward the city centre. To my left, a sombre darkness led to the neighbouring village. The river that flowed within the banks of the shadowed side appeared stagnant, the dark murky colour resembling an oil slick. I shivered in the shadows while noting the contrast in the dappled sparkling sunlight, rich with goodness beckoning from the other side.

Even though the shadows disturbed me, I couldn't help but find them fascinating. I snapped photos of the dancing sable-coloured silhouettes on the pathways and the trunks of the trees. I resumed my walk and noticed a gentle dappling of darkened markings which appeared to my left. Glancing in the far distance to the right, a narrow boat on the river caught my eye. Adjusting my camera lens, I zoomed in. I photographed the boat deck filled with patterned plant pots which extended a sunny welcome to anyone who passed by.

Questions swirled in my mind. I wondered who lived there and if the people living on the houseboat would describe themselves as happy? The cheerfulness of the scene seemed to suggest they were, but I knew from experience that hidden below the surface it could be different. The strangeness I had sensed while in the shadows took a while to leave me.

I had taken about twelve images using the disparity between light and darkness to good effect. I acknowledged this success, but with a glance at my watch, I realised I must make my way home.

I paused and turned, stepping over to the pathway entrance. From the corner of my eye, I spotted two lads who I'd never seen before. The boys hesitated to the left of the trail as if they were hiding in the far reaches of the deepening shadows. I observed as they scrutinised my movements, their eyes never leaving my form. An uneasy feeling crept over me. I glanced over my shoulder to keep them in sight. I felt vulnerable dressed in my short skirt and tugged at it to lengthen the material, but my legs remained on show, bare and exposed. A niggling protestation echoed in my head: 'You should have listened to your mother's warning and stayed away from the river pathway...'

I exhaled, and the voice in my head quietened. I focused on the lads. They had a threatening air about them, and with mounting tension in my muscles, I watched them stride towards me. The taller boy had a dark mop of unruly hair and leering eyes that unnerved me. His friend's hoodie obscured his face, and I couldn't see his features. His presence created a thread of fear in my mind.

Not wanting to appear weak, I strode up the pathway as I headed towards the train tracks. The route seemed to rise to meet my bare legs, and my fear shifted into overdrive as the shadows morphed into beings as if they had taken on their own personality. I swallowed hard and realised the darkness had become like phantoms, their ferocious blackness looming over me like monster bites snapping at my feet. This route had no alternative way home. I had to continue. I had no choice but to keep moving.

The two lads trailed me. I turned back and cringed when I saw their blank eyes surveying me. The surrounding air had grown silent, except for the ferocious pounding of my heart, echoing like a drum. Behind me, I heard their whispering and sniggering. I shivered, and fear clung to me like a shroud. I couldn't shake the feeling they could sense my anxiety.

'Like your sexy legs.'

'Yeah, that short skirt really suits you.'

I swallowed hard, trying to choke back the uncomfortable praise from the boys. I walked faster, and my breathing increased with the quickness of my steps. I heard their approaching footsteps quickening, getting closer and closer.

As soon as I reached the tracks, the shrill whistle of the local train screamed, startling me with the abrupt sound. The barriers came down, thundering into place and bringing the three of us to a standstill. The train's sudden appearance had stopped us from budging an inch. I stood motionless, too scared to move.

The tall boy sniggered, 'Saved by the train.' His eyes trailed over my body.

His friend's cruel laughter jarred my nerves. The train thundered on down the track spewing gravel on the road.

I could take no more. I ran. The boys raced after me, and as hard as I tried to outrun them, I lagged behind their speed. In a matter of seconds, they caught up with me. The tall boy reached me first, pulling at my arm halting me. I attempted to pull away, but he moved so close to me that I could smell the stench of his breath lingering like a sickly smudge on my face. I gulped down short, panicked breaths. Fright hammered in my chest and longed to find a refuge. My hands shook, and I didn't know what to do.

The boy with the dark hair pulled me towards him as he grabbed my camera strap. 'Nice camera you have there, give us a look.'

His eyes drilled into mine. I felt panic rise in my throat. 'No,' I replied clutching my camera to my side. I shook my head in defiance. No way, would I let these two take my camera. I planted my feet firmly on the ground.

The tall, dark-haired boy gestured to the other lad. 'Come on, Mitch, stop standing and gawping. Get her to hand it over.'

Mitch lurched towards me and grabbed the camera from my shoulder. I turned and struggled, holding on to the strap with all my might. That's when I noticed his eyes. They were bright but unfocused, just dark orbs staring at me. Startled, I wondered how his eyes didn't appear as if they belonged to him. I stared closer; in the pupils of his eyes I saw a momentary black shadow. Shaking with fright, I struggled to stand my ground, but I fought back. I gripped the camera strap to my shoulder, tighter, holding it in a vise-like grip.

At that moment, I heard a rustling in the nearby grass. Mitch let go of me, startled by the noise. I turned, still clutching the camera to my side as I observed a young man who appeared out of the shadows near the edge of the path. His appearance caught my attention because he wore black jeans and a faded black tee-shirt washed so often that its original colour had all but vanished. His strange eyes sought me out. I stood gazing into two of the strangest eyes I had ever seen. One shone black as the richest smeared ink while the other glowed green and reminded me of the lushness of a meadow.

'Are these two bothering you?' He rushed toward me, but his question temporarily broke the spell of his mesmerising gaze. I gaped at him, tongue-tied; I couldn't think of a word to say in reply.

The two lads stared at his extraordinary eyes. I noticed that for a moment, they appeared lost for words, too, spellbound by the newcomer's presence.

'I'm Ryder,' he announced, the reassuring tone of his melodious voice flowing, like the gentle caress of a river.

'What kind of name's that?' jeered the taller boy, awakening from his silence and crashing into the discussion with his harsh words.

'A name you'll remember, won't you, Will?' replied Ryder, standing tall, his legs spread apart, dominating the ground at his feet with a show of strength.

'Yes.' Will appeared confused and dumbfounded by a dazzling light. He pushed his dark hair off his forehead and scowled. 'Hey, how come you know my name?'

'That's for me to know and for you to find out.'

'Yeah, I'll find out, all right. Such a weirdo, just look at his eyes,' said Will, laughing and pointing.

Mitch joined in laughing too. 'Yeah, and listen to his posh-boy accent!'

'Thanks for the compliment. Posh weirdos are far more interesting than idiots,' replied Ryder.

'Funny posh-guy, huh? Why are you even here, *weirdo, wacko eyes?*' asked Will.

Ryder remained silent for several moments. I continued to stand, my feet rooted to the ground as I watched the scene play out before me. It looked like Ryder's brain ticked away processing how to respond. I couldn't imagine how he would handle this situation.

When he finally replied to the boys, Ryder chose his words carefully, even though his answer seemed to be addressed to me.

'I often take this pathway.' Ryder spun on his heel and scowled at the lads. 'You never know what treasures you might find along the way.' With a glance towards my face, he scrutinised me as if his piercing eyes gazed into the soul of a priceless jewel. I shivered under his steady gaze. His powerful stare continued to search for a response. When I didn't reply, he softened the tone of his voice and asked, 'Are you sure you're okay?'

'Yeah,' I replied, but my knees were knocking. I tucked a loose strand of hair behind my ear trying to appear nonchalant.

'She's fine; all we wanted to do was…' Mitch struggled for a moment as if he couldn't quite remember what he wanted to say, 'to see her… photos.' He pointed at my camera, speaking to Ryder for the first time.

I felt a subtle shift in the atmosphere. I noticed the two lads' eyes had lost their glassy quality, and no more shadows invaded them. They focused on Ryder and on me as if they were noticing us for the first time. This odd experience left me speechless, but I had to find out what it all meant. The strangeness of this situation shook me to a guarded watchfulness.

'You scared the hell out of me,' I said, edging forward, scuffing my shoes challenging them to say more.

'Sorry I don't know what came over me,' replied Will, appearing genuinely surprised. He scratched his head.

'And me,' remarked Mitch, appearing confused. He thrust his hands into the pockets of his hoodie, shrugging his shoulders.

'Leave her alone. She doesn't want you leering at her, and she doesn't want to share her photos with you,' said Ryder. He stood tall as if defending me against my aggressors.

'Hey! Who says we were leering? We were just hanging out. Bet you're the one who's hoping to get all up close and personal with her as soon as we've left,' said Will. His leering grin twisted, lopsided.

'I hoped to make her acquaintance,' replied Ryder, staring at the boys. 'What of it?'

'Acquaintance? Oh, you're *so* almighty stuck up, posh-boy,' said Mitch, laughing with his friend, his eyes returning to their former glassiness.

'We better leave you two to get acquainted,' added Will, his sarcastic voice mimicking Ryder's posh accent. He pointed his finger at Ryder and me.

'Yes, you had better,' retorted Ryder while peering at the boys as if he wanted to force his thoughts into their minds. I continued to stare and noticed a dark shadow cloud Ryder's face. I acknowledged this subtle yet powerful moment. When his eyes darkened, I swear they flashed thunderous daggers at the lads. Ryder's face locked into a fixed expression as if he prepared to battle. His body became rigid, and his muscles tensed. I stepped back as I observed the hard ground beneath his feet crack, extending in a black shadow as he moved towards the boys. My hand went to my mouth, and I screamed.

PUZZLE PIECE 3:

RYDER WALKS ME HOME

It's a certainty,
Guys like Ryder don't appear,
Every single day,
Weep as you will, but it's true,
'Cause he's lush and forbidden.

I stepped back and stifled my scream. The trembling of the earth continued beneath my feet. I glanced down in horror as I watched the crack grow, spreading tendrils of darkness in an eerie shadow.

I tore my eyes from the trembling ground and glanced at the two boys on the other side of the fissure. Shock and fear registered in their eyes as they met my stare. My heart pounded in my chest, sending a shot of adrenalin through me. I moved as far away from the shadowy cleft as possible, my feet moving with no direction from my mind.

The lads took refuge in glancing at their feet, moving backward from the advancing crack as if they'd thought the strange shadow would swallow them up. I found it odd, but they didn't run. Instead, Will and Mitch hardly dared to breathe. They stepped slowly, stealing away from the edge. Before long I watched as they became two indistinct shapes far off in the distance.

I felt my body relax. The quivering stopped, and the ground felt solid beneath my feet again. I took a deep breath and managed a faint smile. 'Thank you, Ryder.' I could feel the heat of a pink tint colour my cheeks.

'No problem, it's my pleasure,' he replied. He turned to face me, and with an elaborate bow, his face lit up with a confident smile as his eyes met mine.

I grinned back and chuckled when I realised Ryder reminded me of a princely actor. I thanked my lucky stars he had crossed my path. I shuddered to think what might have happened if he hadn't come by when he did. I felt unsettled by that pathway where the shadows seemed to come alive. Those boys were weird. I shook my head, trying to get the image of their blank eyes staring at me out of my head.

A residue of uncertainty remained. Those shadows lingered in my mind, resurrecting buried memories from my thirteenth birthday: an imprint on glass, a charades card, and a young man's beguiling voice bewitching me. I shivered, feeling the coolness of the air. Glimpsing up at the sky, I noticed that grey rain clouds were gathering.

I looked over my shoulder at Ryder. 'I better get back. It's going to rain.'

Ryder glanced up at the gathering gloom. 'I think you're right. If it's not rain, it's darkness that follows me. You never know what's lurking in the shadows. With that in mind, let me walk you home.'

What a strange thing to say, I thought as we turned to walk down the path toward my home. Ryder's words sounded creepy, and I couldn't shake my uneasiness. Perhaps, I should have run away, but instead, I allowed myself to walk with him. I do not understand what possessed me to do so. It must have been the irregular hiccupping of my heart.

Stealing a glance at Ryder, I drew in a sharp breath. I had been so absorbed in the drama back at the river that I hadn't noticed the subtleties flickering like wraiths across his face. I took the time now to note that he had blue-black hair that gleamed in the gloominess of the day. As the rain began to fall, I found myself drawn to his unusual eyes. His inky black eye contrasted with his green eye and had to be his most stunning, and unique, feature. He had long lashes now slicked with raindrops that gleamed in the failing light. Unable to look away, I stared into those captivating eyes as if they were two dark, mysterious pools pulling me into their depths. I imagined myself sinking into oblivion. I felt light-headed as if I'd lost my grip at the top of a high cliff, free-falling, tumbling over and over again, but instead of fighting against this frightening sensation, I welcomed it.

At that instant, I realised that I'd been staring at him for a long time. My unspoken thoughts had said yes, but I hadn't replied to his question. 'That would be very kind of you,' I said, trying to hide my embarrassment. I could feel my face burning an even deeper scarlet than the shirt I wore. Self-consciously, my hands flew to my face.

We both turned and sauntered down the wet path. The walk back didn't last long enough for the blush in my cheeks to subside. I felt them smouldering like two hot red coals. As we walked, I made a silent wish, a desire so insistent that I wondered if Ryder could hear it. When we arrived at my doorstep, Ryder magnified my thoughts by saying, 'Sometimes chance brings together those who might not have met. Let's meet again soon.'

I wondered at the peculiar choice of his words and the odd way he had spoken, but I answered, echoing his final word.

'*Soon*, that would be great.'

He leaned in towards me, sending my pulse racing, a track with no end stop. 'Next Saturday evening at 7 pm would be perfect. I'll pick you up from here.' His eyes lingered inches away from my face as if waiting for a response.

Without a second thought, I repeated his last words again. 'From here? I'll look forward to it.' I turned to open my door but hazarded a look back. It surprised me to see that Ryder had already gone. He had disappeared into thin air. I hadn't even heard his footsteps departing. As I entered my house, I realised that disconcerting feeling I had felt earlier had returned and prickled at the back of my neck.

PUZZLE PIECE 4:

RYDER'S MY SECRET

A secret something,
Draws me to it hugging me,
In a mystery,
That confounds my family,
In this strange life of secrets.

I crept on tiptoes into the house, slipping down the hallway.
As I reached the stairway, my mother Eleanor spied me.
'What are you wearing, Amelina? Is that even a skirt? As for those
tights, they're ridiculous.' I froze, her words piercing and chilling me
to the bone. I drew in a breath of relief that my mum hadn't
noticed Ryder departing. It was easier if I said nothing in reply,
although that just fired her up more. She pursed her thin lips and
scowled at me.

I knew I had stumbled upon a pit of fury as I watched Mum
turn to face me. She exploded like a bomb and shrieked, 'Get out of
that horrible excuse for clothing right now and put on something

decent. You've never worn the black trousers and top I bought you. Why don't you ever wear them?'

I recoiled at her tirade. I had no intention of wearing those horrible, ugly, old lady trousers. I would appear like some sad old person on their way to a funeral. Yeah, it felt like a funeral in this wretched house, but did she need to remind me?

I stared as my dad, Mark, appeared in the hallway, clutching the wall for support and looking so frail and haggard that I wondered if he would collapse. He spoke in a paper-thin, rasping voice. 'What are you and your mother shouting about?'

'My choice of clothes, Dad,' I replied, my voice softening.

Glaring at my mother, I stormed upstairs and slammed my bedroom door shut with an almighty bang. The sound seemed to reverberate throughout the house, shaking the walls until they threatened to come crumbling down. Downstairs, I could hear a commotion. A ruckus blasted from the kitchen as my mum took her daily dose of temper out on her unfortunate pots and pans.

Every nerve ending in my body flooded with a multitude of emotions until I felt like a quivering mound of nervous, trembling jelly. Taking deep soothing breaths, I reached for my headphones to shut out this horrible, senseless world. I craved ear-piercing rock, a vault of high adrenalin noise. That would be sure to do the trick.

I turned up the sound and relaxed, lying in my bed. My thoughts returned to Ryder. What did I know about him? He appeared as a stranger and then surprised me by coming to my rescue. He scared those creepy boys off. I had to admit that I didn't understand him or them either. His personality had switched. One moment he'd been all smiles, and then boom, he'd changed—a scary intensity erupting out of those incredible eyes. I imagined his face staring at me again. He had a mysterious power in him, that much I could see, so much so that even the ground beneath his feet responded to him.

I remembered that Ryder had introduced himself to me but hadn't bothered to ask my name. I scratched my head in puzzlement. Yet he knew who I was. Somehow, he knew those boys' names too. It struck me as strange and unsettling. But one thing I knew for sure: I experienced a trickle of life flowing in my veins. This sensation had long been missing from my life. It heralded an awakening, and I shivered in delight. I felt excited, confused, and more than a little scared. But I felt alive.

I experienced this magnetic pull of some hidden power that drew me towards him. With little difficulty, I realised he was a secret I would be wise to keep to myself. Mum and Dad would go mad if I mentioned that I'd met him down the river pathway. Hero or Prince, they wouldn't understand. Besides, the possibility of keeping dark and mysterious secrets appealed to me. They were the best, most wicked kind.

PUZZLE PIECE 5:

AUNT KARISSA'S GIFT

Hey, unwrapped presents,
Can give lots of surprises,
And these gifts can be,
Chock full of rich mysteries,
So beware, magic, watch out!

A few days after I had met Ryder, a beautifully wrapped present arrived in the morning's post—a gift sent from my Aunt Karissa. My hands shook with excitement because she always sent me strange and mysterious presents. A smile formed on my lips as I opened the parcel. I admired the handsome box carved out of the finest mahogany. My heartbeat grew when I noticed my name intricately carved on top. Little palpitations of excitement fluttered in my chest, quivering like released butterflies.

I opened the lidded box and gasped. Inside was a painting set. A sense of longing came over me as I imagined myself painting with the magnificent brushes and paints. I caressed the fine brushes, noting that the handles were lined with a gold filament. The brush heads were divine and filled with varying thicknesses of real horsehair.

My attention turned to the colour wheel enclosed within the box. I marvelled at the individual crystal paint pots: Purple Amethyst extolled creativity, Red Jade represented courage, Orange embodied joy, Olive symbolised awakening, Green encouraged discovery, Yellow represented enlightenment, Violet depicted intuition, Black symbolised protection, White ice exemplified calcite, and Natural White denoted moonstone. Excitement coursed through my veins at the display of colours—a rainbow of hope.

I couldn't wait to begin. I rushed off to find my half-finished school art project. The new paintbrushes beckoned. I could hear them calling. 'Paint me! Paint me!'

I stopped and looked around the room. Were the paintbrushes talking to me? I shook my head in disbelief. No, they couldn't be! That was impossible. It must be a joke. It had to be an Aunt Karissa speciality—perhaps she delighted in pranking me. I laughed as I mulled over the situation. Confused, I checked for a recording device, but I discovered none.

A crazy theory formed in my mind. Those brushes had to be enchanted! I couldn't think of anything else that made sense. Aunt Karissa must have superpowers. *That figures.* I paused for a moment, wondering what further madness I would stumble upon.

I heard a noise and spun around as my eyes focused on the painting set. The fibres of the paintbrushes were bristling with anticipation. I could hear them whistling in a high-pitched neighing sound I couldn't ignore. The paintbrushes kept rearing up, trying to escape the box, like a bunch of restless horses in a paddock. The whistles and pleading continued, driving me to distraction!

'Okay, okay,' I said, half laughing, and half shaking, 'stop making that chatter, I need to think.' I heard one last neigh and one last pleading note. At that point, all noise ceased, and I only heard complete and utter silence. Now that quiet had descended, I could focus.

I began painting by outlining an image of my house with the paint. I added more detail to make it look more realistic. There were two white shades to choose between, but only one black option. The Natural White Moonstone or the White Ice Calcite could be perfect shades to highlight with.

I tried to loosen the closed lid of the white Moonstone paint. I twisted it, but nothing budged. The whistling, and 'paint me, paint me,' voices started again and became louder and more urgent. I tried to pry the lid open with a paint palette knife, but it stayed shut. Then to my surprise, the pot lid exploded. It burst forth like a delighted champagne cork, whizzing across the room, sending little bubbles of shimmering crystals whirling in the air. I cried out in surprise. I stepped away from the table and gazed at the opened paint jar. Everywhere I looked; tiny crystals twinkled like a multitude of sparkling diamonds. I sighed. 'At last, at last,' the pot cried, and the bristles wolf-whistled.

I reached for one of the paintbrushes, and suddenly I experienced a strange, immediate and blinding sensation. It surged from the end of the brush, radiating an incredible energy up and down my arm. It felt as if the wooden brush had extended, becoming the skin, bones, and muscles of my fingers. An electric sensation blasted its way from my fingertips, all the way to the tip of my head.

In shock, I tried to dislodge the brush, fearful where this might be leading. I struggled, but I couldn't open my palm. The brush had claimed me, and I succumbed to its control. I couldn't escape what happened next. My nails became one with the colour of the brush's fibres, turning a muddy brown in hue. Palpitations of fear and excitement hammered at my chest. I shook my hand again and again. But the brush remained locked in place, possessing me.

An angry voice screeched, 'paint me, paint me,' repeating the words until they echoed in my head. I couldn't stand it any longer. I surrendered. Driven by a buzz of immediate energy that surged through me, I dipped the tip of the brush into the White Moonstone paint. As my paintbrush touched the canvas, the crystal's heady orchid scent hit me in the face full force. My mind raced in an intoxicating whirl. I began to sweat, and the humidity of the room increased, becoming so stifling I could hardly breathe.

Sucking the air into my lungs hastily, the canvas and I became one succession of bold, mysterious strokes. As the painting took shape, I recognised the view of the winter's sky I'd seen through the kitchen window the day I'd met Ryder.

The Black Obsidian paint pot called me next, beseeching me to open it. Just like before, it refused to do so. In frustration, I slammed it down hard. The pot exploded with a loud bang like a child's burst balloon.

As I dipped the brush into the paint, a gripping sensation overcame me. I painted in haste with a multitude of dissolving crystal paint flecks staring back at me from the canvas. A dark grey, bluish black, sinister tinge blemished the artwork. Shades of varying hues moved across the painting, competing for supremacy in a powerful duality of light and darkness.

I tipped over in my chair, toppling to the ground with a loud crash. Wiping the sweat from my brow, I stood and righted my chair. Thoughts and questions swirled in my head. I peered at the canvas and wondered why I'd drawn all those strange black flecks dominating the painting.

My attention turned to the window. The sky had become dark and oppressive, as if etched with the murkiest ink. I felt an uneasiness in the air. It reminded me of the feeling I got when an eclipse of the sun had just taken place. I experienced a dull sensation in my temples.

A swift wave of dizziness and nausea hit me hard. The room spun, and I fought for control. With difficulty, I closed my eyes, willing the strange spinning to stop. Tentatively, my eyes opened, and a narrow tunnel of faded images came toward me in a giddy whirl. First, I saw a misty image of my dad playing his guitar, with my mum laughing by his side. In slow motion, I watched a replay of the day my father had disappeared, followed by the day he returned. The images swirled and blended until everything went black.

PUZZLE PIECE 6:

A GAME OF CHARADES

A missing person,
Disappears, rarely returns,
When they do it's cause,
For a huge celebration,
But not for us, we're tragic.

W hen my sight cleared, I realised that the portrait had taken me back to the dreadful day that my dad disappeared. I remembered that on that day, my thirteenth birthday, we'd been celebrating with music, laughter, and the promise of cake. The vision replayed in my mind, I could see and hear it all, the drum-beats of the stereo, the syncopated rhythm of the music, Dad's flushed face, his broad smile playing havoc with the corner of his lips—but then it all changed...

My family had been dancing in the lounge, doing our own personal boogie, revelling in the music. Dad grabbed me, twirling me around and around until I stumbled in a breathless, giddy whirl. Mum joined in, too, laughing at our silliness. The open fire warmed the lounge, its flames roaring. Flickers of a strange light fell upon Dad's ash brown hair, while he danced in time to the beat of the music. All this exertion had tousled his wavy locks. He stood up, stretching his tall frame to his full height in a series of irregular movements. He picked up his guitar, and we sang, scampering to catch up with the growing tide of his enthusiasm.

Eventually, Dad surrendered his guitar and propped it up on its stand. With a flourish, he opened a bottle of sparkling wine. The cork whizzed across the room, landing with an exultant bang. This became his cue to pour a large glass of wine for mum and a small glass for me.

Excited, I gulped it down in one huge swallow. The hiccups ensued as I struggled to get myself under control. My cheeks flamed red from the wine and the dancing.

Dad shook his head. 'Amelina, it's not grape juice,' he scolded, laughing. 'No more, young lady, even if it is your thirteenth birthday!'

Our laughter filled the lounge, surrounding us in a unifying chord. Sinking down on the settee, I wallowed in the depth of its familiar feeling. Finally, my hiccups stopped. Smiling, I picked at the threadbare fabric. The settee had seen better days, but it felt cosy, like our family. Our sunny life made me feel so happy. We were floating by, drifting on our own chauffeured punt, a strawberry and champagne dream.

Breathless from the dancing and with our faces flushed, we settled down to play a game of charades. Much smiling and laughter continued as we acted out the words on the cards. Dad, always the lucky one, picked the first charade. He played the fool, pretending to eat spaghetti.

As the game progressed, we took it in turns. One minute Dad acted like a snail crawling across the floor, and the next minute Mum impersonated a hiccupping toad. My forehead creased with the exertion of trying to guess the right answer before the sand timer ran out. Nobody stood a chance to guess my next charade. They tried as hard as they could, but they failed.

Dad came to the rescue by picking another card. He turned it over. His face drained of all colour. He stared at the card long and hard, and then he trembled. His shaking progressed from a tremor to a full-on wine spilling. His grip faltered, and the card quivered in his hand. He staggered towards the fireplace and threw it into the burning embers. The fire raged, and a ring of flames circled the card, avoiding it as if it contained the deadly plague. The sand timer ran out. The fire burnt down, leaving its mark on the card with black, singed edges.

I felt a chill creep up my spine. When I searched Dad's face for some clue to his strange behaviour, I reeled back, struck by the sight of a dull emptiness in his eyes. I couldn't tear my gaze away from his face. I thought I spotted a weird reflection in his eyes, maybe a bug, or something that flashed for a moment and vanished. Whatever it might have been, it lingered momentarily; a blink of an eye and it disappeared. I wasn't sure what had happened because no answer transpired. Instead, the features on Dad's face settled into an unfamiliar stony expression. I shivered at his transformation.

Then I noticed the music in the room had begun to jar my nerves, becoming a cacophony of noise. Dad rushed to open the lid on his record player, grabbing the stylus roughly, causing it to scratch the surface of the record. The screeching grated and sent shivers up my arms.

Dad ended the Charades game by closing the lid of the record player. His face remained grim, and his lips stretched across his mouth in a slash of red. I stayed out of his way and hung back watching, not sure what would happen next.

'Are you all right?' Mum asked, reaching out to touch his shoulder. I detected an edge to her voice, a sharp, unfamiliar sound of worry. Her auburn hair appeared to flatten and lose its shape, forming a mask of uncertainty around her cheerful face.

My dad's immediate reply terrified me. The curve of his mouth turned upside down, and his appearance reminded me of a dejected clown with a mouth covered in a frown of smeared make-up. His expression did more than shock me; it triggered a fountain of tears inside. I shook but reached out to touch his arm. 'Dad, what's wrong?' I asked.

'Nothing, it's nothing,' was all he would say. Mum and I exchanged worried glances.

The candles on my birthday cake, a homemade chocolate, strawberry, and vanilla ice cream delight, remained unlit. I gazed at the sweet confection as the ice-cream dripped, forming a multi-coloured puddle, a glossy pastel mess, on the plate.

We should have sung 'Happy Birthday.' My voice hung in the air, unanswered.

The room became hot, yet no fire warmed us. A trickle of perspiration formed on Mum's lip, a tiny moustache of sweat. She frowned and walked unsteadily toward the fireplace. I shivered as Mum added more logs and then re-lit it. The fire roared in the grate, warming the room. I watched as my dad stared into the distance, with unapproachable glassy eyes. My birthday celebration had crashed and burned, and it hadn't even struck midnight. *This had to be a first.* My tears hid just below the surface, ready to erupt.

'Off to bed, Amelina,' Mum urged. A dark cloud slipped over her eyes as if she attempted to hide something. She spoke in a blunt voice I didn't recognise. *She wanted me out of the room.*

'But Mum.' I couldn't hold back the protest in my voice.

Her blue eyes turned icy. When I heard her screech, 'Now,' I knew she meant it.

I shivered again, but this time not from the cold. My limbs were heavy, my heart unsure. I moved down the hallway on silent feet toward the stairs to climb up to my bedroom. I shook my head and puzzled over what had happened and why my parents were acting so strangely.

I opened the door to my room, dejected. I didn't bother to brush my teeth or put my pyjamas on. I climbed into bed fully clothed. I couldn't shake the strange feeling over what had just occurred. It made me feel queasy, so I grabbed my covers, pinching and pulling them tight around me like a security blanket.

Sleep eluded me. I could still hear the sound of Dad's footsteps walking to and fro, pounding the tiles in the downstairs hallway. The thud disturbed me. I noted his unmatched footfalls, one heavy and the other light. I closed my eyes tightly when I heard Mum's voice pleading, while Dad's voice remained silent. I focused my attention on what happened next; on the floor below I heard the sound of a door opening and then slamming to a close. The reverberations shook our house with a strange shock wave.

Rushing over to my bedroom window, I peered into the gloom, searching for the source of the noise. I cocked my head, listening, trying to discern events as they unfolded. The sound of departing footsteps continued and then stopped. In its place, I heard a strange buzzing sound, amplified to an extraordinary level. The intonations echoed as if a bunch of insects were in the midst of a rave in our garden. I witnessed a momentary flash of gold, and two scorching red lights flew away into the sky. The overwhelming silence scared me.

My eyes returned to ground level, following the path that extended into our garden. The trail stretched the full length of our house, encroaching upon a wilderness that lived beyond. I recalled an old tree had fallen days before, its eerie branches curled, almost like its gnarled hands reached out, trying to grab us.

A sick feeling registered in my gut. Perhaps dark creatures of the adjacent forest had claimed him? I shuddered, wondering if maybe a monster had captured him. A terrible feeling of dread settled in the pit of my stomach, sitting there like a crushing stone of worry. I stepped back from the window, and with heavy footsteps, I descended the stairs.

Near the landing, I found Mum huddled in a corner, crying. She wiped her tear-stained face when she saw me. I put my arms around her and held her close. We sat like that for hours.

When Dad didn't return, Mum placed a call to the police to say he had disappeared. But somehow, deep down inside me, I knew the police wouldn't be able to help us. I stood there mute, staring at Mum talking on the phone. I didn't know why Dad had left or for how long he'd gone. There'd been no goodbye. No explanation, just the sound of his retreating steps moving further away down the road, leaving Mum and me far behind.

Our once happy family evoked distant memories, and laughter became a cruel joke. I glanced around and remembered our happy past. I felt it then, the realisation that our house had shrunk, reflecting our sorrow.

With that awareness, the vision I had experienced passed. I slipped outside the front door, gasping for fresh air. Blinking away tears of sadness, I lifted my head and stared at the sky, willing it to reveal its secrets. No stars twinkled in reply; instead, an inky blackness stared back, flooding my senses with despair. My thoughts returned to my painting and the canvas, knowing that this story remained unfinished.

PUZZLE PIECE 7:

DAD'S RETURN

Poetry is my heart,
But it beats,
A single verse, a note of sorrow,
This ruby-eyed, black-hearted curse lives,
A bug-eyed monster continues to torment me,
Staring at my weeping canvas,
I am transported to a time I long to forget.
The time I long to forget was Dad's homecoming.
The irony did not escape me.

It should have been a celebration, but Dad's return reminded me more of a Shakespearean tragedy. I'd just turned fifteen. It had been such a long wait, and I'd hoped for this reunion for so long—but now it ripped my heart apart like a sick joke. It had been no party. As I remembered back to that day, tears of pent-up sadness spilled on my canvas.

I shook the memory from my mind, and I scrutinised my painting. For a second, instead of the image of the sky I had just painted,

I saw my dad's face staring at me. One-half of his image held a youthful aspect, while the other side appeared elderly, forcing me to acknowledge my pain. Yes, my dad had returned, but he'd changed. Time had stolen his youthfulness. His watery eye stared back from the canvas, beseeching me to save him. All the while, his right eye twinkled with a contrasting brilliance.

I watched the left side of his lip tremble. His painted face beseeched me, 'Help me, help me.' The right side grinned and also spoke. 'I'm fine; ignore that wretched old half of me.'

Shaken with the realisation that my precious gift of paints carried a torture buried within its lovely packaging, I shook my head. 'Please, stop,' I cried, my eyes filling with fresh tears.

In reply, the portrait changed. Instead of Dad's face, I now made out the figure of Ryder, in all his youthful glory. His eyes met mine and smiled at me. In the background of the painting, I watched as dark shadows billowed and moved. I drew back when I noticed Ryder's eyelids made up, in a dramatic smoky eye effect one would see during a theatrical production. Dressed all in black, he resembled a Halloween painting. As I stared at him, his meadow green eye turned a nasty red.

I shook my hand, swearing at the paintbrush, hating it for what it was doing to me. I needed this to stop now. However, no release came. So, in desperation, I shouted, 'Release me.'

'Alright, *alrighhhht*,' the paint pots cried in unison. The brush answered with one final piercing whistle and then surrendered, releasing me. The compelling trance came to an end. My fingernails returned to their usual pink colour.

I laughed, but it sounded like a hysterical emission from my lips. Feeling nauseous and disoriented, I rushed off to the toilet and vomited, bile rising from my throat, choking me with its sourness. It was all too much. Even my beloved art tortured me with thoughts and memories I couldn't let go of.

Looking at the drab, colourless furnishings surrounding me in the lounge, I sighed. A sad echo of melancholy reverberated throughout the house like a rung bell. Our bereft home continued, without a soul, just like our family, which now existed without my dad. The heart of our family had been ripped out, erased in one swift moment, replaced by a terrible void.

Our house had always been different, even before all of this. It resembled a mini mansion, a four bedroom with a large kitchen, sliced through with a long hallway, and behind the premises sprawled a wild garden. But for now, the heart of my home seemed to have shrunk to a tiny, compressed space. A room boxed in and filled with despair.

I picked up my favourite photo of my mum and dad where both of them were smiling. It tugged at my heart, making me sad at how faded it seemed. I hesitated, wishing I could turn back the clock, to reset time. I longed for it to be that simple.

Instead, all my thoughts concentrated on that horrible day so long ago when my dad had returned. The memories flooded into my brain and I sat down on the settee trying to decipher my thoughts.

Yet, I remembered that day like it had been etched in glass. I had heard a knocking sound from the front door, a light tapping, persistent noise. I flew downstairs on swift feet. Through the frosted glass of the door, I peered at a hazy silhouette. The knocking stopped. I opened the door a fraction and squinted at the figure that stood in front of me. He gasped for breath, making terrible rasping sounds. His eyes were bleary and bloodshot.

The terrible sight of this man made me cling to the door frame, seeking support, almost mimicking his misery. I wanted to run, to escape this visitor, but for whatever reason, I let him in. I knew it was the right thing to do. One thought gave me comfort; I figured if this stranger turned nasty, I could run faster than he could.

That occurrence seemed so unlikely, I almost laughed. I had this particular feeling that the man had zero chance of going anywhere. Thinking quickly on my feet, I reasoned that if I slammed the door in his face, the poor guy would probably die right there on my doorstep. I sighed. Choice made. *I'm no murderer.* Stealing another glance at the strange man, I winced. He wasn't a pretty sight. He hobbled into the house with a slow, painful shuffle. For some odd reason, I didn't object to him coming in. I didn't welcome this stranger, but I did pull the dining chair out for him. He didn't sit; he collapsed.

I had no clue what to do next. I hovered for a moment, my intention uncertain. The man's breathing continued to rattle in his chest, so I rushed off to retrieve a glass of water to quench his thirst. When I returned, he struggled to hold the glass with his pinkie extended, his hand shaking, and the water spilling on the floor. I observed him through lowered eyes as he lifted the glass to his lips, drinking in gulps that tugged at my heart.

'Amelina,' he croaked, his sad eyes swimming through tears to reach me. The man's eyes drew us together. The shock of meeting his gaze pummelled me with a force equal to a ferocious wave. His voice couldn't say the words he longed to say, those syllables drowned on some faraway shore. I watched him struggle to speak. My name was buried in his heart. I recognised him. It was that tiny finger which reminded me before his voice did. He'd always had trouble bending that finger, ever since he'd broken it.

I heard the sound of the key turning in the front door. It was Mum. He heard it too. He gazed up, his sad eyes expectant, begging for recognition. She didn't have a clue what sight would greet her. She walked into the hallway. 'Amelina, I'm home,' she yelled.

I didn't reply. I couldn't say a word. The sight of Dad's finger held me transfixed. Mum saw us. She staggered and then swayed. Her eyes bulged, two round orbs staring at the scene before her. 'What the, who… is…?'

With trembling hands, the man lifted the glass to his lips. At that moment, Mum recognised the truth. Poor Mum. It was too much for her; she swayed and fainted, hitting the floor with a thud.

PUZZLE PIECE 8:
MIRROR TALK

Better than you do,
The mirror knows your secrets,
Laughter is hollow,
Unless we are free to live,
Beyond our own reflection.

I felt the need to unravel the mystery of my father's disappearance. Somehow, I knew it all began with Esme, a captured victim of a curse who lived in the mirrors of our house and kept out a watchful eye. I could see her, but Mum couldn't. As far as I could tell, neither could Dad. That suited me because Esme was my secret.

I remembered seeing Esme shortly after she had vanished from school, when Dad disappeared two years ago. The memories of that day flooded into me so much that I'd thought I had been hallucinating. Poor Esme. When I saw her reflection staring at me in the mirror, the first thing I did to acknowledge her presence was to grab a flannel and try to wipe her away. Some welcoming! Except she wasn't a reflection, she existed. When she spoke, I almost fell over in shock.

'Hey, stop that,' she scolded. 'I don't need a shower; you're making me all smeary.'

I stepped back and stumbled in surprise. *This is crazy. Bizarre. Extraordinary, how can this be happening?* At that moment, I felt like I had tumbled into a Dr Who mystery. Who else had such a dysfunctional family—a disappearing Dad, an accomplished vanishing cat, a cranky Mum, and now, a girl who lived in mirrors for a best friend? No one!

I recognised Esme as a girl from my school who'd vanished with no explanation, who had then turned up as a permanent fixture in my mirror. I struggled with this reality and closed my eyes, willing her away. My hands shook. I couldn't take much more of this craziness.

When I opened my eyes, she hadn't moved an inch. I fumed, shaking my head in disbelief. She scowled at me as if I'd captured her and put her there myself, like I'd made it my habit to be her jailer. I stumbled down the stairs and ran through the house, checking each mirror. She appeared in all of them—every single one. My thoughts swirled like a nightmare where I had the image of a scowling Esme staring at me with a look of disdain on her face.

I didn't know what else to do, so I spoke to her. It took a great effort, but I acknowledged her existence, even though this whole situation was mental. 'Esme. What are you doing hanging out in the mirrors in my house? How can this even be?' This didn't go down well, and instead of replying, she hammered on the mirror, screamed, and then collapsed in a corner, crying.

I couldn't help but wonder if whatever was happening to my family had reached beyond us and touched others.

Esme answered when she'd got over the shock of seeing me. 'I can't tell you how I got here. I'm compelled to keep that a secret. All I can say is that I'm trapped and can't get out. Whereas you can walk out the door, but you won't be free until you find the cottage.'

Esme smiled. Her blonde hair caught the reflections from the morning light hitting the mirror, leaving a shiny spot on the wall behind me. I gazed at her face and saw that her eyes held the truth: in the sadness, she couldn't hide.

Mum's face showed that same sign of sadness. She had this habit of checking her reflection every time she came in and before she left the house, hoping that one day this ritual would allow her to see a change in her appearance. I would often sneak out of bed in the early hours to catch her talking to her reflection.

Mum's reflection always sent poor Esme into shock mode. I'd watch as she'd sink deeper into the imprisoning walls of the hallway mirror, shrinking away from the disturbing sight of Mum's white skin, her bright orange hair, and sharp features.

Today, I did something that perhaps I shouldn't have done. Mum assumed no one else could overhear her, but I eavesdropped and listened as she talked to herself in the mirror. I could tell Mum didn't realise that she had been spilling her heart out to us both.

What followed could only be classified as fit for an agony column found in a magazine. It might not be as accurate an account because I can't remember exactly what Mum said, but Esme and I remembered overhearing these words…

Mum faced the mirror and smoothed her hair. She peered into the mirror and spoke with careful words. 'I don't feel I can share my thoughts with anyone, not even Mark. Somehow, we've grown so far apart even though we live in the same house. Every time I look at him, I see so much pain in his eyes, and in Amelina's eyes, too, so I prefer to talk to my reflection. It's easier this way, and I like to share my secrets with you. Mirrors don't talk back, argue, or complain. There's something magical in your silent response. It's almost like you wince at the sight of me but understand and deflect my pain.'

I watched the tenseness in Mum's posture as she stood emptying her soul into the mirror. She shook her head and continued.

'I hate who I've become. I'm a bad tempered, ugly mess. My misery's visible to everyone, and I know it. Other people might feel sad, but they can hide their emotions. Not me. When I look at myself, I see the stress from Mark's disappearance and then his reappearance, and how it's chiselled me into something unrecognisable. I feel like a bloody sculpture gone wrong.' At this pronouncement, Mum's voice wavered with emotion. She sighed and wiped a tear from her eye.

She glanced into the mirror and began again. 'I take my frustrations out on Amelina. I feel so guilty. Poor kid, she doesn't deserve it. It seems that ever since Mark vanished, I've felt so miserable. I can't help myself. I lash out verbally. Even though Mark has returned, I can't take my frustrations out on him, so she bears the brunt of it. She must think I'm a bitch.'

I observed Mum as she turned her face to study it at different angles before addressing the mirror again. I could hear the question in her voice. 'Why can't life be kinder? Nothing I do makes any difference—the mental scarring's too deep.'

She paused for a moment and then continued, smiling ruefully at her reflection. 'I feel you're encouraging me to pour my soul to you, mirror. If I remain silent, you seem to reflect more light, as if *you* are lonely and encouraging me to stay and talk to you. I don't know how that could be, but somehow, I feel it is true. At times I swear I hear a noise much like a sigh. I'm not sure if it's me hearing things or if it's someone else?'

Mum shook her head and fluffed her hair; her face hovering inches away from the glass. 'Maybe it's you I hear,' she whispered. She laughed. 'That's ridiculous; mirrors don't sigh. I'm all alone here, mirror.'

Mum glanced down at the floor and over her shoulder before speaking once again to the mirror. 'Everyone's out, except for Shadow. That cat meows, but it isn't a friendly meow. Shadow and I don't get on. There's something weird about a black cat that turns up at troubling times. The bloody cats like a beggar with fleas showing up on your doorstep and claiming squatter's rights.'

Stifling a laugh, Mum surveyed the hallway for Shadow as if she and the mirror were old friends gossiping over tea before she continued her dissertation. 'Shadow often joins me here, mirror. He appears fascinated by his own reflection. Cats are strange creatures. He gives me the creeps. I'd like to shoo him away, but his eyes glare at me, so I don't. You know what that cat does then? He turns his head away from me, all haughty as he continues to stare at the glass. I'm convinced that he's admiring himself the way he stares at his reflection. I believe he recognises himself too. It's odd. Perhaps he's a witch's cat, or maybe he understands what I'm saying. Whatever it is, I can't help but feel like I shouldn't antagonise him.'

Mum scratched her head, peering at herself in the glass. She leaned closer and whispered. 'I'm reluctant to continue talking when Shadow's here, which is ridiculous. Anyway, I filed a missing person report when Mark vanished. It's horrible, but when he returned, I felt even more miserable.'

Tears slid down Mum's face, and she swiped at the moisture lingering on her cheeks. I could tell she'd reached a plateau of upset, yet she kept on nattering on in that way she had. I hoped Esme could stand the outpouring of grief that gushed from her tiny body. Mum continued blubbering, and her voice cracked with emotion. 'Who wants to wake up every morning to this shadow that is my husband? He's hardly living. Sometimes I wish he'd disappear again.'

Shivering from the surge of her words, Mum hugged herself before beginning her tirade once more. 'When you love someone, you can't bear to see them suffer, you know? It cuts away at me, I tell you. Mark's lost his soul. It's not just the aging; his heart has lost its rhythm for life. It still beats a song I love but, only just.' Mum placed her fist in her mouth almost like she longed to stop the words flowing unchecked from her soul. I felt chilled from her admissions and crept a bit closer so I could hear her better.

Crying hard now, her words echoed in my ears. 'My neighbours and friends close their eyes from this horror but pretend that I'm one of the lucky ones—my husband came back alive—what a joke. People can see so little sometimes; they hide from the truth. Mirror, I swear you agree, but I don't hear your answer,' she said bitterly. 'I know, I know. Mirrors can't talk.'

Shadow crept from a corner and sauntered down the hallway,

stopping to admire himself in the mirror. I could tell he'd heard enough. He swished his tail, his reflection following him as he passed in front of the looking glass. With a rueful glance in the cat's direction, Mum said, 'There you are, Shadow. I wondered where you were.'

I watched as my cat spun around and glared at Mum while an evil grin edged with twitching whiskers spread across his face. For a moment it seemed possible that he might be somebody else. Mum's words and Shadow's evil grin had disturbed me, but it didn't stop me from investigating further. I turned to the mirror again to be my source of information.

This time Esme had heard Dad's confession. Perhaps she might have embellished this a little, but who wouldn't under her circumstances?

Dad always spoke to the mirror with the same opening words and repeated them over and over again. That's why she could remember them so well. Not long after Mum's admissions to the hallway mirror, Esme whispered Dad's words to me.

Much like Mum's diatribe, Dad's thoughts repeated many of the same themes. He stared into the mirror and said, 'I don't feel I can talk to anyone…not even Eleanor. Somehow, we've grown so far apart, even though we live in the same house. Every time I peer into her eyes, I see the pain. It's echoed in Amelina's eyes too. So, to preserve them from any more distress, I prefer to talk to my reflection. I still see pain, but at least it's my suffering.'

Esme said Dad seemed uncomfortable sharing his thoughts. Sometimes he paced in front of her and other times he glared at the mirror. Finally, he paused and admitted to his reflection, 'It's weird how I talk to mirrors …ever since I returned. Somehow, it soothes me. And you listen. You keep my secrets, so let me share this dream that's been plaguing me.'

According to Esme, Dad just kept talking. With some trepidation, he said, 'It's become addictive, this talking to mirrors. I have no one else to confide in. So, the mirrors have become my friend, a trusted companion.'

Eerie didn't cover this, but Dad said the same things about

Shadow that Mum had said. I got shivers up my spine when Esme told me what Dad had said. She repeated his words carefully: 'I never talk to the mirror when that black cat's nearby. That animal gives me the creeps, and it's always hanging around. I swear I'm allergic to it, but it's more than skin deep. I just don't trust it. Luckily Shadow's absent today. Perhaps he's out killing mice.'

Esme said that Dad continued his rant while hollering at his reflection and saying, 'I feel like shit, today, and every day. It's like someone's hit me with a shovel and then run off to dig my grave. That sounds harsh, but it's true. I can't see how things will improve. Sometimes, I think of ending it all, and then I feel guilty, because I know that's the ultimate selfish act. But I have considered it.'

Dad's words were scary, but nevertheless, Esme told me every-thing. This time he told her, 'Every night I have this recurring dream that I'm flying through the sky, but an airplane isn't carrying me. This terrible beating sound keeps on and on. Some dreadful winged creature is dragging me further away from my happiness, and my family, but I've no way of stopping it. All I can do is hold on tight and hope that I'll survive.' Esme seemed shook up by Dad's words. She may have been used to my parents ranting about each other to her in the mirror, but this time she said it seemed different.

Dad said, 'Just before the end of the dream, I always hear a loud bang like something's being demolished or dragged from the earth. It reminds me of the deafening sound of the one o'clock gun that I've often heard on Princes Street Gardens in Edinburgh. That's a loud, pleasant sound. This isn't. It sets my pulse racing, like that tormented rollercoaster ride of my past. It disturbs me, and then I wake up in a sweat. It's as if every pore in my body is saturated with fear. I can hardly breathe. Each day starts the same. It's got so bad that I can't bear sleeping, so I stay up as late as I can. I watch TV, read, and do anything so I can stay alert and not fall asleep to relive the dream. Sleeping's become a nightmare. When I close my eyes, dark shadowy shapes crawl into my mind to play horror games. I can't get it to stop. Help me!'

I shivered with a growing sense of horror. Dad's words, '*like that tormented rollercoaster ride of my past,*' made me realise that whatever Dad had been through it had been one hell of a gut-churning ride.

Esme shook her head and shrugged her shoulders, her reflection staring back at me from the mirror in my bedroom. My family was falling apart, and I didn't know what to do…

PUZZLE PIECE 9:

SHADOW DISAPPEARS AND REAPPEARS

Some evil summons,
Made Dad's youth disappear fast,
When Dad returned home,
Black cat Shadow arrived too,
Two strange coincidences.

Today promised the same routine as any other day, and the passage of time had slipped away from me. I didn't know what to do about my parents sneaking around talking to mirrors instead of confiding in each other, or me.

In turn, I crept around, eavesdropping on them or asking Esme to spy for me. I knew we were dysfunctional and one messed up family. It made my head spin, and my heart ached at who we had become. Besides, who else had the spectre of a girl living in captivity within their household mirrors as a permanent sleepover guest? No one. There was no denying it—we were a strange family.

Today, the stifling air in this soulless pit of a house reflected my mood. It held me, an unwilling prisoner. My captivity grated on my nerves like solitary confinement. I lived in a prison with no bars, and that prison had no tangible exit. So, instead of moping, I broke out. I pushed my prison door ajar and inhaled the scent of freedom.

The afternoon mocked me. The way ahead into the garden lay dark and gloomy, all the trees stripped of their leaves and colour like a plucked bird with no plumage. The farther I walked from the house, the brighter everything became. I thought this was odd, just like everything else that had happened to my family. I shrugged my shoulders and forged ahead. It felt good to be outside.

A narrow pathway led to the country park, escaping like a released jigsaw piece with each slab. As my steps quickened, I noticed the wildflowers and grasses grew wilder and more abundant with each step. A strange and silent hush enveloped me, and I realised there were no birds in the trees or animals anywhere. The complete silence meant that I could hear the raspy sounds of my breathing filling the empty expanse of the trail.

Feeling lost and alone, a prisoner in my own tortured thoughts, I noticed the company of Shadow. He slipped next to me, and the only sound I heard was the continuous soft padding of his feet walking towards me. He rubbed against my legs, almost as if he knew I needed a hug. With his blue-black silky fur and white patch on his neck, the cat's vibrant green eyes held my attention. This cat exuded handsomeness, and he knew it. I smiled, glad for his presence.

As I walked back towards home, my thoughts returned to Ryder and how he'd promised he'd take me out on Saturday. It felt like such a long time had passed since I'd last seen him, but it had only been a few days. I had this impression that time had stretched to its utmost point, and it now waited to return to some semblance of normality. I gulped, unsure and unsettled.

Nothing stirred at all in the garden apart from Shadow's panther-like movements, which I watched with a mixture of amusement and trepidation. The cat sat poised at the bottom of the garden fence, and I sensed he lingered, waiting for something to happen. My eyes never left him. Yet, in the blink of an eye, he had vanished from my sight. Confused, I rubbed my eyes and looked again, but no sight of him remained. Shadow had vanished. I paused and glanced over my shoulder. Perhaps my eyes were playing tricks on me? It had all happened so quickly that I couldn't quite believe what I'd just witnessed.

In a flash, Shadow reappeared out of thin air. I drew back and blinked my eyes in amazement. I remembered that he'd done this before. The cat's personality never ceased to amaze me. There was something quite startling about that feline, which added another piece to the mystery of my everyday life. At that moment, I wished Shadow could talk and tell me why he did such strange things.

I bent down and rewarded his reappearance with a pat of his silky fur. 'Hey, there you are, you peculiar, disappearing, crazy cat.' Shadow meowed and sauntered off; his tail raised in the air in the shape of a question mark. I laughed at his composure. I could swear that the cheeky fellow winked at me as he left.

My heart swelled with the love I felt for Shadow. 'Thank goodness, I have you. You don't let me down. Sometimes you disappear, but you always come back. My faithful Shadow.' The cat stopped, turned, and retraced his steps towards me. He arched his back in a graceful curve as he twisted around my legs once more. This time he answered me with a purr in a richer, deeper note that escaped from his whiskered face like a melody. It wasn't hard to figure out that Shadow had understood what I had said.

The sound of Shadow's sweet purring transported me back to the day he'd first appeared at our house… In fact, I realised that his arrival had coincided with the same day that Dad had returned home. I chewed my lip, remembering how my life had changed ever since that day.

Someone summoned you,
Sometimes you will disappear,
You will then return,
In a familiar place,
But you'll be unfamiliar.

I closed my eyes and let that day replay in my mind. Mum had come to from her faint; she'd rose from the floor and locked eyes with poor Dad. This second viewing hadn't been a pretty sight, but she braved it. She didn't cry out. Instead, she hiccupped, swallowing her shock like a bitter pill. Dad had witnessed her hiccupping stare and gulped, lost for words.

Shadow had interrupted us by pressing his nose against the glass, imploring me to notice him. Passing by the patio door on the way to the kitchen, his plaintive meowing had grabbed my attention. Mum had heard him too. That day, she didn't object to my inviting him in. Under normal conditions, she would have freaked out, but that day, she didn't have the energy to tell me no, not with Dad's reappearance.

It seemed like the right thing to do, so; I let him in. The black cat had won. It was funny how he made the decision to stay, fulfilling my wish to keep him.

Dad stayed too. But in his case, it's as if he's not here. He's present, but his mind is somewhere else. It's not surprising. Nowadays he doesn't even join in with Mum and me. By his actions, he might as well be invisible. A statue would be more fun.

Every morning I sigh, and a deep-rooted sense of relief overwhelms me as I recognise the distinctive sounds of his heavy footsteps as he shuffles across the hallway to the bathroom. He might not have disappeared again, but his youthful enthusiasm for life has vanished. Now he behaves like a grandfather, a grumpy relic of an ancient has-been. I can't seem to shake the feeling that his real age laughs at me, berating and teasing me, knowing he's much younger.

PUZZLE PIECE 10:
DON'T CALL MY MUSIC IDOLS UGLY

My three special things,
Music, art and poetry,
Make life worth living,
It's a fact not a fiction,
Of your imagination.

I pondered over Esme's words, "you won't be free until you find the cottage." No doubt this remained in my mind. I had to find the cottage, but how? I hadn't had much luck until now. Esme told me little, but she revealed that the cottage held a vast array of magical crystals which could ward off evil shadows. She mentioned tight security by invitation only, and powerful protectors of the cottage would chase off all intruders using unusual means. I didn't find out more or how she knew this, as Mum chose this moment to disturb our discussion. She came home to chaos. It was the day after my painting episode. She didn't appreciate chaos.

Mum glanced in the mirror and threw an almighty fit. She scowled and glared at her reflection. Today, the sight of her pained likeness upset her. No doubt it bothered Esme too. Whenever she locked eyes with Mum, her face wilted. 'Amelina, what's that terrible noise?' she screeched. 'It sounds like a strangled cat. Turn it off now! It's deafening!'

'I'll turn it off now.'

I wished she hadn't come back to spoil my moments of freedom. That permanent frown on Mum's forehead creased into a thick razor line, which appalled my senses like a caricature character that had come to life.

'What in heavens have you been doing, Amelina? The place smells awful and looks even worse,' she shrieked in a high-pitched, icy voice.

I cringed. 'Sorry, Mum. I opened a present from Aunt Karissa that came in the post yesterday. It appeared to be a box of paint pots. The paint brushes neighed, and...'

'What are you talking about? Don't talk rubbish. Paint brushes don't neigh! Stay away from your aunt's strange gifts. Goodness knows where she gets them. Perhaps they should carry a warning sticker.'

'I'm not sure I can do that, they're so hard to resist.' My eyes twinkled with a glint of mischievousness.

'Yes, but resist you must,' she scolded.

'Did you see that weird sky?' I asked, peering out the window.

'What weird sky? What are you talking about?'

'The sky I painted. It looked like something out of an eighteen plus horror movie, and then Dad's face appeared...'

'Really, that sounds far-fetched even for you.' Mum interrupted me before I could say anything else. 'Stop distracting me with all this nonsense, Amelina. Why is the place such a mess?' She walked into the kitchen and ran her finger down the counter. I knew I pressed her buttons, and I frowned.

'Sorry, Mum. I put a pizza on, and I forgot all about tidying up. Somehow I dropped my glass too.' I hung my head, a disproportionate level of guilt etched in my face.

'That's no surprise, sounds so like you. Clumsy. Oh, you've cut your finger, *again*...'

'Yes, I did.' My eyes drifted to the telltale plaster. 'Sorry for the mess, Mum.'

'Sorry means nothing if you don't mean it. Make sure the kitchen's pristine. Tidy up.' Her sharp words sliced the air, like a bunch of unhinged staccato notes leaping about.

I did what my mother asked—my face couldn't compete with her level of scary. Besides, I knew there wasn't another option. Inside, I was fuming. I pulled invisible faces, simmering at a low boil because of my mother's relentless demands. Silently, I tidied up as fast as I could.

When I finished, I crept upstairs to my bedroom, my refuge, where I could be who I wanted to be. I swore out loud. 'Bloody hell!' Mum drove me mad. I contemplated and breathed in the life displayed on the walls of my bedroom, searching for new energy. Each wall sang a tune to me, awash with colourful, inspiring art, and vibrant music posters glowed with rebellious, tattooed artists, sending me into a much-needed poetic reverie. Inspiration hit me, and I grabbed a pen and paper as the words flowed out of me like a song:

If only time,
Could drive away sorrow,
Life's caricature of pain,
Time takes me journeying,
Music fills my heart,
Art enlivens my soul.

I delved inside my camphor-wood chest, searching for my stash of the bits and bobs I kept hidden away from the prying eyes of my once good-looking, carefree and much-loved parents. Picking up my notebook, I wrote these words: *Sometimes secrets reside amongst the jumble of life's bric-à-brac.*

That became a poem...

Someone's special place,
To hide their thoughts, feelings, fears,
Sometimes secrets live,
Stored deep amongst the jumble,
Of life's hidden bric-à-brac.

That precious time seemed a lifetime ago, yet it had only been two years. *How could that be?*

I shook myself from such thoughts as my gaze once again drifted to the interior of the chest. Inside were my crystal books, little stones, trinkets, a tattoo henna kit, and my drumsticks—all treasures I held dear. I placed the art set, a gift from my aunt, in amongst my precious things and closed the chest tight, longing to protect this part of my life from harm.

Finished, I curled up on my bed in the peace of my room with Shadow. The cat purred and brushed my face with his whiskers. I rewarded his sweet purring with a pat. Shadow rolled on his back and exposed his tender belly for a tickle. I wanted to pick him up but remembered he didn't like this. The last time I'd tried to hoist him into my arms, he'd fought against it. The strength in his tiny body surprised me. His muscles strained against me in such a powerful way, displaying a superhuman strength. Shadow belonged to me, but I sensed he had a past, and he took pleasure in telling me what he wanted. Black cats! They made the rules.

I knew I had studying to do, so I picked up my history notes and read a couple of lines of text. I listened to music and sang along quietly, hoping that Mum wouldn't bother me. The music sent me off to a blissful sleep, but I was disturbed by a presence peering in from my doorway. I wasn't sure if I had been in the midst of a dream or not until I heard the unmistakable sound of Mum's voice.

'Amelina, you're sleeping when you should be studying.' Her voice grated on my nerves, challenging me to answer. Shadow curled into a tight ball. His nose tucked under his paws revelling in upping his game, taking his living arrangements to a new level—hiding. He stirred, braved a peek from one eye, and then hid under his paws again.

'I'm studying,' I said, replying to Mum's challenge, wishing I could conceal my lies. My response fired her up even more. She launched into a full-scale tantrum.

'Amelina! Stop your fibbing! Perhaps you're under the influence of bad, undisciplined people. Why do you have to have all those wild posters everywhere?'

Those last words hit the spot; they jolted me past the edge of endurance. I tumbled over the precipice of war. I couldn't stand it when Mum had a go at my music. I felt anger bubbling up in me. My unspoken words, *You're Dead to Me, GET OUT,* held in my heart for a brief second, two angry messages bursting for release. '*Mum!* Stop it! You say that every time you come in my room.'

'Don't *Mum* me! Cheeky madam! You know I can't stand them, and goodness knows how you can study or fall asleep with all those tattooed, ugly rock stars staring down at you. It would give me nightmares.'

I stared at her for a moment, and she glared back at me like the crazed character of a permanent nightmare. She reminded me of the ugly sisters in Cinderella, jealous and prone to a vicious temper. I felt a bizarre hysterical laughter bursting in my chest, longing to escape.

'You're the ugly one.' I clapped my hand over my mouth. I had shouted at Mum, and now I regretted it. An image popped into my head of her as she appeared every day. I could see her with her hair peeled back from her scalp in a tight bun, not a strand of hair escaping or out of place. The sight of her wearing the same dark grey suits with crisp white blouses that blended into her pallor flashed before my eyes. I cringed at that drowned, victim look she wore so well.

'What did you say?' she screamed, and her face contorted into an ugly expression of anger that set my nerves on edge.

'You heard me. Nothing, Mum.' I retreated into a defence mode, and I curled into a protective ball, hoping she couldn't see me. Shadow did the same, but he didn't hide his intention. He curled his sleek body into such a tight ball that he resembled a sleeping stone. I knew I had few options. If I continued to talk back, the result would be a firecracker of a row, and I just had no energy to do that today. My shoulders slumped.

'That's enough, Amelina. I swear your behaviour will drive me to ruin, first your father and now you.' Mum's sharp voice cut me like a knife.

I sighed and braced myself because I knew what to expect next. Mum could be theatrical at times. She glowered, turned on her heel, and stomped off, sending the floorboards into crisis mode.

I wanted to shroud myself in my covers to escape from my mother's constant criticism, but that wasn't possible. Instead, I gulped down my ugly laughter and said nothing. My mum wasn't a total ogre; she behaved this way for a reason. I needed to remember that, but sometimes I struggled. Sometimes I looked at her and saw someone I didn't recognise or like.

A jangled sense of irritation arose in me. A heady hormone mix surged through me, creating a hot cauldron of suppressed, choked down words and emotions. A regurgitation of sorrow threatened to spill from my guts. I longed to restore my family's former happiness. To cure the curse that seemed to swallow our family whole. *But how could I?* I rubbed my eyes and stretched, wondering if the answer would come if only I could unlock past events. Now, I had to seize the opportunity to investigate the Crystal Cottage.

PUZZLE PIECE 11:

THE TEASING DREAM

A teasing dream, dreams,
You can't forget its message,
It tickles you so,
You wake up longing for bright,
Magical crystal delight.

The evening descended, and darkness filled my room. I couldn't sleep. I tossed and turned, but the stagnant, dead air in the house tightened around my neck choking me. I slipped out of bed and opened a window. It made no difference. Feeling anxious, I noticed a deep sensation of dread forcing its way into my soul.

I often heard strange grumbling voices and laboured breathing coming from the walls of our silent house, speaking in unison, 'Cursed house, dreadful misfortune.' Tonight, no difference awaited me. Those weird sounds seemed to reverberate from the cramped attic room at the top of the house, right down to the ground floor. The hexagonal hallway grumbled as I heard six whispered voices that unified into one loud, persistent groan that amplified, filling the hall with the same repeated words.

I wrestled with alternating tiredness and wakefulness, pushing the sounds away; I fell into a deep sleep. I dreamed. A vision formed and I could see the pathway ahead lay deserted, not a soul in sight. The dead of night beckoned, and an eerie silence magnified every rustle and quadrupled every whisper in the breeze. The gentle sound of trickling water soothed my disturbed senses, but I couldn't find the source. I fought a strange feeling that someone followed me. Yet, when I glanced over my shoulder, no one seemed to be there. No footprints, no churned-up earth, nothing. I walked faster, but my steps lagged, like a clock pendulum moving back and forth on a predetermined journey, yet moving in slow motion.

As my dream continued, the whispering winds grew louder. I forced myself to turn around and confront my growing fear. I saw the shadow of a man, and he was following me. Disconcerted, I tried to run and stumbled as if this shadowy man's long limbs were reaching forward to trip me up. Just when I couldn't take another step, the winds stopped. The shadow revealed itself in a flash of light and vanished. My eyes blinked, captivated by blue-black hair, but I couldn't see his face. I stood transfixed by a bright light followed by an immediate darkness.

With the shadow's departure, the deep-rooted sadness trapped within my soul subsided. The dream seemed so real I felt expansive breaths of liberating air fill my lungs. I walked forward with the image before me that I'd walked this path many times before. I felt the muscles in my face relax; my jaw slackened, and my eyes softened. I lifted my outstretched arms and took slow, deliberate steps.

I sensed a change in the dream when a strange creature appeared. His body and features fused together with rotten flesh, matted mud, skin, and protruding bones. The creature did not speak. His silent presence terrified me, and I shivered.

The beast stood motionless and pointed a bony finger at the ground. Fear clenched at my heart. A flood of messages bombarded my brain. Warning signals went off, suggesting a multitude of horrible intentions that the creature may have had in store for me.

A tremor shook my body, and my teeth chattered. My ears rang with the sound of the earth cracking below my feet. It meant that I had left it too late to run. My eyes fell downwards as the world tilted on its axis, and the realisation came to me that the only way out was via a slide that suddenly appeared at my feet.

With one glance, I could tell the slide had a definite beginning but no visible end. I placed a tentative step onto the slide. The minute I touched it, I knew there was no time for fear. I swallowed hard and plunged into the darkness, sliding into oblivion. Every emotion I possessed had compressed into mere seconds—a momentary adrenalin rush. Sensations continued like the aftermath of the wildest rollercoaster ride. Fuelled by fear, it sent my senses reeling, the ultimate blood-pounding, stomach-churning thrill.

I slipped down the slide and landed on a stone floor, yet it cushioned my landing like a silky feather down quilt. No longer afraid of the shadows, I felt welcomed, at home. With wide-eyed astonishment, I took in the magnificent interior of the Crystal Cottage. Gems in a myriad of welcoming shades—purple Amethyst, white Quartz, red Jade, blue Topaz—covered the walls. A riot of colours reflected in the facets of the crystals, which welcomed me with their brightness. This magnificent display promised more, luminous lights twinkled and burst forth from each separate gem in a firework-like extravaganza. I gasped. My breath caught in my throat, and I glanced down at my hands. They were sparkling as if they had touched an enormous glitter ball. A crystalline light bounced off the walls of the cottage, finding a resting place on my face. The brilliant light caressed me.

My heart filled with wonder at this miraculous event and I wished the exquisiteness of the moment would last forever. I willed this spectacle to carry on and on, but the glowing display tapered off. The colours became darker, and glimmers of the crystals' bright lights darkened to a menacing black, then lightened to a grey, washed-out colour before turning a muddy brown.

In horror, I could feel the skin on my face puckering like an orange peel stripped of all moisture. My body shivered, and I shook. I stirred in my sleep, suspended in the haze of the dream. I struggled to remain, not wanting to leave the beauty and comfort of the Crystal Cottage. So I remained, floating in the abyss, fearful but longing to find out more.

In my dreamy state, I lifted my head and looked up. All I could see was the strange creature a short distance above me, standing as if he waited, but for what I could not tell. He held a ladder—two long ropes connected by short crosspieces made of skin and bones—which he dangled down. I grimaced, but with no other choice open, I reached out and latched onto the gruesome ladder device. The creature hoisted me out, and we stood side by side, motionless for a second. We exchanged no words. Once again, I felt the ground beneath my feet shudder and crack wide open into a large gash of exploding brown earth. I stepped back, afraid of the black void looming in front of me. I shrieked as I observed the creature as he plummeted into the depths of the earth, the whole time reaching his arms out towards me as he fell.

The image of the cottage grew distant, swallowed in its entirety; each stone, pillar, and column disappeared from sight. It continued to spiral until it became a tiny speck of inconsequential dust. An unnatural silence descended around me. A great rumbling shook the earth, and the mound of unsettled earth closed shut. The creature and the cottage had disappeared. No signs remained that they had ever been there.

My heart fluttered like a caged bird. A brooding sense of dark-ness enveloped me, and a curtain of melancholy fell over me. My body shifted as I stirred. I opened my heavy eyes. The dream had ended, and reality clawed its way in.

I lifted my heavy head, punched my pillows, and sat up. It had felt so real. The cottage had been within my grasp, but now it had gone. My disappointment was tangible. I'd had a glimpse of the magic within the cottage, but now that wonder had vanished. I couldn't believe this strange episode had presented a reality so cruel, a dream that had teased me with its beauty but had shattered me with its truth. I shrunk down into my twisted sheets, sobbing, resuming my daily existence, a living nightmare with no escape.

PUZZLE PIECE 12:

ESME TALKS TO ME

Think you know someone,
No, you don't know anyone,
We're all cheerleaders,
Carrying our false pompoms,
The mirror captures our truth.

After the strange dream, I felt drained and at a total loss as to what I should do next. I slipped out of bed and observed myself in the mirror. Purple shadows lined the skin beneath my eyes. My disturbed sleep had made my face appear old, like Mum.

Esme edged forward in the mirror. She frowned. 'You look awful, Amelina.'

'Thanks, Esme.' I rubbed my eyes.

'Sorry, but you do. Are you okay?'

'Nope. I had a nightmare. I met a strange, creepy creature who scared me to death. I don't know how for sure, but that thing helped me reach the cottage.'

'Oh, now you are having nightmares too. Poor you! Tell me

more.' Esme peered through the glass, standing up on tiptoes. Her eyes gleamed with a morbid curiosity as if we were chatting about some sinister TV drama.

I didn't want to talk about it. So, instead, I played it down, saying, 'As you know, the Crystal Cottage invited me to visit.'

'You must go,' said Esme, stretching to her full height to give weight to her words. 'It's a sign—dreams often are.'

'Maybe. I dreamt I had set foot within the cottage, but it was just a dream, and I still haven't found it in real life. I so badly want to escape, though. This house imprisons everyone, not just you, Esme.'

'Yes, I know, but it's worse being inside this glass, *believe me.*' Esme pointed at herself, and I watched as her face fell, inch by inch, a chilling avalanche of sadness.

'Yeah, it must be,' I said, feeling guilty.

'That's okay. It sucks for us all. I'm locked in a mirror, and you're locked in a time you don't want to be in.'

'What?'

'You hate your present and want to be part of your past once again.'

'That's true,' I replied, observing her curiously. I mulled over the fact that this Esme was much deeper than the girl I remembered. I realised that glass imprisoned her and her thoughts too.

I turned from the mirror. It was time to get organised, but I didn't feel like moving. My coat, bag, and school uniform lay dumped in a confused heap on the floor. A trail of several days' rubbish extended across my room in a chaotic but familiar pattern. My mum would be cross if I didn't tidy up, but I had more important things to do—like sleeping. I yawned and stretched, not willing to face the day ahead.

I'd made my decision, and back to bed I crawled, shrouding myself in sleepiness. I willed the covers to hide me for a few hours more before Mum would discover me and yank me out of my warm bed. Shadow joined me, purring his approval of my decision.

No such luck today, though. I heard Mum's footsteps as she entered my room. I sighed. She didn't even bother to knock. Typical. Shadow raised his head, his whiskers twitching their disapproval at her untimely arrival.

'Amelina, your bedroom's a full-scale health hazard in here.'

I glanced up and caught sight of Esme smirking at me from the mirror. I wanted to give her an almighty smack. 'I'll tidy up, Mum.' I gave her my word as I stood glaring at Esme.

'You sound like an actress delivering a well-rehearsed script, and who are you glaring at young lady? It better not be me!'

'Of course not...'

'You better tidy up. But before you do, I have something to say. What's this I hear about you going down the river pathway? How could you?'

I glowered at my mother, my face challenging and unrepentant. It irritated me that she always had such an uncanny knack for discovering what I'd been up to.

'How did you find out, Mum? Spies?' I challenged her to respond and propped myself up by placing a supportive hand next to my pillow. Out of the corner of my eye I could see Esme press her nose against the glass, desperate to hear more. Shadow swished his tail in annoyance and did a quick exit. The tension in the room had driven him away.

Mum exploded with irritation. 'Don't be ridiculous. What were you doing down there? You know it's unsafe.' Mum's face tightened with an unguarded fear that caught me by surprise.

'Don't get all panicky, Mum.' I shifted in bed to watch her from a better angle.

'I'm not.' Mum's voice rose shrilly, and she fidgeted, picking fuzz from her trousers.

'Why don't you want me to go there?' I punched the stuffing of my pillow with a fist.

'I can't and I won't say.' She dug her heels in, scarring my wooden floor to make a point.

My teeth ached with tension. I wished Mum would stop making such unfounded statements. 'In other words, it's nothing, and you're just afraid I'll run into stupid delinquent boys,' I retorted.

Mum spun to face me and placed her hands on her hips. 'What do you mean, did something happen when you went there?'

'No,' I lied, my voice rising in anger. I might as well have shouted "yes" from the rooftops. A convincing liar I was not. I knew what had happened. Ryder had happened. I feared if I wasn't careful, Mum might drag the truth out of me. From my vantage point on the bed, I watched as Esme's expression changed. A dark shadow crossed her face. It disappeared almost as soon as it had appeared. I couldn't help but think that amounted to an odd reaction for my mirror friend to make.

My mother glared at me in exasperation. 'Get up, Amelina. You can't achieve anything by lingering in bed and staring at yourself in that wretched mirror all day.'

Esme recovered from her momentary shadow, and she pulled a face and giggled. I nearly responded but stopped myself. I didn't want any hassle, and Esme's predicament had to be the last thing Mum needed to know about.

Mum glanced at her watch, frowned, and disappeared down the stairs. This was the normal time for her to get ready for work. I sat up and swung my legs over the side of the bed. Mum's departure did nothing to lift my deep sense of frustration.

I felt like screaming; Esme was in for it. But I had to get out of bed before I could tackle her, and that meant a supreme effort. As soon as my tired limbs were vertical, I grabbed my dressing gown, adopting it like body armour, as if I intended to battle with the philosophising mirror girl. I advanced towards her. She stepped back, but she had nowhere to go, nowhere to hide. At that moment, I knew for sure she existed. She wasn't just some delusional figment of my unhinged imagination.

Esme adopted a shamefaced expression. 'Talk to me, Amelina, it's so lonely trapped in the mirror, please don't desert me.'

'Hmmm, after that show you put on for my mother, you want *me* to talk to *you*? You've got nerve. I have better things to do.' I turned my back on her dejected image. Esme collapsed. She slid down the edge of the mirror and hung her head in misery. The realisation that Esme sat trapped within the mirror's glass, day after day, unable to escape, hit me hard. What had she done to deserve it?

Esme's dejection worked. 'Shit, sorry. I know it must be terrible trapped in that mirror day after day, unable to do anything, go anywhere or have any fun.'

Esme perked up at my comments and placed her face against the glass. 'It's beyond terrible. No parties for me or any boyfriends to chase after. It's enough to make a girl cut herself, but I have no knife to do it, no sharp object to smash this glass.'

Esme backed up and made repeated cutting motions on her arm, which scared the hell out of me. The expression on her face terrified me. My voice rose in alarm. 'Stop it, Esme. Don't say or do that. It's horrible and disgusting.'

Esme jerked her head up and spoke with sadness. 'Sometimes that's how I feel. It's like I want to mark my skin with sharp lines to let people see the pain I feel.'

I shuddered at the thought of ever wanting to hurt myself. 'Did you cut yourself before? You know, before you were locked in the mirror?'

'Well, yeah. Duh, of course I did. Everyone thought I was "Perfect Esme," but I wasn't. I'm Esme, the girl who cuts herself,' she said as she hung her head in shame.

'No, you're not. That's not true. You're Esme. Everyone wants to be like you. You're the most popular girl going.' I paused for a moment, unable to make sense of it all. Then as gently as I could, I asked the question lingering on my lips. 'What made you cut yourself?'

Esme stopped and thought for a moment before she replied. 'It released the pain, and it bled out. Now I can't do it, and everything's so much worse than it had ever been before.' Her attractive face stared back at me, and she hung back amongst the shadows of the mirror. Her blue eyes brimmed with tears and her hair drooped around her shoulders, creating an aura of sadness.

'Esme, I'm so sorry, I never realised.'

'Yeah well, you know now.'

'I do. We can talk anytime you want, Esme, I mean it. Really, I do.'

'Thanks, Amelina, that means a lot.' Esme's face brightened with a look of hope.

'Anytime you want to hang out, just let me know.' I paused for a moment, letting her confession sink in. What a shocker. But I knew what I wanted to ask next. 'How did you end up locked in the glass?'

Esme shook her head and gazed at me. 'I cut myself deep, so deep I could feel my life bleeding away. I accepted the offer of a chance to live, if you can call it living. In exchange, I promised to keep a terrible secret. Now I'm bound to this mirror for all eternity unless someone can break the curse,' said Esme, tears flowing from her pretty blue eyes down her face.

My hand flew up to my throat. I had to know more. 'Who cursed you?'

'Whoa. That's a secret I can't share. But believe me when I say trust no one.'

'Trust no one?' I brushed my hair away from my face, uncomfortable with Esme's answers. 'That's terrible. If I couldn't trust anyone, I'd be lonely.'

'That's me,' Esme said, pointing to herself. 'I long to free myself and you, too, but you *have to listen, Amelina.* You're in danger.' The word 'danger' clung to her lips as she released the words in one tense, heartfelt moment.

'Danger?"

'That's what I said. Danger.' Esme glared at me from the other side of the mirror.

I scratched my head, perplexed at her suggestion. 'From what?'

'I can't say.'

'Oh, right, you're no help at all. There's no way you can protect me. You can't even jump out of the glass if I need you. And you can't even tell me what's going on,' I said, shaking my head in exasperation.

'I can't. Don't you understand? Didn't you listen? I'm stuck here. A prisoner, forever.'

Esme's tears fell again, and they reminded me of tiny, captured raindrops on the mirror's glass. She paused for a moment to think and then placed her fingertips on the glass. She stared at me with an urgency written on her face. 'Don't go out today, Amelina. Keep me company. A storm's coming, I can feel it.'

I felt a shiver of apprehension run up my spine. 'What's that? A weird Esme prediction? Why are you talking like that?'

'If you'd poked around in this mirror for the time I have, you'd sound like me too! It does strange things to you.'

I nodded. What more could I say? The threat of danger Esme spoke of sounded real. Poor Esme, how wrong I'd been about her. I couldn't believe what she'd just told me. What a confession! Esme, the girl everyone longed to emulate, cut herself. That had to be the strangest, saddest news I'd ever heard.

PUZZLE PIECE 13:

ESME'S REFLECTION

Some siblings can't help,
Escape the prison they're in
What do siblings do?
Whether they are real or not,
They're always there for you.

E sme had the habit of talking to her imaginary friend, her
perfect reflection—Sunflower Esme. She did this whenever
her emotions threatened to crumble. Today, I caught her doing it,
and without meaning to, I slipped into eavesdropping mode again. I
lay on my bed, pretending to sleep, listening to her discussion with
her own reflection.

Esme stared at her reflection shining back at her from the other
side of the glass. 'You're cruel. Stop it. Stop showing me my cuts.'

'No!' her reflection screamed.

'Why did you have to show me that? My healed cuts peeling
open, bleeding like I've just cut myself.' I watched as Esme covered

her eyes with her hands, trying to obliterate the sight of her cuts. I could see the horror in the wide-eyed shock of Esme's reflection.

Her distressed reflection shrieked another question, mimicking her voice. 'Why did you do it?'

'No one understands!' Esme wailed, addressing her reflection. 'I cut to bleed my emotions out. I'm not doing it because I want attention. People say that, but it's untrue.'

Her reflection replied by shrugging her shoulders as if she didn't get it. 'I couldn't understand why anyone would cut.'

Esme tried to explain, the tension showing in the lines around her mouth. 'I can't control my emotions. It's the only way I can release my pent-up feelings. I have to release them somehow. For a moment, I feel like I'm in charge. Can't you understand? It's me deciding—how to cut, where to cut, how deep to go. I know it's wrong, but I can't stop doing it. It's my addiction. Everyone hates me, but they pretend to love me. Who could blame me for this one failure?'

Esme's reflection cried, but Esme ignored her. She carried on, and I almost wished she could take back her words so I could reverse what I had just seen and heard. I remained silent, listening to Esme's painful words as she continued speaking.

'I might have been the most popular girl in school, but my skin yelled no. It itched to tell me that I was the worst. Everyone thought I could do it all, the dancing, acting, singing, sports, and academic stuff. I swear they'd expect me to be the school circus act, you know, the best juggler if it came to it. I had the fittest boyfriend, the perfect family. But it was all lies. I was a lie. I couldn't hack it. I take that back. I don't want to sensationalise this. I want no one to suffer like me. Please listen. I can't bear anyone to suffer, to torment themselves like I've done.'

By now her reflection had collapsed into a sobbing fit. I blinked back a tear, fighting the overwhelming urge to cry too. Yet Esme's words continued.

'This familiar black place has no exit door. I slide down an imaginary cliff face, and when I reach the bottom I gasp for air, my heart hammering in my chest. My frequent palpitations of anxiety drown me in sorrow.'

Esme clutched at her heart in a dramatic fashion. I peeked through half-closed eyes, and I could see the message written in her reflection's beseeching eyes; they were imploring her to push through, to fight.

Through a veil of black words, Esme continued. 'I couldn't cope with the pressure, and the hidden hatred everyone had for me. Who wants to be friends with the girl that can do everything? Nobody.' Esme seemed to rally and stood taller as she continued her diatribe at her reflection in the mirror. 'They pretended to like me. The depression didn't just go for my brain; it bit me in the throat. Dark thoughts reached the redness of my heart. Soon everything turned black, everything except my blood.' Her reflection's eyes glowed with the intensity of hot coals. Esme paused for a moment, sucked in a deep breath, and then said, 'We all need to be loved; we all need to be saved.'

Her reflection nodded, so overcome with emotion that was all she seemed able to do. 'I'm stuck with you, imperfect sunflower girl,' she sobbed. Moments passed and turned into an eternity. Esme said nothing. I couldn't help wondering if perhaps she didn't have the strength to say another word. However, her reflection continued to fight, with eyes burning like two tornados of whirling pain, willing Esme to be strong.

Esme swallowed her sobs, gaining the confidence to say one last thing. 'This bloody mirror's a prison to you, and me, reflection. I can't cut anymore. I can't do anything. I can't feel the wind on my face, smell flowers, skinny dip, snog a boy, or lick an ice-cream. I can't even bite my nails; every time I try, the mirror engulfs my fingers with a slippery glass fluid restricting my movement. The mirror's in charge and I've lost control. This is the worse punish- ment ever. All I have is Amelina, and she's my only hope to save me.'

Her reflection nodded in agreement, finally understanding the full degree of Esme's horror. I said a silent promise to myself that somehow I would find a way to save her. Then I heard the words burst from Esme's mouth that I would never forget.

'If Amelina saves me, I swear I'll never cut again.'

Esme's sad reflection whispered two barely audible words: 'Me too.'

PUZZLE PIECE 14:

THE QUARTZ CRYSTAL

Tell me what to do,
I will do the opposite,
I'm stubborn you say,
It's my least endearing side,
I strongly must disagree.

I realised I had two options: I could admit to Esme that I had overheard her shocking conversation with her reflection and try to help her, or I could pretend I hadn't heard her words. My decision was easy, and I chose the latter. I did not understand what a dreadful mistake it would be. Until you see the scars, you can't appreciate just how terrible and distressing it is. But I'd failed her, I had zoned out. Sometimes when your own life is in such turmoil, it's easier to pretend a friend's suffering isn't happening because you don't have the energy to focus on someone else's mess. I couldn't cope with her problems and mine too.

Somehow my silence drew a wedge between us. As this awkwardness grew, the atmosphere in the house drifted from awful to abysmal.

In the meantime, Esme's prediction about the storm turned out to be right. The sudden change in the weather echoed my downcast mood, and the clouds shifted across the sky, threatening a downpour.

The ceiling above me pushed down and squeezed out the air as the oppressive weather boxed me into a tiny space with pockets of humid, breathless air. I longed to escape, to run away from my pathetic failings, even if it meant risking the storm and the potential wrath of Esme's warning. I felt imprisoned in a stifling glass house. Claustrophobia gripped me. My palms became clammy, and my heart rattled against my ribcage.

I ran down the stairs, eager to open the front door and escape. A gale blew in, pushing me towards the wall. I pushed against it, forcing it to retreat. I closed the door as the wind spewed leaves, twigs, mud, and debris into the breeze, hurling them around me without mercy. I pulled my coat tighter and pressed on.

The force of the wind filled my lungs with sweet, liberating breaths of much-needed freedom. I danced a merry jig, which uplifted my downcast mood. I ignored Esme's words of warning: 'Don't go out today. A storm's coming, and change with it.' I listened to the dance of my heart. It won. I risked it.

I followed the pathway that I knew led to where I had last seen the Crystal Cottage. Buffeted like a kite on gusts of wind, I continued, but the strength of the storm didn't carry me to the cottage, as I'd hoped. There was no sign of it anywhere.

Amidst the wailing winds, I detected a footstep, a clue. Once again, these footsteps were following me. I guessed the cottage teased me, playing hide and seek, and those footsteps were part of the game. I peered around at my surroundings, trying to figure out what to do next. The steps stopped and went silent. The winds of change bellowed and, with one final gust, died down.

Dismayed by this unfortunate turn of events, I sighed and turned back. As I walked into the house, I caught a glimpse of myself in the hallway mirror. I looked a fright. Esme shook her head at me to say, I told you so. Rushing upstairs to the bathroom, I picked up my brush to untangle the mess of my unruly hair. The knots refused to budge as if they tangled on their own each time I ran the brush through the strands.

Esme laughed. 'Oh, my God! What a state you're in, Amelina! Ha, Ha! It serves you right. I told you a storm's on its way. You're lucky that nothing bad happened while you were out. Your mum's going to have a fit if she sees you.'

For a moment, I forgot all about Esme's problems. All I could think about was this growing frustration at not being able to find the cottage. I regretted when I had told her to get lost. To make matters worse, I followed it with these hurtful words, 'I swear that being stuck in that mirror has liquefied your cheerleading brain. Stop following me all around the house, or I won't talk to you anymore.' Immediately, I hated that I had spoken to Esme like that and wished I could gulp back my thoughtlessness.

I was about to say sorry when she said, 'Knock it off, Amelina. Stop being such a bitch and stop twiddling with your hair! It might be a pretty blonde colour, but it's only *hair*! Can't you see that I'm lonely? Don't you care? You're my only friend. Can't you at least try to imagine what it's like to have only one friend that doesn't want to talk to you?'

'I'm sorry, Esme, I …' Esme glowered at me. She shone an unflattering light on my face, which shadowed my reflection in the glass.

Her face crumpled, and she continued to vent. 'I can't follow you anywhere, Amelina. I'm trapped. You should know not to speak to me like that. It's cruel.' A single tear escaped from Esme's eye and landed in the palm of my hand, leaving behind a shimmering quartz crystal.

I stared at the gem in astonishment. The quartz crystal came to life and vibrated in my hand. The unmistakable hum encouraged thoughts to swirl in my head. *This proves that Esme is linked to the Cottage. Somehow, she has to be, but how?*

'Esme, you just cried a fricking crystal!'

Esme forgot all about her anger. She stared at the gem in my hand with wide-eyed astonishment. 'What the heck? That's spectacular. How on earth did I do that? I wish you could give it back to me, Amelina.'

'Me too.'

'I wonder what it means?' she said, wrinkling her nose while a perplexed frown creased her forehead.

'I don't know, Esme. But it appears that when you get upset, you produce crystal tears.'

I scowled a guilty frown, remembering my recent unkindness. 'I'm sorry about being so mean. I shouldn't have said what I just did; it sucks. I'm so stressed. Nothing makes sense. It feels like I live in a glass house of unhappiness,' I said, wishing I could reshuffle all my selfishness and rearrange it somehow.

'Me too,' replied Esme sadly.

We weren't biological sisters, but we shared a sisterly condition, and that said it all. I tried to cheer Esme up by sticking my tongue out at her sad face, wiggling it around. The house answered us and echoed with trapped laughter. Esme laughed a hollow laugh. I wanted to hug her, but I couldn't, so I offered her a reassuring grin instead.

PUZZLE PIECE 15:

THE PAINTING - THE CREATURE

Sometimes it happens,
That art and life intertwine,
Together in time,
The result a dead creature,
Dead, earthy, not of this earth.

I put the quartz crystal, which had been one of Esme's tears, away in my camphor-wood chest. That mystery would have to wait. While the chest remained open, I rummaged around searching for my art equipment. I felt guilty abandoning Esme to her solitary prison, but I had to finish my most recent painting.

Grabbing the paint set, I descended the stairs and entered the kitchen. I set out the pots of various colours and placed the paint-brushes on the kitchen table.

I opened my art book to survey the page where my teacher had written a comment on a post-it-note, '*Great atmosphere, maybe you could add people to the painting.*'

I paused, wondering whether to chance using the gift of my

aunt's paints again. Eventually, my curiosity got the better of me. Mum's advice could stew. I grabbed the first brush, and as before, an unusual sensation transmitted from the brush to each of my fingers. This time the sensation felt stronger, and my hands shook as the room spun around in a woozy circle. I experienced uncontrollable dizziness that threatened to overwhelm me. Regretting my decision to use the paints again, I tried to pry the brush from my right hand. My panic level arose when I couldn't get the brush to budge. *Now what?*

The paintbrushes were silent and so involved in creating they didn't have the energy to talk. My hand moved of its own accord. Breathing deeply, I calmed down a little. The brush continued to make progress. Before I knew it, the black splodges of paint I'd painted during my last session had moved together to form a dark, ominous creature dominating the centre of my painting. I couldn't believe my eyes. It was the creature from my dream. The face scowled at me, and I noticed a suggested movement as if the creature contemplated leaping out of the canvas in my direction at any moment.

This terrifying being deserved the term: hideous. No other word would do it justice. Lumps of earth were matted around its skull, convincing me that it wore dreadlocks. Worms fed on the rotting skin that hung from its skeletal frame. Many insects collected in the recesses of the creature's decaying body.

Surprised at the painting's transformation, I knocked over my paint pots in shock. Paint spattered across the kitchen table. My mind raced. I questioned how I could have painted such a revolting thing? *Am I hallucinating?*

Without warning, the floorboards beneath my feet rattled. I tried to throw the paint brush away, but it clung to my hand like extra strength super glue. After several attempts, I succeeded; my fingers released the paint brush. I ran into the lounge in a panic, leaving my art stuff scattered all over the table. This calmed me down a bit, and I slowed my pacing. The thudding of my heart grew so loud I heard it pounding like an overzealous gong in my ears.

With the continuous sound of the beating of my heart, it wasn't long before I heard the house joining in with a chorus of shouts and yells. The rattling floorboards continued moaning out their sorrowful tune.

When the doorbell rang, I sprung up to answer it thinking it could be my dad. Just in time, I remembered what he had always said: 'Make sure you check who's at the door before you open it.'

I turned on my heel and sprinted upstairs to the first-floor landing, where I could observe the transparent window above the doorway. This window allowed an excellent view of the front of the house.

To begin with, I saw nothing. I considered the doorbell ringing must have been kids playing a prank. I was ready to turn away when there followed a flicker of movement. My eyes darted left and right, and I couldn't believe what I saw standing on the doorstep. There in all its glory stood scary dreadlock dude, the creature I'd just painted, the same creature I had met in my dream, standing on my front doorstep like a visitor at Halloween.

A family of rats sat perched on its head, biting at the last remnants of meaty flesh from around its eye sockets. Closing my eyes, I hoped that he was just some wild figment of my imagination. However, when I re-opened them, I saw that my fears were justified. The being resembled a horrible hellish beast transported from a Halloween Underworld Party who had paid me a trick or treat visit! Except, I saw no sweets, instead a bunch of worms and rats were making a mega meal out of him.

I heard distressed sounds coming from the house as it registered this unwelcome visitor at the door. Weird noises echoed from within the walls, and the floorboards creaked like they would crack wide open. The central heating pounded a protest like an agitated heartbeat.

Beneath my feet, Shadow's black fur stood on edge. He hissed and bared his sharp fangs at the sound of the unwelcome visitor at the door. The strange being continued knocking. I freaked out. I feared the door threatened to tumble down. The sound of splintering wood shattering filled my ears. I imagined the creature racing up to get me; the rats tucking into my painted toenails, and the worms feasting on my mascaraed eyes.

Terrified by the mental pictures I had created in my head, I dashed toward my bedroom. Within her captive mirror, Esme stood on tiptoes, wide-eyed and curious at all the commotion. Shadow had vanished into thin air. *Some rat catcher!* I knew one minute he'd been hissing, and now he had gone.

My breathing wheezed in my chest as I squeezed myself as flat as possible to crawl underneath my bed. I remained hidden for ages until finally, my ragged breath slowed, and I forced my body to slip from my refuge. I tiptoed down the hallway. Shadow miraculously reappeared, following me, winding around my ankles. 'Shadow, stop that,' I whispered in a trembling voice, my legs shaking with anxiety. The cat stormed off in an almighty huff, his tail swishing in irritation.

When I reached the window, I peered outside to see if the weird creature still occupied the same position. I noticed that the creepy thing remained poised like a street performer still standing on the step. He stood motionless, not moving an inch. Yet I remained convinced that he was about to do something. I could feel it in my bones.

Sure enough, it reached forward with a bony hand to knock on the door again. An expectant hush continued. The silence hung in the air, sounding abnormal to my ears. The hideous creature's hands moved forward, and parts of his body unravelled as its mouth gaped wide. The creature's fists crumbled into dust before he made contact with the door.

Unable to batter the door anymore, the heinous being bellowed with fury. 'You must open the door, Amelina. Come with me!' Each syllable it uttered sent little parts of its decaying body flying in a multitude of different directions. Its chin jutted forward until piece by piece the creature disintegrated before my eyes, tumbling into a mess of leaves, debris, and mud. The rats fled in terror. The noises ceased. The house sighed, and a deafening silence followed.

I stood silent, unable to take in what I'd just seen and heard. The roof of my mouth felt dry, and my pulse raced. My stress levels had hit the top of the crazy scale. I shook, and my heart rate continued to speed out of control.

I drew in slow, deep breaths, struggling to get back to normality. With trembling limbs, I made my way downstairs to check the damage to the door. There was none. Not a single splinter, not one broken panel, nothing. I glanced over at Esme, expecting her to appear as shocked as I felt, but she seemed unperturbed. She smiled at me, that crazy mirror girl.

'What are you smiling for? Didn't you see that rat-infested thing that looked like a demon? What about its door battering magic trick? Don't tell me you didn't hear or see that.'

Esme shrugged. 'The wood didn't mind. That thing could do no harm.'

'Huh… Are you for real? I can't believe what you said! Who says the wood didn't mind?'

'Me.' Esme stood proudly, a smug grin on her face.

'This is the weirdest conversation. Esme, forget about the fricking wood for a moment; let's talk about that infestation that just dropped by.'

Esme shook her head in defiance. 'You have zero sense. Sometimes scary beings aren't half as scary as you think. Talk to the wood, it'll tell you I'm right.'

My mouth gaped open at this exchange. I flipped my hair over my shoulder in annoyance. 'Geez. Now you're telling me to ask the wood whether that thing's a nice guy!'

'While you're at it you could ask him what he knows about the crystal cottage. I bet he is Mr Knowledgeable. I bet he knows just how magical the cottage is.' Esme didn't have time to elaborate further because Shadow slunk back into view.

'Where've you been, Shadow?' I asked the cat as if expecting an answer. 'You're no use at all. You didn't even protect me from those rats. I need a guard dog, a Rottweiler or something.' Shadow meowed and for once let me pick him up, but this weakness in his armour only lasted a moment. Then he protested and squirmed out of my arms.

For some strange reason, my thoughts returned to Ryder, and I remembered that it seemed like an age since I'd last seen him. So much had happened since our first meeting. It appeared life had crawled by until I met him, and now it speeded up.

I walked into the kitchen and mulled over the happenings of the afternoon. Could the weird creature be conjured up from my art set? Is that even possible? Or could its presence be a punishment for never doing as anyone told me?

Guilt pricked at my heart. My mother had told me not to use the art set again, and to tidy up my room. I had chosen to do neither. With a heavy heart, I picked a few mouldy items up from the kitchen counter and popped them on top of the bulging trash bin.

Nobody would believe me if I told them what had just happened, least of all my mum. She'd insist on taking me to the GP and then moan about it interfering with her busy schedule. I had no choice but to keep the weird creature a secret for now. My only hope was that it wouldn't make a return trip again with all those bugs, rats, and worms in tow. Even if Esme defended him, proclaiming him to be a harmless, wood loving batterer.

PUZZLE PIECE 16:

THE CRYSTAL COTTAGE

Beauty has to hide,
From the shadows to survive,
Light and dark, yin, yang,
Sweet heaven which is hidden,
Deep within the earth itself.

I struggled to understand what the weird creature had meant by saying, 'Come with me.' He'd risen out of the earth to ask me to follow him, but why? After painting the creature, I felt compelled once again to find the Crystal Cottage, even though the desire to do so now mixed with anxiety at what I might find. I reasoned that the answers to all these strange happenings lay hidden within the cottage's walls. There was no other answer. Even though I didn't know where to look, I sensed that perhaps now would be the time to find out.

I slipped out of my house and followed the deserted pathway to the trail I had taken before. It appeared eerily quiet, and not a soul was about. With each step I took, I had a mounting sense of unease and fear. I glanced at the view to the right towards the train tracks and saw nothing to reassure me. The patch of land stretched into the weary landscape. I noticed abandoned and distressed old buildings which seemed to cling to the ground with broken, jagged windows pierced and pointed, peering outward on the world. Nearby in a field, agricultural vehicles lay silent in their death throes. The sad and lonely atmosphere whispered a fearful disquiet in its breathless warning.

The pathway to the left unfolded before me like a delicious puzzle, full of mystery and hope. I admired a large grassy field; a light and breezy place where horses roamed and lingered near well-kept fences as if waiting for a chance visitor to pass.

My supercharged hearing detected the silent whispers in the breeze, which echoed as did the sound of trickling water, and the vibrations of the earth below my feet. The sounds propelled me forward down the road. In no time, I had stumbled upon the same spot where I'd discovered the cottage of my dream. I shrieked in excitement, shocked when the sound echoed, forcing its way beyond the tranquil horses to the far reaches of the empty field.

A series of moss-covered steps led below the ground to a gaping hole. The cracks and loosened stones surrounding the hole resembled a brain teaser, almost like a challenge, waiting for me to solve the mystery. Curious, I stared into the inky darkness. The silence held me enrapt in a motionless grip. I hesitated, not sure what to do next. Until the earth beneath my feet moved a fraction of a centimetre. I heard a loud cracking noise and jumped in fright.

The sound reverberated, and a large zigzag crack formed in front of the steps. Startled, I moved away from the edge of the steps, fearful of falling in. In a brilliant flash, the cottage appeared before my eyes. My first thought was that it resembled a treasure entombed, rising out of the earth, shaking off its muddy cloak of slumber with a high-pitched wailing sound reminiscent of a banshee who'd just been awakened from an endless sleep.

My mouth gaped open in surprise. I had waited so long, and here it finally was. I couldn't contain my excitement, and my hands shook in anticipation of my visit. I breathed in, saturating my lungs until they felt they were about to burst with the deliciousness of this moment. I pondered the realisation that since it revealed itself to me; I sensed that the cottage had made me wait. But why?

I shook off my questions and marvelled instead at the beauty of the quaint old cottage. It had a gated door leading into the garden where many varieties of roses and a fragrant patch of herbs grew. The smells were heavenly. In the front, I spotted a large courtyard filled with bird tables and bird feeders hanging from the trees. Breathless at the beauty, I stood, marvelling in the sights.

I revelled in the sight before me. The cottage sported a round, arched front door. The tiny, shuttered windows and door were a pastel green colour which blended into the landscape, and the stone cottage's brilliant white exterior colour gleamed. An ornate plaque with angels clustering around the edges like a halo hung next to the door frame. To the right of the door hung another plaque, engraved with gold lettering displaying the name: Crystal Cottage.

I swung round when I heard a sound. The doorstep mat lifted from the ground and spun towards me like a magic carpet. When it reached my side, its coarse bristles formed a mouth that spoke. 'Open your eyes and you will see.'

I couldn't believe what I saw. This whole extraordinary experience had me brimming with excitement. I reached out to touch the mat, but it frowned. 'No touching!' it said, stiffening. Seeing my confused expression, its bristles softened. 'Come in! Come in!' it urged.

I blinked. I struggled to comprehend that I had arrived at the Crystal Cottage of my dreams. I followed the mat's advice and stepped through the door. Everywhere I looked, a reward of beauty met my eyes. Light reflected off the surfaces of the many crystals and bounced around the room in a kaleidoscope of colour. A myriad of gemstones twinkled at me, winking in a musical symphony of colour, brightness, and warmth. The walls of the cottage twinkled with crystal faceted gems. Their names leaped out at me in quick succession. There were Amethysts, Black Obsidian, Bloodstone, Merlinite, Red Jade, and Honey Calcite, to name a few.

Skylights in the ceiling let in rays of sunlight that reflected on the crystals, creating a dazzling display.

The remarkable sight made me feel like crying. I turned in circles, delighted with the sights and sounds. The deceptively large inside of the cottage hid an array of bird cages, housing doves who were bathing in cups filled with rose water. I peered further into the cottage and locked eyes with the owner. She appeared as a delicate, almost bird-like wisp of a person I wouldn't have noticed if it hadn't been for her colourful streaked hair. She stood amongst the bird cages, whispering to the doves in a gentle, chirpy sing-song voice.

The tiny woman caught my eye and smiled. 'I am Leanne, the owner of this dear cottage. Welcome, Amelina. It's so wonderful to meet you at last! You have been a welcome visitor in my dreams.' The woman bowed, and smiled wider, adding, 'No longer a stranger, for here you are before me.'

'Thank you, Leanne. It's wonderful to be here at last. I struggled to imagine that I would ever find the cottage. Now I'm here, I have so many questions I want to ask you...' I stopped talking when Leanne raised her hand to silence me.

'Before you say another word, show me the crystal you carry.' Leanne reached forward with cupped hands.

I didn't know how she knew my name or how she knew I carried Esme's tear, which had turned into a Quartz crystal, but she did. Not sure what to think, I wished I could read her mind before I handed the crystal to her. Filled with curiosity, I popped the gem into her waiting hands.

'Ah, a Quartz crystal, and a powerful one at that, often used in time devices,' she said, lifting it up to the light while staring at her multifaceted reflection that mirrored her face in a facet of the gem.

'In time devices?' I swallowed hard, wondering what she meant.

'Yes, well. I think I might know where you found it, but humour me. Tell me anyway,' Leanne said with a chuckle as her multi-coloured greying hair floated around her shoulders like a mantle.

I hesitated before answering and chose my words carefully. 'This sounds crazy, but a girl from my school called Esme spends her days trapped within the mirrors of my house. She appears to be a prisoner and can't get out. One day we argued and when she cried, this Quartz gem formed from her tears. It sprang from the interior of the mirror and ended up in the palm of my hand, like magic.'

Leanne nodded her head, and a smile lit up her face. 'Nothing is crazy. Everything is possible. How delightful. Now, do not despair, Amelina. It is a sign that your friend is no ordinary girl, and in time you will free her.'

'No ordinary girl?' I scratched my head in disbelief.

'That's right. To produce such a specimen is extraordinary. It suggests that perhaps Esme is a Quartz Krystallos. She is a child out of kilter with the present; her time should have been in the past. This will cause her grave problems, and anxieties living in present day Britain. But that's enough to focus on today. Now is not the time to discuss Esme's freedom or her status as a Krystallos. There is much to do.' Leanne turned and walked back toward the bird cages.

'But… you must help me. I need to free Esme. She…'

Leanne spun around and said, '*No*, we must not discuss this any further, Amelina. It is a delicate matter…'

'But my dad…' I let my voice trail off. I didn't know what to do, so I stood facing Leanne, waiting to hear what would come next.

'Again, revelations will come in time. Be patient, dear Amelina. The crystals will help you reach your goals: happiness for your father and freedom for Esme.' Leanne smiled, and confidence filled her face as she straightened her tiny body and stood taller.

'My darling beauties wish to join you on your journey. It will please *them* if you choose a crystal,' said Leanne, gesturing to the spectacular array of gems that blazed in intensity from the walls of the cottage.

'*Them?*' I gazed at the stones, wondering if she meant the crystals themselves.

Leanne grinned and pointed at the crystals. 'The defenders of this dear cottage, oh powerful one.'

I had never considered myself to have powers before. The tiny lady's eccentric demeanour and her gushing words suggested that she was a tad loopy. Yet, I took comfort from her words about Esme and my dad. They sounded truthful, even if that freedom and happiness she promised lay buried for now. Besides, I longed to find out more about the crystals and the defenders, whatever that meant. If Leanne could help me, then I would be more than happy to fulfill her request and select a crystal.

'There are so many delightful ones. How do I decide which one to choose?' I turned in a circle, trying to take in the dazzling gems as they spun before me.

'Many of the stones have healing properties, but you must follow your instinct and find one you know is right for you. The defenders of the Cottage will guide you.'

Again, I wanted to ask about the defenders of the cottage but left the words unsaid, and they remained stuck in my throat. A jumble of incoherent sentences tumbled around in my thoughts.

Unsure of how to proceed, I followed Leanne's advice, running my fingers up and down the crystal wall, caressing the gems. I felt a warmth generating from the crystals as my hand brushed over them. I stifled a giggle when they tickled my fingertips. Eventually, a crystal responded to my touch by easing itself from the wall to find a new home in my palm.

Mesmerised by the experience, I realised that above all else, the feeling of the stone on the wall had guided me to choose it. I sensed that the gem belonged; it spoke silent words of encouragement as if it claimed me. I relished the feeling of power that emanated from the crystal as it radiated a warming light that caressed my skin, hugging me like a dear old friend.

'Wonderful choice, my dear. The Red Jade is a lucky crystal. It is the most passionate and stimulating of the Jade stones. It will urge you to go beyond your comfort zone, to be courageous.' Leanne beamed a bright smile and stared deep into my eyes as if she would find an answer to some unanswered question there. With an abundance of confidence in her voice, she continued. 'There are those amongst us, corrupt souls who will try to follow you into the cottage. So, you must take care. The cottage will rise up to greet you, but you must not encourage others to enter, or terrible things might befall them, so beware.' With those words of warning ringing in my ears,

Leanne turned back to tending her birds, dismissing me without a goodbye.

I knew this was my cue to depart, so I moved toward the door. Placing a foot outside, I felt the beginnings of an earth tremor beneath my feet. I jumped as far as I could, dreading that I might fall to my death in the crack that appeared. There was no way I could have leapt so far, and yet somehow, I had. The magic that bound me to the cottage lifted me high in the air and ensured my safety. In a blink of my eye, the cottage drew back, claimed by the depths far below. Nothing remained of the old ramshackle building apart from a few loose pebbles scattered on the ground where the cottage had stood only moments before.

————

With an unpleasant jolt, I made my way back to reality. I walked home, not sure if the whole experience had happened. I staggered back into my house and made my way upstairs. Back in my bedroom, I shut my door and trembled from a sense of loss and sadness. Compared to this reality, the blissful cottage seemed far away.

Esme smiled a welcome from the mirror, flashing a wry smile. I heard the heavy tread of my mother's footsteps downstairs, signalling her arrival. A profound sense of disappointment engulfed me that the waiting game continued. Patience had never been one of my strengths. The cottage and all it promised seemed a distant treasure, hidden far away.

Opening my fingers, I took comfort from the Red Jade crystal that sat housed within the palm of my hand. Sunlight sifted through the open window and glinted on the gem, red hues bouncing around the room. The house moaned with a murmur of delight and seemed to approve. I sighed with deep satisfaction.

This crystal held a promise of magic within its grasp. I had collected many before, some just small trinkets, but this treasure made all others pale in significance. The Red Jade bewitched me with its astounding beauty. It throbbed in my hand, pulsating with a life I could not understand. But Leanne's words of warning echoed in my mind. These were no ordinary crystals and the power they held, contained a danger too.

As before, I added this treasure into my camphor-wood chest and shut the lid tight. An overwhelming feeling overcame me, with the reminder that today would be a day I would never forget. It hadn't been just a dream! It had happened, and the proof, my Red Jade crystal, lay hidden in my precious chest of secrets.

PUZZLE PIECE 17:
THE BAND SESSION

Sometimes notes can jar,
Music's unexpected tunes,
Blended harmonies,
Driving out the sadness vibes,
Sweet silent stringed perfection.

The next day, after my memorable visit to the Crystal Cottage, I felt supercharged, buzzing with energy, ready for my pre-arranged band session with my friends. The crystals had triggered my creative energies. Today, I had music on my mind. Things were looking up, and meeting Leanne had given me hope that life could only get better.

My mobile rang just before I had intended to set off. I couldn't believe it, it was Ryder. I hadn't heard a word from him since our last meeting. He surprised and perplexed me by asking if he could join our band session. How could he have known our practice was today? I hadn't mentioned it to him, yet he seemed to know about it.

I couldn't stop debating how odd this revelation felt. In the end, I agreed he could join us.

The prospect of seeing Ryder again thrilled me. Nevertheless, I wondered if this was the best time to get together. I couldn't wait to tell my friends about him, but I wasn't too keen on him meeting them now. He'd somehow taken the choice right out of my hands.

My mind journeyed back to the day I'd first encountered him. Ryder had appeared down a pathway that my mum had warned me not to travel on. My first experience with him had been swift, and he had disappeared just as fast. Then, there was that weird experience with the portrait of my dad turning into the haunting image of Ryder. I sensed danger. There was something different about him compared to other boys, eerie almost, but I couldn't decide whether to trust him or to stay away from him. The threat from those other boys and their intentions that day had vanished with his unexpected but welcome arrival, and yet my concerns suggested he'd been shadowing me, following me for some reason.

———

After mulling these thoughts over for some time, I returned to the present. In fact, I wondered what my friends would make of Ryder. I loved visiting my friend Jade for weekly band practice, but a deep bout of depression often followed. It was like taking a shot of happy hormones or escaping from prison while on parole and then crashing down to reality with a loaded injection of back home misery. Jade's house brimmed with bright cheerfulness, such a wicked contrast to my family life. Sometimes I couldn't help but feel jealous as Jade's parents exuded happiness and normality like two complementary switches.

Mum had agreed to drive me to Jade's house, and I sat sullenly in the front seat. As my mother pulled into the drive, I peered out of the window at Jade's home, Shamrock Farm House, named after Jade's favourite horse from the Cottenham Bridge Farm Riding School. Set in a wooded area with a long driveway leading up to it, Jade's horses could be clearly seen in the large field to the left of the house. To say Jade had inherited a lucky gene to live in such luxury was an understatement.

I jumped from Mum's car and ran toward the stable. I spotted Jade mucking out her horses' stalls while wearing skinny jeans. Fashion conscious, she often wore jeans or leggings and lived in shorts in the summer. Jade had a perfect figure, and she could get away with wearing anything and still looked good. She stood with a tall and slender grace and had luxuriously long, jet black hair. Her almond-shaped eyes were bright and intelligent. I had no doubt Jade could wear a bin bag and still hit the glamorous list.

My friends Joselyn and Ilaria arrived shortly after Mum had dropped me off. Their presence kicked off a buzz of excitement as they helped Jade and I set up the equipment for the practice session. Jade's parents, Peter and Alice, allowed us to play in their large shed at the bottom of the garden. My drum kit sat in permanent residence at Jade's; my parents would have had a hissy fit if I had suggested band practice at our house.

Before our music session started, I told the girls about my walk down the path by the river and the two boys who had threatened me. I waited until last to share about the mysterious young man who'd appeared named Ryder.

'How did he appear out of nowhere?' asked Jade, wide-eyed with excitement.

'I don't know,' I replied, shaking my head at the girls. 'One minute the barriers descended, trapping me with those two idiots, and the next moment he appeared out of thin air. I reckon I must have been so engrossed in trying to get away from those boys, that I didn't see or hear him coming.'

'You didn't hear or see him at all?' asked Joselyn, raising an eyebrow.

'No. It was the strangest experience I ever had.'

Ilaria propped her guitar next to the amp, looking every bit the rock chick. She had short, brown hair cut in a spiky, cropped style, and always wore unexpected combinations of clothes that no one else could get away with. Today was no exception; she wore her ripped jeans with a studded belt and a black crop top.

'How mysterious; tell us more,' she urged with a wicked gleam in her eyes.

I hesitated for a moment, prolonging the anticipation. 'Well... this mysterious guy tops the hunk of dark, dangerous handsome list, and he has these amazing eyes and a wicked smile!'

'Hmmm. Amazing eyes?' asked Jade, wiggling her eyebrows up and down in a suggestive way.

I chuckled. 'I've said too much. He'll be here soon.'

'Sounds so curious... What time is this mystery guy getting here?' enquired Joselyn, tentatively looking around the room.

'He should arrive any time now,' I said, glancing at the time display on my mobile phone.

'I hope he's not coming empty-handed. Is he bringing a mysterious friend with him?' asked Ilaria before anyone else could. That got a laugh.

Jade chuckled and said, 'I hope so. I could do with a bit of excitement. Is he, Amelina?'

'I'm not sure,' I replied, pausing for a moment to gather my thoughts. 'I think it might be too much to ask. He seems kind of unreal as it is, and knowing my luck he'll not turn up, or else he'll be all looks and no personality.'

'Oh, shut up, Amelina! Stop spreading such a doom and gloom vibe. I know things are horrible back home, but maybe this is your chance. Y'know, to liven things up a bit?' urged Ilaria. She placed her hands on her hips and smiled at me.

'I wish.' I let out a sigh of relief.

Joselyn fidgeted. I had a terrible feeling that she teetered on the edge of having an anxiety attack about something. I realised that she thought I'd forgotten to bring the song lyrics. 'I've remembered them.' I laughed before Joselyn had a chance to ask her question.

Joselyn smiled. 'You did it again! You mind reader!'

I wasn't really a mind reader, but I had missed band practice for the last two weeks. The atmosphere at home had been so bad that I didn't have the energy to move, let alone practice. In fact, I'd been avoiding our music sessions because I just couldn't hack the after-effects of missing the happiness vibe I felt from visiting Jade's house.

The happy atmosphere made me realise that my family categorised as even more dysfunctional. That really hurt.

Now, I was about to pay the price for all those absences. I hoped that I'd be able to play the song well, particularly as I expected Ryder to come to this session. I didn't want to make a complete fool of myself.

It occurred to me that I was a double fool. I'd been so engrossed in getting ready for the band practice that I'd forgotten to give Ryder Jade's address. What an idiot. How would he ever find us? I brushed my hair back in agitation. I couldn't believe my stupidity.

The girls were ready to start, and just as we were about to tune up, Ryder appeared. I watched him walk toward the group like some kind of magnificent mirage. What an extraordinary thrill! He had found us. How? I'll never know.

The sight of Ryder kick-started my sluggish mood with a powerful blast as if I'd just been hot-wired to a car battery. Excitement coursed through my veins. My first memory of him more than lived up to my expectations. I could swear that the immediate hush in the room had fallen due to his arrival. Seeing our reactions, Ryder walked towards us and smiled confidently.

I returned his smile, but my brain couldn't quite process how he had got here. 'Hi, Ryder. How did you find us? I realised that I'd forgotten to give you Jade's address.'

'No worries. I have an unusual ability for solving mysteries. Call me Sherlock Holmes,' he replied with a bow as he pretended to take off his deer-stalker hat.

His response didn't explain a damn thing, but it made me laugh.

I pointed at my friends and said, 'Meet my fellow band members, Sherlock. This is Jade, our main singer, Ilaria, our lead guitarist, and Joselyn, our bass guitarist. And me—well, you already know me.' My cheeks flushed with embarrassment at this admission.

Ryder paused for a moment. I noticed his eyes lingered on Jade longer than was necessary. My friends couldn't help but stare at Ryder's bizarre eyes. His long eyelashes lured you into his lair, lush and moist with a hint of raindrop darkness. I pulled out of my reverie, but it felt a long way out.

'Hey, can't wait to hear you play,' he said as he effortlessly unfolded one of the garden chairs and sat down. Ryder exuded a comfortable air and glanced at us with an expectant look on his face.

The four of us didn't reply but laughed nervously. Taking this as my cue, I picked up my drumsticks and settled into my seat. I felt an electrifying surge of energy work its way through my body, causing a tingle from my fingertips extending into the tips of my drumsticks. Ryder's presence made me feel inspired. It was an odd reaction considering I'd felt depressed, and now that feeling had disappeared, replaced by a Ryder induced euphoria.

Ilaria concentrated on tuning up her guitar, waiting for the rest of us to begin. Strangely, we all began playing in unison. Instinctively, I immediately knew what to do. My drumsticks had a mind of their own as they fiercely hit and rebounded off my drums, creating a perfect accompaniment to the music.

Jade's powerful voice rose and fell as she sang her heart out to the lyrics of our new song, *Rock Crystal*, inspired by my love of crystals and the group's love of rock music. The words slipped like silk off her tongue:

You are my rock crystal, rock crystal,
Your light fires me up like an ever-glowing ember, so bright and warm in
December,
Your crystal eyes so bright twinkle as they give me insight,
I am your rock crystal, rock crystal,
A jewel of light, your rainbow of red, yellows, oranges, blues and greens, irides-
cent and warm as ever I've seen, a kaleidoscope of shades that will never fade,
Everlasting Rock Crystal, Rock Crystal.

I noticed that Jade sang to Ryder alone; her eyes kept drifting off in his direction. The words continued to slip from her lips, and she channelled all her energies into pouring her heart out while staring at him.

. . .

Here from the dawn of time, so fine, love of mine. You are every colour of the rainbow, plus much more besides.

Ilaria's guitar belted out each chord almost like it would be its last. Joselyn seemed to come alive as she played her bass guitar, and for a moment all of her shyness and insecurities vanished. As a group, we had never sounded so great.

When the song ended, Ryder stood up and clapped. 'That was unbelievable!'

We all looked at each other in amazement, and Jade's face glowed with his praise. 'That was brilliant, Amelina. How did you play so well? You haven't had time to practice. I thought a horrible illness had stricken you?'

I blanched at Jade's words, and my face flushed. 'M'fine. I have no idea how I did it, it just came to me,' I replied, frowning.

Jade whispered in Ilaria's ear. 'She must have enchanted the drumsticks, the song lyrics, and Ryder! I'm so jealous!'

The whispers had failed. I had heard Jade's words loud and clear, and in response, I blushed a fierce pink. Ilaria sniggered and whispered back, 'Perhaps it's Ryder who's enchanted her and our music too. Y'know, we've never played like that before.'

'What are you two whispering and sniggering about?' I stood with my hands on my hips and flashed a defensive glance in their direction.

'Nothing.' They giggled conspiratorially.

I spun around and detected that Ryder now stood next to me, yet I hadn't seen him move. He must have crossed the room with lightning speed. I felt a buzz of nervous energy crackle between us. Feeling awkward, I pretended to tidy away the music equipment so I wouldn't have to deal with how he made me feel.

Ryder joined in folding chairs and lifting equipment, moving with lithe, panther-like grace as he continued to charm everyone with his disarming smile and smouldering eyes. 'Have you ever thought of recording your music on YouTube? I bet you'd be a hit.'

'No, haven't thought of that.' I smiled at his interest in our group.

'I could help out. I have access to an excellent video recorder.'

'That would be awesome, Ryder,' I replied with a smile bright enough to light up the interior of the shed. Ryder's mobile buzzed, interrupting our conversation. He paused for a moment while he stood reading his text message, and a faint smile registered on his lips.

'Sorry, Amelina, but I'll have to go. See you soon.'

I wondered what his mysterious text message had said. Instead, I tried to appear cool and replied, 'Oh, okay. We can hang out another time.' I hated that he had to go, but I walked Ryder down the garden pathway and waved as he sauntered off down the road.

When I returned to the shed, I peeked inside to witness my friends huddled together in gossip mode. Jade had centre stage, her eyes bright with mischief as she led the conversation. I crept to the side of the door and eavesdropped. I was a pro at eavesdropping at home, so I decided I might as well do it with my friends too.

'Well, Amelina goes from hardly noticing that boys exist to finding the hottest, most incredible guy in the universe. Now, how's that possible?' asked Jade.

'Yeah, I know. It's so unfair. My jaw dropped like a broken elevator shaft when Ryder walked in the room!' said Ilaria.

'I'm glad Amelina's luck changed, but, um ... I'm not sure about Ryder,' remarked Joselyn.

'What d'you mean, Joselyn?' asked Jade with a puzzled expression on her face.

'His voice is weird, and his eyes are beyond freaky,' answered Joselyn, looking perturbed.

I had to stifle a laugh at that remark. I placed my hand over my mouth to keep from laughing out loud. The conversation continued.

'His voice and eyes are freaky, but sexy too!' said Jade, winking.

'I'm not sure about sexy. I just found those two different coloured eyes and his voice to be creepy-freaky!' said Joselyn, frowning.

'Joselyn, shut up! Can't you see he's fit?' said Ilaria, shaking her head. 'He's perfect for Amelina.'

'I don't know. Ryder's too perfect—sort of unreal. There's something in his eyes, a touch of hardness that I just don't like,' said Joselyn.

I imagined her biting her lip, chewing on it mercilessly. Typical Joselyn, she always saw things the rest of us sometimes ignored.

'Stop being so boring Joselyn. You never trust anyone; you should get a job in the police force,' remarked Ilaria. And that was so Ilaria, always the smart ass. I held back my laughter and rolled my eyes. This overheard conversation fascinated me more and more.

'Maybe I should! But there's something about him that freaks me out. That's the last thing that Amelina needs. Her life's trashed as it is,' said Joselyn.

I gasped at the truth of Joselyn's words. *Thanks for pointing that out, Joselyn. Trashed, yeah, that just about sums it up.*

'I disagree. I think Ryder's appearance is a sign that Amelina's luck is changing,' said Jade.

'Yeah, Jade's right; I think you're exaggerating Ryder's freakishness, Joselyn. But it's true that her life 'til now's been rubbish. Haven't you heard the rumours about her family? A curse?' whispered Ilaria. I swallowed hard. I wished they wouldn't talk about this because the curse lay in the off-limits zone. But I remained hidden, wanting to know what my friends really thought about Ryder. I hovered closer to the door, listening intently.

'Yeah, I have. Poor Amelina, she's got it rough,' remarked Joselyn.

'There must be some truth in this curse theory. You only have to see her parents. That's evidence enough. Like a pair of wax horror exhibits in Madame Tussaud's who've undergone some weird time shift, aging them, wrinkles and all. As for Amelina, she's strange too. Haven't you heard that nutty story? You know? The one about her holding up her newborn head as soon as she arrived?' asked Jade, her eyes twinkling with mirth.

I couldn't believe it. Jade had crossed the invisible line of friendship. I'll give her Madame Tussaud's! As for that head thing, what a load of rubbish…

'Yeah, my mum told me she arrived exactly on her due date as if she knew when to join the rest of the human race,' joined in Ilaria, bursting into laughter.

I felt the rumbles of anger bubble to the surface. *Hey, I can't help it if I'm always on time, Ilaria!*

Then, in between bursts of giggles, Jade added to the conversation. 'She took ages to talk because she was already cleverer than everyone else.'

It stunned me to realise what Jade really thought of me. I brushed my hand over my eyes, willing my body to remain quiet so I could hear the rest of their harsh words.

'No doubt about that!' said Joselyn.

'No wonder she's landed a hot guy. She's got brains, beauty, and a touch of magic on her side!' said Jade, doubling with laughter.

Enough, I had to stop this. I walked around the corner, slipping from my hiding place. 'Okay, knock it off. Don't you know you're not meant to talk about friends behind their back?'

'We've been talking about how amazing you are, Amelina!' said Ilaria with a mischievous grin.

'You witches! Gossiping more like,' I said, pulling a face.

I turned around and Jade's mum, Alice, entered the shed to welcome us girls, saying, '*Selamat Datang,*' in her quiet voice. She always greeted us in the same way, using this Malaysian expression. She'd prepared a lovely Chinese meal, which she carried in on a large tray. We all gobbled down the excellent fare in no time at all.

Shortly after the meal, the girls gathered outside, waiting for their parents to arrive to take them home. All except me—I had no alternative but to rush to the end of the driveway, not stopping to say goodbye, because my mum exuded control punctuality freak like no other. She was also a cleaning freak and a tantrum monster. In my house, being late wasn't an option. That kind of behaviour would set off the erupting volcano of Mum's temper.

I relished the snatched seconds of laid-back atmosphere, wishing I could stay longer. I felt different at Jade's house happier and lighter, as if a weight had lifted from my shoulders. I despised the thought of going home. I tried not to dwell on it, but whenever I spent time at Jade's house, my situation became clearer. The only way to describe my family life would be to define it with one word. Tragic.

I hung my head in dejection. If only my mum and dad could be like they used to be. A heavy depression settled like an ominous black cloud, threatening to engulf me. I gulped for air.

PUZZLE PIECE 18:
THE YOUTUBE RECORDING

I feel jealousy,
Mounting reaching a high note,
And I don't like it,
Boys—cause a string of problems,
Beware boyfriend who plays lead.

E ven though Ryder had made promises at our last band session, I didn't hear from him. In fact, he seemed to have disappeared without a trace. The depression I often suffered following a music session settled deeper, eating away at me. I lost all sense of time. The days rolled from one to another as time continued to pass me by. Living in the real world was a dream I longed for. Trying to cope, I ate, slept, and repeated each day like a hamster stuck on a treadmill.

When I decided that I'd reached rock bottom, Ryder finally turned up. His long disappearance annoyed me, but I was desperate to have fun, so I gave him another chance. I couldn't let the opportunity to record our songs get away from us. Also, there was no way that Ilaria, Jade, and Joselyn would let me, anyway. Those girls had been relentless with their calls and texts. They tried everything to lift my melancholy mood. Guess what? It worked.

I cheered up, glad to be back amongst the living and excited about the new opportunities ahead of us. Later that same day, Ryder arrived at Jade's house in perfect timing to the sound of us tuning up. I smiled, glad to see him and even happier that he had remembered his promise. He ambled into the shed carrying a professional-looking video recorder. I chuckled at the girls babbling at each other in excitement, reserving my opinion for later. If Ryder's boasting suggestions were true, our band would soon be on YouTube. Now he would have to live up to his promises.

'Hey, I can't wait to hear your new song,' said Ryder as he set up the video equipment. 'What's it called?'

'*Drifting Shadows.*' My heartbeat in my chest so loudly that I was sure Ryder could hear it.

'I like the name. It conjures up an alleyway of wickedly evocative thoughts,' said Ryder with a devilish smile. He turned and gave me a wink. My breath caught in my throat; his devilish smile captured there for a moment more.

'Yeah, I agree,' said Jade, returning his wicked smile. Ryder laughed.

Joselyn winced and met Jade's eyes as if she was taking this as evidence of his guilt in a court of law.

'We'll play it for you now. See what you think before we record it.' My aim was to cut off Ryder's laughter in one swift move. I didn't want him paying too much attention to Jade.

However, Ryder's immunity to my tactics surprised me. Instead, he agreed with me, saying, 'Oh cool. I'd like to set the video to self-timer so I can introduce the song for you as we record it if that's all right?'

He had said it as a statement more than a question, and I paused for a moment, reflecting on his words before I asked, 'Are you planning to introduce *Rock Crystal* too?'

'Let's try *Drifting Shadows*, for now, just in case it goes wrong.'

Ryder fiddled with the equipment, adjusting the volume and other buttons.

I turned away, searching for my music. 'Okay.'

'Amelina's singing this one,' said Jade. She glanced at the other girls with a smile on her face.

Ryder glanced over his shoulder at me. 'You sing, too, Amelina?'

'Yeah, I do the haunting, edgy numbers because they fit my doom and gloom personality.' I flashed a wry grin in Ryder's direction.

Ryder had stopped tinkering with the buttons on the recording equipment and had turned to face me. 'I don't see doom and gloom, Amelina. I see sunlight and talent.'

I smiled. He knew how to charm a girl. My heart fluttered when I met his eyes. *Those crazy eyes.*

'Hey, how do you drum and sing at the same time?'

God, he was gorgeous. I cleared my throat and beamed him a smile. 'C'mon, that's easy. I'm a girl; we multi-task with ease!'

I walked over to join the girls, and we finished tuning up our instruments. Ryder set the recording on a self-timer mode and joined us on stage to introduce the song. The recorder emitted an atmospheric sound, which filled the room with a haunting, reverberating echo.

As we played, the lyrics of the song sounded distant as if they were flowing down a long, dark tunnel. Out of nowhere, my voice echoed and drifted back, filling the room with a hypnotic and haunting sound. It reminded me of several voices singing in unison like a choir, instead of my voice alone. My drums were at the back of the shed in the shadows, and without warning, a strange sensation engulfed me, and my spirit felt like it soared, wild and free. The beats of my drum dominated the musical piece, creating a powerful recurring pattern of sound. The melancholic quality of my voice matched the lyrics of the song:

Your fragments of light cast drifting shadows,
Cloaking my eyes so I can't see,
Dark demons hide in your beguiling eyes,

Wading in the deep waters of my mind,
Your darkness and light a glimmering candle,
Too brilliant, too exquisite to ignore,
Shadows of your soul linger in my eyes,
Too mischievous and alluring not to adore,

The music flared in pitch and volume, filling the darkening room. Shadows teased us with patches of flickering light and darkness. The vibe increased as the wavering shadows danced in time to the rhythm of the rave-like music. I felt amplified, **flying** on the ultimate adrenaline high. I sang with all my heart, sucking energy from the other band members as I watched their illuminated faces staring back at me.

Your voice like milk and honey,
Rich, flowing, and tender,
Never forgotten,
Whirling in my mind,
Bewitched and intoxicated I am,
Please hold me once more,
Please hold me once more,
Forget all the others you have held before,
Forget everything you have ever known,
Trust me,
Trust me,
My voice,
Alone.

At the end of the song, I wiped the sweat from my brow, exhausted but triumphant. I had sounded good. We milled around, sorting our music and stretching. Ryder left the stage and set up the video recorder to record *Rock Crystal*.

By now, the rest of the girls seemed to be under the same spell that controlled me. A blinding, ethereal light worked its way into the room as we played. Crystalline images projected on the walls behind us as Jade's voice found the words to the song. Colour and warmth permeated the room, calming us after the frenzied beat of the previous song, *Drifting Shadows.*

When we finished recording, we huddled together in a tight knot. Our voices rose in excitement as we chatted about the miraculous recording session we'd just taken part in. Ryder stood off to the side and uploaded the two songs. I flashed an angry look at Jade when she walked over to his side. I knew she was vying with me for Ryder's undivided attention. I shook my head in disgust as I observed her bubbling like a spring of teenage hormones on full alert.

'That was awesome, Ryder, but did you see those strange shadows and crystalline images flashing on the walls? Wasn't that surreal?' Jade's face flushed and her eyes glimmered.

'Crystalline images, no. Shadows? Yeah, I always see them. I think the crystals must have been your imagination shuffling off into hyper musician drive.' Ryder chuckled as if he had shared a joke.

We all glanced at each other with shocked looks on our faces. I cocked my head and stared at Ryder's back. 'But I saw them too,' I said, butting in.

'And me,' agreed Ilaria.

'It's odd, but I did too!' remarked Joselyn.

Ryder turned around and stared back at us with a strange glint in his eyes. 'Maybe I'm not as creative, or maybe my perception is lacking compared to you girls.'

Our voices broke out in an angry chorus of disagreement as we said in unison, 'You must have seen them, Ryder? We all did.' Joselyn and Ilaria nodded their heads in agreement.

'I didn't see them, and *I don't lie,* Amelina,' said Ryder. A hurt edge crept into his voice. It was light, almost hidden, but it was there, like a knife edge waiting to take its first slice.

My face paled at this declaration. I stepped back and steadied my voice, trying to calm my thoughts. 'I didn't mean that, Ryder… Thanks for helping; you did such a fantastic job.' I accepted his words as if set in stone.

'Thanks, girls, it's my pleasure.' Ryder, forgetting his hurt, appeared to bask in the glow of my praise. He brushed his ebony hair away from his forehead with a practised grace.

'You look great in the recording, Ryder,' said Jade, blushing. Her body language said more than I wanted her to say.

Joselyn rolled her eyes. I said a silent, *oh, my God, stop it, or you're dead, Jade.* But Ryder and Jade didn't pick up on my pissed-off vibe. The heat of anger rolled off my skin in an invisible steam.

'I pale into insignificance next to you,' he said, his kiss-me eyes lingering on Jade's flushed cheeks.

I turned toward my friend, my usually gentle eyes sending a deliberate warning glare in her direction. An unpleasant feeling of jealousy came over me, threatening to burst from the top of my head. *Maybe he prefers Jade.* The more I thought about that possibility, the more jealous I became. That would be typical. Could things get any worse? Perhaps this was my secondary curse, to have hot guys always falling for my best friend. *Great.*

Ryder's next words singled Jade out for even more attention. It wasn't so much the words he used; it was more the way he focused his attention on Jade.

He stared into her eyes. 'You should record your songs. I think it would be a big success.'

'We were thinking of doing that,' replied Jade, staring back at him, seemingly captured by his magnetic personality.

I didn't butt in, and I frowned at Jade, even though no one seemed to notice.

Ryder still held Jade's gaze with his mesmerising eyes. 'I could help. I have contacts in the music business. You could sell them at school and then do a concert once you have your fan base,' he said, skirting closer to Jade's side.

That was it! I had enough. I spun around and let a telltale edge of hurt creep into my voice, betraying my emotions. 'You two have it all figured out by the sounds of it.' I felt a burning in my cheeks, and my temper flared as I stood fuming over the turn of events.

'You could do worse, you know. I only want to help,' answered Ryder, his eyes searching mine for forgiveness, his voice echoing the sentiment in his eyes.

I wanted to scream, but his smouldering panther eyes were too much for me. I buckled under their stare. My knees shook. Why did he have this effect on me? I reconsidered, realising I'd let the jealousy vibes get the better of me. I took a deep breath and exhaled. 'Okay, your help would be great, Ryder.'

As soon as the words left my lips, I felt an overwhelming desire to curl up and go to sleep, as if I'd just stepped off a plane after a long-haul flight suffering from jet lag. *What could that be about?* I knew it wasn't true, but I felt like Ryder had slipped a drug into my drink, turning me into a cute girly-girl who always does what she's told. I hated this feeling. His next words floored me. They were only five words, but they affected me profoundly.

'Y'know, I aim to please,' he said, with a winning smile that melted my heart.

I couldn't help but soften, even though I remained wary. I just wasn't sure about Ryder yet. He seemed to know everyone. Nothing appeared to be difficult for him. The word 'obstacle' didn't exist in his vocabulary. *No*, wasn't a word you said to Ryder.

I heard a noise and turned to the door, watching as Jade's mum, Alice, walked into the shed, breaking the magical spell Ryder had cast upon us. Both of her hands were full, and she carried a tray filled with an array of Asian foods. When she spotted Ryder, she stopped in her tracks, and an expression of surprise lit up her features. Just in time, she caught herself—she had nearly tipped the food off the tray into Ryder's lap. Embarrassed, Alice turned away from Ryder before he could notice the flushed look on her face.

I grinned as Alice recovered with ease and smoothed down her tailored dress. 'Oh, how nice to see your new friend, girls.' She smiled at Ryder and said, 'Please stay and have some food. You're more than welcome.'

Ryder's face turned into an instant mask, appropriate for parents only. 'Sorry, I'd love to, but I can't stay too long; I have to return the video equipment.'

'Oh, that's such a shame. You must come back again. Thank you so much for recording for the girls,' said Alice. 'I'm sure they appreciated you helping.'

'It's my pleasure,' said Ryder. He enunciated slowly, and the word *pleasure* lingered in the air, like a caress.

The girls stood rooted to the spot, watching the scene play out before them. I couldn't believe the exchange between Ryder and Jade's mum. In fact, all our mouths hung open in surprise. Alice appeared to be on the verge of a spectacular hot flush. Without a doubt, she looked like she could do with one of those Chinese fans to cool herself down. Instead, she resorted to calming her heated emotions by welcoming us in her usual manner. 'Selamat Datang. Lunch is ready.'

As was her custom, Alice had prepared a feast. Displayed in brightly coloured Chinese bowls were spring rolls, dainty curry pastry puffs, orange-coloured prawn crackers, garlic prawns with a chilli dipping sauce, and little bowls of tasty fried rice. Alice handed out chopsticks and tiny cups of green tea. The aroma overwhelmed me, and my stomach growled, anticipating the meal.

Jade's dad, Peter, even appeared. He glanced at Ryder and said a brief, 'Hi.' He seemed more interested in the incredible array of food. He grabbed a spring roll and took a bite. 'You know, it's a wonder that Alice is such a good cook, considering her aunt brought her up, and she couldn't cook at all!' Peter hovered, crunching his spring roll and gaping, his mouth salivating.

He bent down to pick up one of the garlic prawns, but his wife rapped his knuckles. 'Not for you, Peter. You got slimline salad back at the house. Come.' He pulled a long face and followed his wife back out the door. I couldn't help but feel sorry for him. *Poor Peter!* Punishment for mentioning Alice's aunt, no doubt!

Jade giggled and rolled her eyes. 'Oh, my God! They're gone. Hurrah! Aren't parents embarrassing?'

'You could say that,' answered Ilaria. The girls clustered around the fragrant dishes, filling their plates from the bowls filled with food.

It was strange, but I didn't feel hungry. A moment ago, my famished stomach had grumbled, yet now I felt distant and preoccupied with my own thoughts. My eyes were heavy and my limbs even more so. Exhaustion settled in my bones. I sat in a chair to rest and watched the girls begin their meal.

Once Ryder finished uploading the recording to the machine, he checked his phone. On cue, his phone pinged, signalling an incoming text message. All at once, his demeanour changed. Ryder paced in agitation and announced that he needed to leave straight away. I watched his strange behavior and wondered why he didn't say where he intended to go.

The more I thought about his abrupt departures, the more I realised he was always rushing off. Ryder walked toward me and stood beside my chair. I looked up at his face, closing my emotions off to him. I knew what to expect next.

'I'm sorry. I have something I must do. Amelina, I promise I'll make it up to you. Next time I'll take you to a fantastic restaurant for dinner. In fact, I'll take you to a secret venue that is out of this world.'

I sat quietly. I eyeballed my friends as they returned my gaze like the Envy Goddess had bitten them hard, all except Joselyn, whose forehead burrowed into a worried frown.

I sighed deeply and studied Ryder's face. 'A secret venue,' I said, turning into that girly-girl mush, wistful twat once again. 'All right. I'm a forgiving girl.'

'Me too. If Amelina comes down with the flu, I'll join you in her place,' teased Jade. She grinned and flashed him a winning smile. Ilaria giggled.

I spun around in my chair and gave Jade a dirty look. Ryder winked at Jade but reached down and pulled me towards him, his velvet lips brushing my cheek. He kissed my other cheek, lingering for a moment in the embrace. I hadn't expected him to kiss me, and I'd responded in a hopeless manner. I'd failed to return his second embrace. I remained standing, paralyzed by my stupidity.

God, it couldn't have been more embarrassing. I felt certain that Jade thought I was a complete idiot. How could I have messed it up so badly? Now, without a doubt, I suspected Ryder would prefer Jade. No way would Jade have been so unsophisticated. And I knew she wouldn't have any trouble kissing Ryder from the way she had acted tonight.

Ryder didn't appear to notice my discomfort, and instead, he lightened the moment. 'Au revoir,' he said in a sexy French voice. He swivelled on his heel and blew a kiss in the girls' direction.

I watched Ryder exit the shed and walk down the path toward the driveway. In the background, I heard a chorus of goodbyes fill the room.

PUZZLE PIECE 19:

RYDER VANISHES

To vanish so fast,
In plain sight makes me dizzy,
Mocking my senses,
Wish Jade would disappear too,
No chance—she's too boy crazy.

I stood at the door of the shed and blinked. Slowly my overwhelming tiredness lifted, and a delicious sense of power enveloped me. I hugged myself. I had Ryder all to myself, and only my eyes had seen him leave. Ryder continued unaware that my eyes followed him; his face grew stern, so different from a moment ago. It made a momentary shiver travel up my spine like I was looking at a different person. He hurried as if he'd calculated each step to take him further and further away from me.

Then to my complete and utter astonishment, Ryder vanished. I saw a flash of grey and a hint of black light, a twirling piece of fabric, and then nothing. One moment he stood before me, and the next he vanished. I scratched my head. It made little sense. A worm of anxiety worked its way into my thoughts. Maybe he walked so fast that somehow my vision couldn't keep up. It occurred to me that Ryder and Shadow had that in common—disappearing.

I walked back toward the table, replaying Ryder's steps like a slow-motion reel in my mind. Perhaps he'd bewitched me. That would explain it. Either that or maybe I was going mad? I didn't welcome either of these explanations. I sat down at the table where the girls were busy enjoying Alice's meal. I didn't eat or join in the conversation.

Alice walked into the shed and interrupted my thoughts. She caught my eye and smiled. 'I've come to tidy away the food. Are you alright, Amelina? You seem very distracted. That young man is a distraction. You didn't eat anything.'

'M'fine, Alice, just tired, I guess.' I brushed my hand over my face. I *had* been behaving in an odd, dream-like manner, and I needed to get my act together. It's true that I hadn't eaten Alice's lovely food, and guilt gnawed at my heart. I said the first random remark that came into my head. 'I love your new dress.'

Alice appeared pleased and touched. She wasn't a stranger to compliments with her slim figure, attractive short black hair, and elegant, manicured nails. But this compliment must have seemed random.

'Thank you,' she said, smiling as she stacked and cleared the plates away.

Jade devoured the last morsel of her lunch and licked her lips. '*Ummm*, Ryder's delicious. I'm impressed.'

'Knock it off, Jade,' I replied. I was not in the mood to discuss Ryder's looks with her.

'Come on, Amelina. I'm a natural flirt, you know that. I wouldn't steal my best friend's boyfriend, now would I?' She wiggled her eyebrows in an attempt to be funny.

I stopped to pause, wondering whether Jade would stoop so low. Remembering the way Jade had eyed him, all encouraging and wide-eyed looking. The prize was too precious. To say that the odds stacked in Jade's favour would be an understatement. With her looks and personality, she always got the guys. Somehow, I knew I would have to keep the two of them apart, or else I didn't stand a morsel of a chance. Then my life would really be a double-headed curse.

Words to a future song swirled and etched in my heart:

A shadow blots my landscape,
Black-hearted drifter,
Vanishing deceiver,
Bewitching fellow,
Alluring hero,
Blight on my heart.

PUZZLE PIECE 20:
AUNT KARISSA'S VISIT

Persistent chatter,
Eccentric mannerisms,
That gossipy style,
Barrage of words swallowed, gulped,
Silenced by sweet Earl Grey tea.

I didn't feel comfortable talking to my parents about sensitive issues. Instead, I often turned to my Aunt Karissa when I needed someone to confide in. I loved my flamboyant aunt, and I couldn't wait to see her.

I always knew when Aunt Karissa had arrived. Strong perfume announced her entrance, wafting from every pore of her body. Her loud booming voice vibrated the rafters as she walked through the door. Whenever she visited, the house woke up and appeared alive again. The central heating hummed and light drifted into every part of the house from the otherwise murky windows.

My Aunt Karissa's passion for dogs culminated in her choice of a dashing red setter called Toby. He had a difficult temperament due in part to my aunt's inability to train him. Luckily, Shadow was out hunting mice when Toby bounded into the house in search of adventure.

Karissa Flavell ticked all the boxes that my mum Eleanor had crosses for. My eccentric aunt flourished whilst being an enthusiastic gossip. She always wore colourful, exuberant, large clothes that hung like an ill-fitting wardrobe, a few sizes too big for her. Karissa's weight fluctuated so much that sometimes I would have to do a double take to make sure the woman before me was my aunt. Today I saw a trace of chocolate at the corner of her lips and a telltale widening around her hips. I smiled. Once again, her sweet tooth had got the better of her.

Karissa enveloped me in a tight, corset-cinching hug. I broke free and gasped, struggling for breath. Toby barked, wagged his tail, and leaped against my legs to garner my affection. Aunt Karissa peered into my face. 'How's my favourite niece? You're so thin. You need a large slice of home-made apple pie, my dear. Has your mum been starving you again? Where is she?'

Karissa didn't seem to notice the effect her breath-squeezing hug had on me. She didn't even look for Mum. She absently patted Toby's head to settle the dog and waited for my response. I felt light-headed, but I recovered enough to say two breathless words in reply. 'Food shopping.'

Aunt Karissa shook her head and clucked her tongue. 'Oh dear, I wish I had time to bring something with me. That means we're in for Eleanor's specialities—burnt supper, or, even worse, microwave cuisine.'

I squeezed out a laugh. Toby carried on, seeking attention like a demented puppy. I pushed the dog away, trying to curb his jumping fit.

'Well, the place is tidy,' Aunt Karissa said, glancing around the lounge. 'How does your mum do it? I'm terrible for clutter myself, and I can't seem to get on top of things. As soon as I tidy up, more mess appears out of nowhere and makes matters worse. I wonder what her secret is. Perhaps she has a male cleaner that pops in every day to clear away the clutter. I bet your mum doesn't want to admit it. Maybe he's ridiculously handsome,' said Aunt Karissa with a wink.

I rolled my eyes at my aunt. 'I doubt that. I don't think she'd notice. She never stops cleaning.'

'What a shame! Life is too short for tedium. That's my motto. Make it yours, my dear; it's much more fun.' With a deliberate smile, she opened her mirrored compact and teased her eyelashes with mascara. With flair, she flipped her hair over her shoulder.

Aunt Karissa always came with a gift for me, and this visit was no exception. She rummaged around in her enormous handbag and pulled out a two-tiered box of chocolates wrapped in silky paper, tied with a bow, and handed it to me.

'Thanks, Aunt Karissa. Another present! The art set, ahem, it was… extraordinary, and now this.' My aunt smiled. That bit of chocolate stuck in the corner of her mouth made her curved smile remind me of a chocolate orange slice.

I tore the wrapping off of the box and passed the treats to my aunt, but she politely refused. 'I'm on one of my wretched diets, *quel dommage*! Amelina, you must keep them for a very special occasion. I'm sure you'll know when it's the right time to indulge yourself. Besides, I've no doubt you will find *the right time* to share them. They're not for the likes of me.'

I wondered what my aunt meant by saying, '*the right time*.' Was this another of her coded messages? I closed the lid and placed the dubious chocolates on the kitchen table. What a temptation for Toby. The dog couldn't resist sticking his long muzzle on the table and sniffing them. I knew chocolate was bad for animals and pushed the box further from the nosy dog's reach. Aunt Karissa caught him in the act and pulled him away. Instead of telling him off, she reached into her pocket and pulled out a doggy treat as a reward for not gobbling the box down straight away. Apparently, in my aunt's book, sniffing was okay! Discreetly, I placed my hand over my mouth and stifled a laugh.

I longed to share with her all the strange happenings of late, and of course news about Ryder, but I didn't get a chance. Aunt Karissa talked nonstop about all manner of things, including the local gossip from the town of Ely.

'Well, my neighbour's wife has run off with someone half her age, can you imagine it? It caused quite a stir. The woman seemed like such a quiet, reserved lady. The funny thing was she kept going out every evening while her husband worked the night shift. He continued working, and she was otherwise engaged!'

I listened with one ear and thought about how anybody listening to my aunt would believe Ely ranked amongst the most notorious places to live in the UK. I tried to change the topic of conversation but didn't succeed. Stopping my aunt's rattling on about the town was like trying to slow down a billowing, hot-air balloon after it had managed to soar into the sky. Finally, in frustration, I resorted to gently tapping her shoulder in a desperate attempt to get her attention. 'Aunt Karissa, there's something I wanted to ask you.'

'Of course there is, dear, I can't wait to hear your news. Oh, where was I?' She smoothed her hair out of her eyes and added, 'Oh, yes, it's always the quiet ones that get up to mischief,' she concluded with a gleam in her eye.

The shrill ring of the doorbell sounded, and the ringing persisted nonstop. I jumped at the sound and heard Mum shouting loudly when there was no response. Toby took this as a sign that he had every right to jump up and down, barking like crazy until someone let her in. Aunt Karissa carried on talking at full throttle, oblivious to everything else, and I couldn't move away from her without seeming rude.

I heard the key turning in the door. Mum stormed into the kitchen like an erupting volcano, nearly treading on Toby. 'Why can't you come when I ring the doorbell, Amelina? I couldn't find my keys. Don't just stand there, come and unpack the groceries.'

Mum exchanged a brief hello with my aunt, who tried to placate her. 'Eleanor dear, I'm so sorry. I got so engrossed. Amelina and I were having a lovely chat, weren't we, dear? Oh, heavens, what was it you wanted to tell me, Amelina? I got side-tracked. I'm such a dreadful chatterbox.'

I gave my aunt our private signal *for not now, let's talk later*. I met her eyes, and Karissa registered the signal and winked at me. I unpacked the groceries while Toby kept on trying to steal anything that looked vaguely edible and getting in the way of everybody, especially Mum, who resorted to giving him the evil eye when Karissa wasn't paying attention. At long last, the groceries were safely deposited away. Toby lay down, his red tail fanning the floor in a gesture of defeat.

PUZZLE PIECE 21:
SNORES, DATES, AND BRIBERY

It's bribery time,
Sweet form of tea and biscuit,
Estimate will win,
It almost formulaic,
Taste buds always surrender.

As I considered my date that night with Ryder, it dawned on me that I would have to tell my mum. Any changes to her schedule were always unsettling, and even more so when Toby visited. The dog irritated her, so I knew there was only one way to get on her good side. I resorted to sneaky bribery, a cup of tea and Mum's favourite biscuit.

When I offered to make tea, Mum's beady eyes surveyed me with a curious look that said it all. I knew it was hard to get anything past her. Mum and Aunt Karissa sat down at the kitchen table while I made the tea. Aunt Karissa continued to jabber on and on. I peeked out of the corner of my eye and watched Mum as she nodded in agreement with a glazed expression fixed on her face. I smiled to myself realising that butting into the conversation would be a challenge.

Eventually, I succeeded—even Aunt Karissa couldn't talk with her mouth full of biscuit. I cleared my throat, and a bubble of nervous tension accumulated in the pit of my stomach. 'Mum, I forgot to tell you I'm going out tonight with a friend.'

'You forgot? I doubt it. What friend's that?' asked Mum, picking up her cup and gulping down her tea.

'His name's Ryder.'

'I haven't heard his name before, Amelina. Where did you meet him?' Her eyes narrowed and her lips stretched in a thin line across her face.

I fidgeted and looked at my aunt for support. I shifted my eyes to Mum. 'Oh, one day when I stumbled upon him down the river path, and he helped me.'

'What do you mean? Helped you how?' Curious now, she placed her cup down on the table with a clatter.

Nervous, I opened my mouth to respond. No sound came out. I swallowed hard and said, 'I fell, and he helped me up.'

Mum slammed her hand on the table. 'Amelina! I knew it. Well, I'm glad that's all that happened. I've told you countless times how dangerous it is along the river pathway. What were you doing down there?'

'I was taking photos for my art portfolio.' I lowered my eyes and stared at the tabletop.

I lifted my head and returned her stare through my eyelashes, but she didn't look impressed. I knew I had to get on her right side, so I choked down my guilt and fixed my gaze straight into her eyes. 'I'm sorry, Mum, I should have listened to you.'

My mum's reaction didn't surprise me. She did livid like no one else, and the fact that I had ventured down the river path on my own made her even angrier. She asked more questions than I had answers for.

'Where does he live? Where does he go to school? How old is he?' Each question followed the other, hammering me without mercy. Not once did she say that she was glad that Ryder had helped me. No, she did what she did best; she continued to tell me off for going there.

'Amelina, answer me!'

I shut my mouth. I couldn't take any more. I'd had enough. Yet I stood my ground. Mum wasn't about to stop me from having a tiny morsel of much needed fun. No way. Judging by the expression on my aunt's face, she appeared to find this conversation amusing beyond belief. She sat riveted to the edge of her seat, behaving like she was watching some TV drama. I could see Esme staring at me from the looking glass down the hall. Her expression wasn't filled with amusement; it was filled with horror.

Aunt Karissa contemplated me curiously, as if she knew there must be more to the story. She raised a quizzical eyebrow. Meanwhile, from the mirror, Esme's eyebrows knotted together in a hairy fit of anxiety. My aunt rested her ample bosom on the table; the weight of her substantial assets must have been too much to bear. 'How romantic, and you met him down the river path. What an appealing mystery. I imagine it must have been a stunning day, my dear. What does he look like, all rugged and handsome?'

Mum frowned, and an ugly red furrow deepened across her forehead. She shook her head with displeasure and glared at both of us. Aunt Karissa had gone too far. She knew it and I knew it. Mum's glare was enough to send her off, so she retreated upstairs to the guest bedroom to put her suitcase away. I watched as Toby followed her, his eyes downcast and his tail drooping as if he'd been the guilty troublemaker.

The sound of my mobile beeping saved me from further questioning. I grabbed my phone and hoped it was Ilaria getting back to me about the sleepover for Joselyn's birthday party. Sure enough, Ilaria's text message read: *It's okay for Sunday night, hope you can come.*

I wondered what Mum would say about me going out on Sunday night as well. I sighed deeply.

'Mum, Joselyn's birthday party sleepover is Sunday night. Ilaria needs to know if I can come.' Mum crossed her arms and leaned in towards me as a withering look spread across her face. I recoiled and edged away.

'Really, Amelina, first you arrange a date with a boy I know nothing about.'

'Mum, I…'

'And then you want to go to a sleepover on Sunday night while your Aunt Karissa visits. You know how your aunt's visits are, um… stressful what with her dog, and her endless talking.'

I heard a sound and turned to look behind me. Aunt Karissa had crept downstairs in time to overhear Mum's admission. A pained expression lingered on her face. From the hall mirror, Esme's sad reflection demonstrated her disappointment that she couldn't go with me to the sleepover.

Mum jumped out of her chair and fiddled around, picking up ornaments and putting them back as a way of avoiding an apology. Aunt Karissa stood there, not sure what to say either.

Ready for any kind of interruption, I heard Dad letting himself in the front door. His laboured breathing echoed and came in quick gasps as he made it down the hall to the lounge.

'Fancy a cup of tea, Dad?' I asked, making my way out of the kitchen as I headed straight for the lounge and pulled out a chair for him. He looked like he needed one.

'Yes, please,' he replied, sinking into the chair.

I returned to the kitchen to prepare the tea, and Aunt Karissa popped into the lounge and greeted Dad with a brusque nod as she settled into a chair. Down the hall, I could see Toby had settled at her feet, nuzzling his face on the carpet, ready for his nap. I heard Mum join them, and she said a quick 'Hi' to Dad. I never heard Dad's reply.

I gathered up Dad's cup and walked down the hall. The adults weren't talking. Even Toby joined with this conspiracy of silence. *Great. Fantastic.* I paused and wondered how I would get what I wanted? Seizing the moment, I walked into the room and handed Dad his tea. I took a deep breath and gathered my courage. The time had come to discover my mother's decision, but I was afraid to know the answer.

'Oh, Mum, please can I go? It's Joselyn's birthday.' I pleaded my case, looking at Aunt Karissa for much-needed support.

I glanced over at Dad, but he had already fallen asleep, his drink untouched beside him. A gentle snoring escaped his half-open lips.

'Well, it would have been nice to get some notice. You must have known about this ages ago, Amelina,' growled Mum.

Aunt Karissa took this as a cue to interrupt the conversation before it turned nasty. 'I hope you don't mind me butting in, Eleanor dear. I know I do prattle on a bit... um... Toby and I are sorry if we upset you earlier. We don't mean to, we're just excited to visit. I'm sure in all the commotion of our arrival, Amelina forgot to tell you. You know what young people are like, heads like sieves full of youthful daydreams. I don't mind if she goes out; after all, you're only young once.'

I looked at Mum with a hopeful glance. How could she say no to that? What a hatchet ice breaker. Aunt Karissa held the title of best aunt ever.

A hesitant smile hovered over Mum's lips. 'Okay, that's um... very, kind of you Karissa. Oh, what a racket. Stop snoring, Mark!'

I rolled my eyes in horror as Dad took that admonition as his moment to snore even louder. Mum shook her head but did nothing to stop the continuous drone of his snoring. 'All right, Amelina, if you must go, do. In that case, maybe you'd better see that young man some other time.'

'What young man?' Dad cleared his throat and sat up.

'Now you wake up! What a racket you've been making. I could hardly hear myself think.'

'I don't snore,' replied Dad. He ran his hands through his hair.

'Neither do I,' added Aunt Karissa, laughing. 'I just rumble sweetly.'

I turned in amazement to witness Mum as she rolled her eyes and threw her hands up into the air. I swear Mum's eyes spun around loosely like a washing machine cycle on fast spin. 'Amelina has a date with someone she met down the river path.'

Dad's face wrinkled further. I observed as deep grooves made a subterranean home in his prematurely aged skin. His voice wavered as he spoke. 'Oh, I don't like the sound of that. All sorts frequent that pathway. It's not safe, you know; hasn't been for a long while.'

Aunt Karissa shook her head. I felt sure that my aunt would have wagged her finger if she could get away with it, and Toby would have joined in fanning his tail, but he was still asleep. 'Oh, you can't keep her wrapped up in cotton wool forever, Mark. For heaven's sake, let her have some fun! This place is like a clean and tidy morgue.'

In the mirror hanging over the settee, Esme was mouthing silently, 'No,' repeatedly, and then nodding her head and saying, 'Yes.' That Esme continued to do my head in. Perhaps she was saying 'No' to Ryder, and 'Yes' to the morgue bit. Who knew?

I silently watched as Dad wandered off down the hall. His slow progress made me grimace. His shoulders curved downwards, and I imagined a defeated expression was firmly planted on his face. Toby woke up and stood, shaking his entire body as red fur floated in the air. The dog lowered his head and followed Dad out of the room. The dog's erect ears pressed against his furry head as he mimicked Dad's slow steps with his own sleepy ones, walking in a sympathetic solidarity of dog and man.

Aunt Karissa turned towards Mum and spoke in a coaxing voice. 'Let her go. He sounds like such an interesting young man. He came to her rescue.'

Mum's grim features tightened into a mask of determination. Aunt Karissa saw the fierce reluctance but knew how to win her over. 'I've got an idea. Why don't you and I go for a girl's night out? It would be fab, just like old times? It's been ages since we last went out. I'll treat you to dinner.'

I smiled. Aunt Karissa had the winning formula. I also knew she couldn't abide Mum's culinary inability and was praying for an opportunity to eat out. Mum hated cooking. It was the perfect solution.

Toby and Dad sauntered back into the room. I noticed Dad carried a tiny glass filled with an amber liquid, a shot of alcohol. Toby licked his lips as if he had just received a naughty treat. Dad paused next to his chair and sat down, his knees creaking in noisy protest. Toby copied each of Dad's moves, right up to adopting a weary expression on his face. Dad unfurled his newspaper, creasing it at the crossword page. Toby sat by his feet, his big brown hero-worshipping eyes never leaving him.

Aunt Karissa noticed the hero worship but didn't seem to mind. 'If you don't mind, Mark?'

'Mind what, Karissa?'

'If Eleanor and I go out tonight?'

I spun around to see the look on Dad's face. I had to hear his response. Dad glanced up from his crossword. I could tell from his relaxed expression, the prospect of a night in with no interruptions delighted him. His wrinkled face creased into a disconcerting trench of a smile. Toby licked his hand.

'No problem.' He reached down and patted Toby's head in a reassuring manner. Dad grabbed the shot glass and tossed back the amber liquid, flinching as the alcohol took his breath away.

Mum paused for a moment to consider. An evening out along with the bonus of not having to cook must have sounded too tempting to her. She beamed a rare smile. For a moment, I worried if that meant she'd get terrified looks from passing strangers. I knew Mum was used to how folks talked about us. She'd lived with it for years. She'd developed a thick skin.

'Alright, against my better judgment, your aunt has convinced me.'

A great sense of relief flooded through me. I hugged my aunt and bent down to scratch Toby between his ears. He whirled around in a circle, barking and wagging his tail in an excited response.

'Thanks, Mum. And you, too, Dad.' Mum nodded, and Dad's only answer was a grumbled 'Humph.'

My Aunt Karissa whispered in my ear, 'Don't forget to tell me all about Ryder when you get back! I promise I'll be all ears. A sleepover, too, what a weekend! Oh, I do wish I was young again.'

Luckily, I had won this battle. I smiled at my aunt and rushed back to text Ilaria the good news.

PUZZLE PIECE 22:

ANXIETY ATTACK

Parents can crush love,
With tragic withering looks,
Bewitched I may be,
But am I doomed to remain?
Alone, in this misery.

My initial elation turned to a full-scale anxiety attack when I surveyed my surroundings. What would Ryder make of my strange house, and my even more bizarre parents? I hoped he wouldn't walk in, see them, do a massive freak out, and disappear. I shivered in anticipation and climbed the stairs to my room.

Now wasn't the time to have a worry fit—now was the time to get ready. I had to make a good impression; Ryder was a year older than me. I didn't want to appear like an innocent schoolgirl. A sense of anxiety welled up in me. At only fifteen, and one of the youngest in my year group, I felt inadequate next to this sixth-former. I had to look my best, and I knew makeup would help. I clicked on my computer and selected my favourite YouTube makeup video. I needed inspiration and a bit of confidence right now.

A great noise sounded from downstairs, disrupting my concentration. I rushed down and witnessed the return of Shadow. Poor Toby. The dog was beside himself. Shadow glared at Toby with disdain, his tail swishing, his black fur exploding around him resembling a spiked ball flail. Toby yelped and barked in fear, but his hind legs shivered as if Shadow posed a significant threat. It was so bad that we had to separate them. Aunt Karissa helped by offering to take Toby out for a walk. I agreed, realising my aunt was a godsend to sense the issue.

Shadow revelled, once again free to roam the house. The cat slinked around the corner, and I could swear that he smirked. He followed me back upstairs and watched my various wardrobe choices as I tried on each selection and then discarded them on a heap on my bed. By 6pm I had a messy pile of clothes accumulating, and I was no closer to choosing. Shadow took this as his cue to plonk himself on top of the pile of my clothes. He purred, enjoying being in the centre of and surrounded by my best outfits.

I wagged my finger at him. 'Shadow, you'll get fur everywhere.' He stared back at me, his green eyes glowing rebelliously. I gave him a gentle nudge. He replied with a short, reproachful meow and settled himself on top of my laundry basket, his glistening eyes watching me.

I had to make a decision. Delving into my wardrobe, I snatched the perfect dress: a lovely, simple dress, constructed of a luxurious, exotic red fabric. I added a black belt, matching shoes, a long-beaded necklace and a pair of crystal earrings. From the bed, I noticed Shadow's whiskers twitched in approval. Rushing, I applied my makeup and attempted to tidy my room.

I glanced into the mirror and realised that this made me seem at least a year older. *Success.* I smiled in approval at my reflection. Esme smiled back, but the half-smile she gave me disturbed me.

'Please tell me you aren't going out with that strange guy you met down the river?'

'I am,' I replied.

'No, you mustn't!'

Her face blanched. I glanced at my watch. I didn't have time for this; I was going to be late. Esme would have to take a chill pill. She'd been spending too much time listening to my mother.

'Bye,' I said, allowing one last glance over my shoulder at my reflection in the mirror.

'Amelina you mustn't go,' Esme shouted after me, but she had left it too late; I'd already started to make my way down the stairs. I made a mental note not to encourage Esme's histrionics. She excelled at putting a downer on everything.

When my aunt saw me, she passed comment. 'You look fantastic, Amelina; I love your dress. I'm sure your young man will be smitten. You're so lovely.'

'Thanks,' I said, smiling. 'I thought I was never going to get ready. Shadow was such a nuisance.' *And Esme acted all overanxious, like a second mum.* I purposely didn't glance in the mirror to see Esme's angry scowl.

Aunt Karissa laughed. 'Shadow's a bit of a rascal. Just like my Toby. But that seems to be his appeal, a bit like boys really!'

'Yes, the cheeky ones are always much more attractive.' I giggled.

'Do tell. What's Ryder like?' asked Aunt Karissa, rolling her eyes like a schoolgirl.

'Heart-stoppingly handsome! The butterflies in my tummy are so horrible, I swear they are doing triple somersaults and multiple backflips.'

'Oh, you poor thing, got it bad, haven't you?' Aunt Karissa smirked and glanced at me with a gleam in her eye.

'Judging by Jade's, reaction so has she.'

'Oh dear, sounds like competition,' said Aunt Karissa with a sympathetic grin.

'You could say that,' I replied with a heavy sigh.

Mum and Aunt Karissa went upstairs to get ready for their night out. I heard a few stray giggles make their way down the stairs. The unfamiliar sound made me smile; Aunt Karissa knew how to make everyone happy, even Mum. I waited in the lounge, my nerves increasing with each passing moment. At 7 pm the doorbell rang, and I rushed to open the door. My heart pounded so wildly that the sound must have carried all the way to Ryder's ears. His wicked good looks left me gaping.

'Hi, Amelina.'

I stood at the door with a silly smile plastered across my face. There was no way that I could hide my delight at seeing him again. My brain practically short-circuited working overtime in the love department, and my body didn't have a hope of catching up. I stumbled, lost for words.

It was then I heard the unmistakable sounds of Mum and Dad approaching, which added to my already dangerous levels of embarrassment.

Ryder didn't bat an eyelid when he spotted my parents. In fact, he showed no reaction whatsoever, which didn't make any sense at all. I couldn't help thinking that nobody could be that unfazed; it wasn't possible. Yet it was. Ryder was a law unto himself. Perhaps he had heard about my dad or read the newspaper article, and that was why he didn't seem surprised, but even so, his lack of reaction ranked peculiarly high.

Turning to greet my parents, Ryder literally spoke in a clear, confident manner. 'Hello, you must be Mr and Mrs Scott. I'm Ryder. I trust you don't mind if I take Amelina out for dinner?' He beamed a beguiling smile in my parent's direction.

Ryder's laid-back attitude and the formal way he spoke seemed to make Mum hang on every syllable he uttered. Her unnaturally made-up red lips quivered and gushed. 'Of course, we've heard all about you. We're only too happy for you to take Amelina out. We must thank you for stepping in and…'

'It was my pleasure,' interrupted Ryder, stopping my mum in mid-sentence.

Dad's reaction couldn't have been more different. He narrowed his eyes and stared at Ryder long and hard; his concentration wouldn't have been any less if he had been dissecting an unpleasant insect. This wasn't going quite the way I had expected.

'Haven't we met somewhere before?' asked Dad, looking

perplexed like a man incapable of solving some strange mystery. 'Perhaps I know your father or something… your face is horribly familiar.' Dad scratched his head and glanced at Ryder again. 'Do you go to the same school as Amelina?'

'No, I'm at sixth form,' answered Ryder, seeming oblivious to Dad's critical demeanour.

'Oh, yes, you seem older…' said Dad, continuing to look challenged, trying to work out where he had seen Ryder before. His eyes held Ryder's in a steady glare.

I watched as Mum openly stared at Ryder until he returned her stare at full torch strength. She diverted her attention away, apparently unsettled by his nerve. She patted her hair and smoothed her dress, managing to compose herself. 'Are you going anywhere nice for dinner?'

'Aphrodite's,' Ryder answered, in a tone of voice that suggested he held an air of authority in such matters.

Dad raised an eyebrow, stretching his creased skin around his eyes even further than I thought possible. A frown pulled at the corners of his lips. Mum elbowed Dad and then gave him one of her famous stares that said, 'stop it.' She swivelled and turned her attention back to Ryder. Mum seemed envious, even though I'm sure she'd never heard of Aphrodite's. She said no more, though her thin lips pursed into a tight line.

I heard the sound of hurried footsteps as Aunt Karissa rushed downstairs. Her wet hair dripped a flurry of drops on the floor. Driven by curiosity, she had leaped out of the shower to catch a glimpse of Ryder. My aunt smirked and hung back in the corner of the hallway.

Meanwhile, Dad sneaked another suspicious glance at Ryder, his face puckering into a worried frown before he slipped away. 'Sorry, got to get back to my work. Oh, and make sure you bring my daughter back at a reasonable time.'

'I will. Time's drifting away. Amelina, we have a seven o'clock booking. What time is it? Your clock must be wrong. Your mantel clock shows it's ten thirty. How curious! I think your timepiece isn't working. It has lost its grip on reality,' observed Ryder.

'Oh, we like to judge the time by other methods. It's ten past seven,' replied Mum. She scowled, and it was evident by her expression that her broken clocks were not a subject she cared to discuss.

'How time flies. Off so soon. Have fun,' remarked Aunt Karissa, eyeing Ryder.

I rushed out the door, shouting a quick goodbye, hoping that Ryder would follow me.

Behind me, Aunt Karissa mumbled, 'I knew I should have dashed out of the shower earlier! Oh, my! He has such a captivating, mature voice for one so young.'

Ryder paused and surveyed his reflection in the hall mirror. I turned from the doorstep outside and hazarded a look. Esme's reaction astonished me. Her mouth formed the shape of a ringed doughnut of fear. As I watched, Esme's skin turned a perplexing and unnatural shade of grey, clashing with the bright yellow of her hair. How odd. Why had Esme reacted to Ryder in such a way?

Ryder appeared oblivious to Esme's distress. As far as I knew, nobody could see Esme except me, so no great surprise at his reaction.

'Why are you in such a desperate hurry, Amelina?' enquired Ryder, in a bemused tone of voice, as he joined me outside. We left the house and walked down the road.

I didn't answer. I continued to wonder why Esme had looked so frightened. Ryder glanced at me with a deep, penetrating stare that unsettled me. It was as if he'd crawled into a cavity of my mind, taken up residence, and had started playing an elaborate computer game, with me as one of his players.

'You all right, Amelina?' His words pierced my thoughts. 'You look like you've seen something that's disturbed you?'

'No, of course not, I'm fine,' I lied. 'It's my Aunt Karissa. She'd have bombarded you with a multitude of questions if we stayed any longer. I knew we had to get out of there.' I glanced over my shoulder at Aunt Karissa peeking out the window as if she had been cheated out of the latest gossip opportunity.

'She's a bit curious!' said Ryder, his face softening into a laugh.

His laughter calmed me. It filled my thoughts like a soothing elixir, and I relaxed. I laughed and glanced at Ryder. 'You could say that. Aunt Karissa's curious, embarrassing, crazy, inquisitive, but lovely all the same!'

Ryder paused and thought for a minute. He chose his words carefully. 'Your parents are, *very, um...* different from you.'

I roared out a harsh laugh. 'That's the polite thing to say. Most people can't hide their shock. I know they resemble a scary carica-ture that's gone wrong. Sorry, I should have warned you.'

'No need, I don't get scared by much. Not even Stephen King.'

A pause in the conversation ensued as I considered his last words.

'C'mon, Aphrodite's, here we come.'

I could tell Ryder wanted to change the topic of conversation by the way his voice changed. 'Sounds interesting; what kind of restau-rant is it?'

Ryder raised an eyebrow. 'You've never heard of Aphrodite's? Oh, it's *the* in place to go for lovers of romance.'

He smiled and shifted his eyes to meet mine. His glance entwined me in a magical embrace, and he added, 'You *will* adore it.'

PUZZLE PIECE 23:
APHRODITE'S RESTAURANT

A fascination,
With the exquisite or strange,
Is hidden away,
In a strange tucked away booth,
No room for intimacy.

After Ryder's words had such a mesmerising effect on my brain, my thoughts ran away with the strange images of what I perceived the restaurant to be like. I imagined the interior of Aphrodite's Restaurant to contain whitewashed walls, a sky-blue ceiling, and private booths tucked away in dark alcoves. Somehow, I knew this romantic restaurant would fit the drop-dead gorgeous bill since its namesake was the Greek goddess of love, beauty, and fertility. The tumultuous waves of Cyprus Bay allegedly gave birth to Aphrodite.

Ryder's voice broke into my dreamlike reverie. Those crashing waves in Cyprus Bay fizzled out, and his words flooded my senses.

'Y'know, I think I may have forgotten to mention we're meeting a few of my college friends there.'

That got my attention. My happy sense of anticipation now lay at the bottom of the bay, drowned and buried. But instead of voicing my feelings, I answered with a succession of words that didn't seem to belong to me. 'Oh, yeah, right… it'll be nice to meet your friends. I'm looking forward to it.' I berated myself. What a wimp. Why had I even said that?

I carried on even though I was feeling peculiar at the change of events. I could swear that I lingered on the verge of fainting. Struggling to get rid of this strange sensation, I took several deep breaths, but it made no difference.

We had arrived at the front of the restaurant by then, and I strained to recapture control of my drifting mind. Ryder held the door, and as I walked inside, I focused on the restaurant's interior. Aphrodite's presented everything I'd expected and much more. The waiter seated us next to an exquisite painting of the waves crashing against the cliffs of Paphos Bay. We slid into our very own private booth.

A snow-white Aphrodite statue stood in the centre of the restaurant as a focal point. Her exotic and mysterious image enthralled me. No wonder she deserved the title of the Goddess of Love. The realistic statue captured my attention. I almost expected her to step towards me and crush me with her stone arms in an over-enthusiastic embrace.

Large elaborate fish tanks lined the walls, housing exotic fish, including coral and ferns. I glanced around at the pictures of white doves which dotted the walls.

My eyes travelled to a painted likeness of the Golden Apple of Great Renown. I remembered the goddess Eris had written 'for the fairest' on the side of an apple. Both Zeus's wife, Hera, and his daughter, Athena, as well as Aphrodite, claimed they were the fairest. But the Prince of Troy, Paris, couldn't choose between them. The rest is history. Paris fell in love with Helen, which led to the Trojan War. I had been paying attention in history class after all. I reflected for a moment on what a bitter-sweet and ultimately destructive force love could be.

Ryder edged closer to me in the booth. He brushed a strand of hair away from my face. I could feel his breath on my face. A hot, sweet, intoxicating murmur that caressed. 'You're so lovely,' he said, his voice coaxing me to come even closer.

I couldn't resist his advances and snuggled closer to his side. He cupped my face in his hands and leaned in towards me, planting a lingering kiss on my cheek. I closed my eyes and leaned back, allowing his lips to brush my neck. My skin tingled with a strange heat where he'd left a trail of kisses. I longed for more. He ran a finger over the top of my lip. It was such a thrill; I trembled and my breath caught in my throat. I could hardly breathe. Catching my breath at long last, I inhaled him, my lungs filling with his heady aroma.

As suddenly as his kisses had begun, they ended—the moment was lost. Ryder's eyes darted toward the approaching figures of his friends. He disentangled himself from my embrace.

'This is Kyle and Emily,' he said, breaking the spell. He turned, nodded at me and said, 'Meet Amelina.'

I blinked, coming out of the moment. 'Hi.' My words tumbled out as a whisper. I could have kicked myself; I sounded like a twelve-year-old.

Ryder stood up and peered through the dimness, searching for something. 'This booth is on the small side; I'll see if a waiter can find us a new table.' I felt myself sigh inwardly at this statement. Ryder waved a waiter over, and we were moved over to a nearby table with four upright chairs.

Ryder flashed me a questioning 'forgive me' smile as he sat down. I accepted it, but I wasn't happy with the choice of seating arrangements.

Emily gave me the once over. 'Hi, Ami, love your dress, wher-ever did you find it?'

Was she being bitchy? By the looks of her, she could have bought ten designer dresses in one shopping trip. She reeked of money. As for calling me Ami, what had she meant by that? Nobody called me

Ami. I might be younger than her, but I wasn't half of an Amelina. I wanted to be known as one hundred percent the full version, and one of a kind.

I intended to launch into a tirade of my thoughts, but I caught Ryder's gaze. 'I got it in the vintage boutique in town,' I replied, biting my tongue, surrendering my unspoken words.

'Oh, yeah, thought so,' said Emily, flashing a half-smile in my direction.

Emily's response suggested that my first impression of her was spot on. Emily looked every bit the part of a prize bitch. The girl had a petite frame and a fragile, protect me style. With her long blonde hair and green eyes, I could see why the guys would vie for her attentions. I surveyed her perfect choice of dress, shoes, and handbag and ended up feeling even more self-conscious and inadequate. I hated comparing myself to this bitch.

Turning my attention to Kyle, I noticed he couldn't have been the more opposite of Ryder. Rather than dark, he was fair-haired, of medium height, with green eyes.

Ryder smiled and gave Emily the once over. 'Well, I see Emily's immaculately turned out as ever. You never cease to impress,' enthused Ryder, giving Emily a hug.

Kyle continued the praise. 'Yeah, she's drop-dead gorgeous.'

I felt a stirring of jealousy. Were these two competing for Emily's attention? The thought pricked at my brain, and I shook it off.

Kyle glanced my way. 'As is Amelina.'

I blushed at Kyle's shy, complimentary remark but felt gutted when Ryder added none. Kyle focused his green eyes on my face, paying particular attention to my eyes. I looked away and smirked. No surprise there as I'd often heard that my crystal blue eyes had an enchanting and soulful aspect to them. I enjoyed the compliment. Besides, Ryder didn't seem to find my eyes engaging, neither did he compliment me; instead, he turned his attention to the menu. *What a cheek!*

'Well, Amelina, let me choose.'

I studied Ryder curiously. How did he know what I wanted to eat? Did he think he was a mind reader or something?

'I know just what you'd like,' said Ryder, his deep voice flowing rich and dark, like melted chocolate. He closed the menu and placed it on the table.

'Okay,' I answered. I sat there and listened to the conversation, engulfed by a strange stupor.

Ryder carried on talking as if he pitched for custom like a sales rep for the restaurant. 'Yep, it's a haven for seafood enthusiasts, and they offer lobster, crab, prawns, mussels, and about every type of fish you can imagine.'

The waiter sauntered over to our table, and Ryder spoke first. 'Lobster for everyone?'

I glanced sharply at Ryder's silhouette. How odd. It wasn't the type of feast a bunch of teenagers ate. Pizza was our usual diet. I listened to the small talk and jumped in surprise when the waiter appeared with our meal. It seemed like only minutes had passed.

As I ate, my stupor lifted. My senses bombarded by the visual beauty of my meal and the aromas and textures. 'Wow, this tastes like its fresh caught today in Aphrodite's Bay. The lobster's amazing.' I smacked my lips in delight.

'Couldn't agree with you more,' enthused Emily.

'Yeah, it's great. I've never tasted food like this anywhere else,' agreed Kyle.

'Do you remember the last time we ate here, just after our exams? That was incredible, wasn't it?' remarked Ryder, raising his eyebrows. A smile played around his lips.

'Yeah, it was fantastic. We stayed up late, drank too much, and couldn't get up the next day,' Kyle said with a laugh.

'I couldn't get up either, although I think mine resulted from eating too much,' added Emily, as she played with her food.

'Really?' replied Ryder, digging into his lobster with relish. Butter dripped from a claw he held in his hand.

Emily shifted uneasily in her seat. 'Seafood isn't everyone's cup of tea,' said Kyle, coming to Emily's rescue. He patted his lips with his napkin.

'Tea isn't everyone's favourite drink either, and I prefer something fuller bodied. Aren't I right, Amelina?' Ryder spoke directly to me, his face markedly challenging.

'I feel like I could do with an energy drink.' As soon as I said 'energy drink,' the heavy feeling in my body returned. I slumped even further down in my seat. Ryder didn't respond.

Kyle caught the mood and tried to change the subject. 'Ryder's told me all about your band, sounds awesome. I'd love to hear you play.' Tired beyond belief, I managed to lift my head and glanced gratefully at Kyle. 'Yeah, that would be great.'

'The YouTube recording was a huge success, receiving lots of likes and hits. *Drifting Shadows* takes the crown for being the best,' said Ryder in a voice that suggested it was all his own doing.

I dragged myself out of my stupor once again to reply. 'Don't forget *Rock Crystal*, too.'

Again, Ryder swiftly changed the subject of conversation. 'What are we going to have for pudding? The menu is mouth-watering. How are we to decide?'

'I couldn't eat another bite, Ryder, just a black coffee for me,' said Emily. She smiled and laid her fork down next to her plate.

'Same,' said Kyle. 'If I eat anything else, I will be in danger of needing a crane to lift me off this seat.'

'Oh, c'mon, eat something.' Ryder glanced at each of us, waiting for an answer.

In that instant, I felt like my head was being spun around in a churning cement mixer. My swift reply sounded like it belonged to a stranger, a greedy stranger. 'I'd *love* a pudding.'

'Great. Let's have a rich, chocolate dessert, my favourite,' urged Ryder.

'I've changed my mind, Ryder. I'll have a tiny piece,' said Emily.

'I should've known! What a change of heart. I knew you couldn't resist!'

'Yeah, me too,' said Kyle. He rolled his eyes and looked over at Emily.

. . .

I couldn't believe what I'd heard. What was going on? I sat there, my mouth gaping open at the weirdness of this conversation.

The rich chocolate dessert indulged in every way I had hoped it would. After we had finished eating our hefty meal and the decadent dessert, the four of us prepared to leave. The cool night chilled us as we walked back toward my house. Ryder continued to be disturbingly quiet towards me.

Standing on the road in front of my house, I sensed that Ryder would say that he didn't want to see me again. To my surprise, he turned towards me with a winning smile. 'Hey, we must do this again soon. Let me *suggest* that you bring your fellow band members next time.'

I nodded my head even though I had mixed feelings. I felt a sense of relief that Ryder wanted to see me again, but it annoyed me that he wanted me to invite my friends, especially Jade. When I thought about Jade getting closer to Ryder, the churning in my stomach got a lot worse. My feelings settled into a block of cement and hardened into a thick mass inside my tummy. I didn't like where this was going.

I agreed with his suggestion even though I knew it amounted to signing my love abdication warrant. I couldn't understand why I behaved this way. No boy had ever had this impact on me before, but then Ryder couldn't be categorised as an ordinary guy. That much was certain.

With a startling intensity, Ryder's piercing eyes locked on mine. 'I'll call you. We can arrange another get-together.'

I thought about his choice of words, 'get-together!' That didn't sound romantic, in fact, it sounded like something he would arrange with his mates. Not a solid foundation for a date. Was he toying with me? At that exact moment, I felt myself slipping off the mental love cloud and crashing to the ground with an almighty bump.

To make matters worse, Ryder delivered the second crusher. 'Afraid Emily and I have to get back. I promised that we would do some revision together, but I'm sure that my best mate Kyle would be more than happy to keep you company.'

Kyle dug his hands deep into his trouser pockets and stared at the ground. He mumbled, 'Of course,' but his cheeks flared with embarrassment.

My mental love cloud evaporated—poof, gone in a second from Ryder's stark words. He paused and kissed me briefly on each cheek in a sudden absent-minded way. Without another glance in my direction, he and Emily gave us a reluctant wave and walked away.

As soon as Ryder and Emily left, I felt a vast change in my mood. It was like I'd partially woken from a deep sleep. The adrenaline that had been pumping around crashed, sending me into an even deeper lethargic slump.

'You don't have to if you don't want to.'

'Don't have to what?' I replied, almost forgetting Kyle's presence.

'Ask me round…'

'No, it's fine,' I replied. I was going back to an empty, gloomy house, with only Esme for company, at least Kyle might cheer me up a bit.

The so-called date had been a dead loss. The kisses had been over almost as soon as they'd begun. I felt more than a bit jealous that Ryder had left with Emily. Why hadn't I said something? I didn't often find myself tongue-tied. A niggling thought crossed my mind: was Ryder a player?

PUZZLE PIECE 24:
KYLE COMES ROUND

Ryder leaves, Kyle stops,
Two very different guys,
One dark other light,
I eat cookie dough ice-cream,
Chilling confused emoji.

After Ryder's departure, I felt dazed. I could have written these words: *Good-looking unfathomable guys mess with my cookie dough emotions, chilling me to pieces.*

I wanted to curl up in my room and console myself by eating a ridiculous amount of cookie dough ice-cream, but instead, I was polite. I asked Kyle in. As soon as I did, I wondered what had prompted me to do so.

After all, I hardly knew Kyle, but there was something about him that made me feel comfortable. He seemed trustworthy. Yeah, Kyle seemed okay, whereas Ryder couldn't have been more different —dangerous and alluring.

Those stolen kisses at the restaurant kept slipping back into my mind, reminding me of Ryder. Somehow there had been an edge to them. They had been kisses that had left a passionate mark, a mental imprint. Self-consciously, I touched my neck. It still tingled where his lips had touched me. The tingle had turned into a heated ache, a burn that couldn't heal.

I shook my head. Trustworthy Kyle was no antidote to the situation. As soon as I stepped into the hallway, my whole body felt heavy where each step involved an effort, an unbearable trial to bear. I knew I was home again.

Kyle glanced at me with an expression of confusion. He couldn't hide his dismay as we walked into the house. 'It's... a bit... um.... dark?'

'Yeah. Welcome to my gloomy dungeon! Bring a torch next time —light is in short supply.'

'That sucks,' said Kyle, squinting.

There in the hall mirror, Esme stood up, her eyes wide with a mixture of curiosity and apprehension. No doubt she was wondering what I was doing coming home with Kyle. She drew in a breath of relief and gave me a quizzical look.

The house was quiet apart from the sound of Shadow meowing. I realised that I'd forgotten to feed him, so I opened his favourite cat food and placed a generous serving in his bowl. Poor Shadow, he was starving and lonely. I could see no sign of Dad. He must have gone out.

Shadow twirled around Kyle's legs, winding round in figure eights as if he claimed him as a plaything. Kyle bent down to pat him, and Shadow purred. It was a deep, throaty sound of sweet satisfaction. The cat rubbed his head against Kyle's leg.

'What's his name?' asked Kyle, continuing to pat him.

'Shadow.'

'What a cool name.'

'Thanks. I think it suits him.'

An awkward silence followed. The house sensed that there was a visitor, and the room became warmer, the sign of a welcome yet unexpected change. I led the way into the kitchen.

'Hey, what sort of music do you like?' asked Kyle, breaking the silence with a question that grabbed my attention.

'All sorts, especially rock.'

'Me too.' A faint shimmer of sweat beaded on his brow.

I noticed Kyle's uncomfortable demeanour, so I flashed a smile in his direction. 'Would you like to listen to music or watch a DVD?'

Kyle's face lit up. He wiped the sweat away and unzipped his coat. More at ease now, he draped it on the back of a chair. 'Great. Music sounds great.'

'Would you like to listen to *Rock Crystal?*' I asked.

'Yeah, sure.' Kyle sat in the chair and glanced around the room.

I hurried upstairs to get my laptop, which I had left in my bedroom, on permanent charge. Lately, all my electrical equipment seemed drained of energy and needed a super charge to work efficiently. If only I could supercharge myself! I took off my cardigan. It was strange, but the atmosphere in the house continued to brighten.

'Hey, Amelina. Who's the cute guy?' Esme asked, licking her bottom lip with excitement.

'His name's Kyle.' I noted her rising levels of lip licking with amusement.

'Hmmm. Kyle has a nice ring to it. Sweet.'

'Ha! Not as sweet as all that licking you're doing. Yuck! You'll end up with chapped lips if you do that anymore. See you in a mo...'

'No, wait... I thought you were out with the scary river dude?'

'I was, but it's a long story... I've got to go, Esme.' I grabbed the laptop with a quick backward glance at Esme, who peered at me from the mirror as I traipsed down the stairs.

I placed the computer on the table and together with Kyle, we watched my band's performance of *Rock Crystal.* Kyle's eyes stayed riveted to the screen. I couldn't help but warm to his obvious love of music. I kept thinking to myself that anyone who liked my favourite bands and appreciated my music had to be more than okay.

After the *Rock Crystal* track had finished, I put on my favourite playlist. I motioned for Kyle to follow me into the lounge. He smiled and jumped up from the chair, eager to join me. We settled down on the settee to listen. Shadow cruised into the room on silent feet. He jumped up and sat on Kyle's lap, purring while he stroked him, his eyes closing into slits as he drifted off to sleep. Reflected in the lounge mirror, Esme looked like she'd fallen asleep too; the music must have lulled her to sleep. I had to smirk at the thought.

As a rock ballad played, my attention drifted back to thoughts of Ryder. I was desperate to find out more about him. It was then I noticed that the atmosphere in the house darkened, and the room grew cold. I shivered. Kyle remained quiet, dumbfounded by the sudden temperature change in the shadowy room. The stifling silence between us continued.

I couldn't stand it any longer, and I broke the unbearable quiet with a question. 'Emily and Ryder seem kind of close?'

In the corner of the mirror, Esme woke up. She pressed her hands against the glass, and her mouth opened as if she wanted to speak.

Kyle hesitated, choosing his words carefully. 'Oh, right, yeah… They used to be together. Now they're just good friends.'

'Oh. Ryder never mentioned that.' I gazed directly at Kyle, unable to keep a touch of resentment from creeping into my voice. Esme gave me an "I told you so," look from the far corner of the mirror. She shook her head and clucked her tongue in sympathy. I glared back at her interruption.

'Ryder doesn't like to talk about it. It all ended badly. Emily took the breakup hard.' Kyle stared at his feet as if his boots were the most fascinating things he'd ever seen.

I jerked my head back in Kyle's direction. 'Emily's over him now?'

'Yeah, she is now, but she was ill after they broke up. She became anorexic.'

'No way! Anorexic? She's way too thin even now and eating looks like torture for her.'

'Yeah, it's clear, isn't it? Ryder blamed himself for her anorexia. He felt guilty.'

'That figures.' I paused for a moment, also choosing the right words for my reply. 'Ryder acts like… um… they're still together.'

Esme bent forward, taking in Kyle's words as if she wanted to jump out of the mirror, land on Kyle's lap and ask him herself. I discreetly rolled my eyes at her.

'Old habits, I suppose. Ryder's a difficult one to figure out. He's a loner who often disappears and doesn't stay in touch. That's what happened with him and Emily. He kept on disappearing, and Emily couldn't cope. His vanishing games were too much for her.' Kyle's eyes became heavy with sadness, and he added, 'she wanted his undivided attention.'

'What about you and Ryder… Are you…?'

Kyle shifted in his seat awkwardly. He looked so uncomfortable that he jumped in before I'd had a chance to finish what I was saying. 'I haven't got a girlfriend at the moment.'

I hadn't meant that at all, and realising my mistake, I hastily added, 'Sorry… that wasn't what I meant. I was asking if you two are um… alike.' My face flamed a bright red colour as embarrassment oozed from my pores. Esme rolled her eyes. From the dirty looks she was beaming my way, I could tell she thought I was making a right mess of this.

Kyle glanced at me in a hurry to get the words out. 'Well, we are alike in some ways, but Ryder tends to be the moody, difficult one. Although, he wouldn't hesitate to help if you were ever in danger. I tend to be less complicated.' He smiled, and a thoughtful grin spread across his handsome face.

'I think the ladies like Ryder, though, and even some guys too! You know, it's the dark, brooding type that appeals to all. The guy looks the part! Did you know that he spends ages in front of the mirror perfecting his hero look with the latest hair gels?' Kyle shook his head and laughed loudly. He pointed at his chest. 'I'm low maintenance, and with me what you see is what you get.'

Kyle grinned, and a slight smile touched his lips.

A feeling of warmth encircled my body. After Ryder's drama, Kyle was refreshing. I liked his sense of honesty and those promise of spring green eyes. Kyle smirked at me and moved nearer on the settee, our legs touching.

Esme inclined her head forward, and her eyes widened in surprise. She blew a succession of pretend kisses, mouthing the word 'Kyle.' I glared at the mirror in disgust. I knew this was getting out of hand, what with Esme, and now this too cosy scenario with Kyle. *I didn't want him to get the wrong idea.*

A sudden thought entered my mind. Maybe Kyle had thought that I was asking him if he had a girlfriend. My eyes widened in surprise, and I noticed that Shadow joined in. The cat curled into a tight ball and snuggled deeper into Kyle's lap. Oh, oh. I peeked at Kyle through my down-turned eyelashes. I had to shift the mood, and fast.

'Would you like a drink?'

Kyle's face fell. It was clear from his expression he'd hoped to continue this shared moment of closeness or even to take it further. Instead, he picked up his wounded ego and answered me with a half-smile. 'Thanks, a cola would be good.'

I got up and walked past the lounge mirror. Esme stood on tiptoe, taking in the turn of events. I could see she wanted to join in or to flirt with Kyle, but there was no chance of that. As I walked down the hallway to the kitchen, I became more and more confused. I couldn't understand why Kyle wanted to make a move on me. What was with all these sixth form guys taking an interest in a nearly sixteen-year-old? It didn't seem Kyle's style to dive in so fast. Especially when his best mate had shown an interest first. So much for loyalty! Trustworthy Kyle? I scratched my head in wonder.

While I busied myself getting drinks, I muddled over Kyle's strange lack of loyalty. I was almost finished filling glasses when I heard Dad turning the key in the door and his slow shuffling foot-steps stumbling into the house.

'Hi, Dad, where've you been?' I walked out of the kitchen into the hallway with the drinks.

'Your mum and Aunt Karissa are out, so I ventured out to the pub,' he replied, down the hallway, undoing the buttons on his jacket with slow, painful movements.

'You okay, Dad?'

'Just the usual. When I go out to have fun, I end up exhausting myself.' Dad sighed, and his voice slurred. 'I need to get a walking stick since alcohol and old bones do not mix.'

I looked at my dad's ashen face and sighed. He traipsed down the hall and made for the lounge, where he collapsed into the nearest chair. He didn't realise it, but he'd chosen the chair opposite where Kyle sat. Toby had been hiding somewhere—far away from Shadow—but when the dog saw Dad, he joined us, lying down by Dad's feet.

Dad glanced at Kyle with knitted brows and then back at me. 'Dad, this is Kyle. He's Ryder's best friend.'

'Hello, Kyle, I'm pleased to meet you.' Dad struggled to catch his breath.

Kyle's bottom jaw dropped, and his eyes popped open in surprise. Obviously, Kyle hadn't known about my dad. Or read the newspaper column. His expression said it all. He looked like he was staring at a walking corpse out of an eighteen-plus horror movie. I handed Kyle his drink, reacting quickly because I knew I had to. It was up to me to spare Kyle any further embarrassment by answering for him.

'Dad, Ryder had to get back, but Kyle wanted to stay and listen to music.' Kyle continued to stare at Dad.

Dad raised an eyebrow and said, 'Ryder seems a very unusual young man.' He turned to Kyle with a stern expression on his face. 'But I expect you know him better, Kyle.'

Kyle picked up his cola, took a big gulp and recovered enough to say, 'Yeah... I've known Ryder since we were little; he's very different from anyone I've ever met before.'

'I'm sure,' replied Dad, his heavy-set eyebrows knitting together into a fragmented line as he frowned.

Kyle turned his face away, indicating another attempt to hide a wince. Toby watched the scene with sad eyes. I ignored Toby and scowled at my dad. I didn't like how critical he was toward Ryder. That was my job!

Dad changed the topic of conversation. 'Are you a fan of Amelina's music? All her friends seem to like the same kind of music. She has quite a following.'

'Yeah, I am,' replied Kyle, though he seemed lost for words. He sneaked another painful glance in Dad's direction. 'She's an amazing drummer.'

'She is, but unfortunately, we've no space for a drum kit, so I haven't heard her play.'

Kyle shifted uneasily in his seat. 'That's a shame.'

I smiled. Kyle glanced at his watch. Seconds later, he stood up. His swift movement resembled the springing motion of a jack-in-the-box toy. I took it as a desperate bid to make an escape before his face could betray his emotions anymore.

'Sorry, Amelina, I've got to get back. Thanks for the drink. Hope to hang out again soon.' He turned to my dad and inadvertently winced again, but redeemed himself by saying a quick, polite 'Bye.'

Dad stared at him for a second and then replied, 'Goodbye.'

I smiled at Kyle sympathetically. 'Bye, Kyle. See you soon.' Toby leaped up and followed Kyle to the door with his tail wagging. Knowing Toby, he probably thought Kyle would take him for a walk.

'See you later,' said Kyle. Toby took this as a no, and his tail drooped as his eyes reverted into sad mode.

I opened the door wide, allowing for Kyle's exit while I held onto Toby's collar just in case the dog tried to make his break. Esme watched Kyle leave. Her sad eyes followed him out the door. Toby was frantic. It was a job to yank him back in. I shut the door and walked back into the lounge.

Dad watched my entrance with interest and said, 'Well, I've never heard of a young man taking you out on a date and then leaving you with his best friend. Most peculiar.' Toby barked loudly. Dad shook his head and left the room before I had a chance to respond. This time Toby didn't follow. I reckon he still hoped someone would take him out.

Esme saw this as her opportunity to vent. 'Yep, hate to say it, but your dad's right. Can't you see Ryder's playing you like a pretty

pawn in his chess set?' She pointed her finger at me as if she wanted
to emphasise her point.

'Leave it, Esme, I don't need it from you too.' I was angry at
Ryder for the way he had treated me, but I didn't want to hear any
more.

'Amelina, Kyle's so much cuter. Why don't you drop Ryder and
hang out with Kyle more? That would be the smart thing to do.'

'Hmmm, I get it. You don't like Ryder. But you like Kyle?' I
giggled, cupping a burst of unexpected laughter with my hand.

'Whoa. Oh. How did you, um… guess that?' she asked, blushing
a bright scarlet.

'Ha!! You've got to be kidding? It's obvious.' I stepped closer to
the mirror to see whether she would tell me more.

'All right. I admit it. I do. Or at least I think I do. I've only just
met Kyle, but he looks hot.' Esme's eyes gleamed like two fireballs of
excitement.

I couldn't believe my ears. 'You and Shadow should form an "I
love Kyle fan club."' I shook my head in disgust at the course of the
conversation. Toby lifted his head at that remark. He didn't bark in
agreement. Instead, he lowered his head back down to his paws.

'I'd be happy to join Kyle's fan club. But just so you know, Ryder
is a pleasing piece of poison.' Esme got the last word in before Dad
returned. I heard his laborious shoes clunking down the hallway
coming toward the lounge.

Before I responded to Esme's remark, Dad walked in and joined
the conversation. Dad exhaled a lengthy moan as he sat down, and I
knew it was coming. He inhaled, and I heard it rattle in his chest.
He paused for a moment to catch his breath. Before continuing, his
voice echoed in his ribcage, 'I've nothing against Kyle; he seems a
decent enough lad. But I'd be careful if I were you, Amelina. My
instinct tells me there's something about Ryder that doesn't quite
add up.'

Anger flared in my heart at Dad's words. I kept silent. Annoyance had replaced misery. First, the curse. Now this, Dad's instinct.
What did he know? Half the time Dad didn't even voice his opinion
about anything that happened in my life. In fact, his overblown

reaction made me even more determined. I gritted my teeth. I had no intention of backing off with Ryder. No way. Dad would have to accept my decision. I wasn't his little girl anymore. I could make my own choices.

As far as I could tell, Ryder deserved the benefit of the doubt. My emotions swirled as I tried to reason the situation out in my mind. All right, so Ryder had left with Emily, and he'd been out with her before and hadn't shared that fact with me. But that didn't mean he was a cheating rat. If what Kyle said was true, then Ryder was acting like a good friend to Emily and looking after her. So that left Kyle. Maybe as a friend, Kyle would help me in gaining Ryder's affection.

I knew nothing for sure, and it certainly wasn't black and white. My head hurt. Yet, I needed to figure out a way to squash the curse, restore my dad to the way he used to be, and reactivate my mum's happy mode. More than anything, I wanted to become a normal teenager again. In the meantime, kisses—even weird ones—made the curse a whole lot more bearable.

PUZZLE PIECE 25:

AUNT KARISSA'S NIGHT OUT

Grown-ups staggering,
Leads to the craziest fight,
I'm picking my way,
Through all the smoke and the flames,
No way out? No, I'm weeping.

There was a great commotion when Mum and Aunt Karissa came traipsing in after their girl's night out. My aunt stumbled into the lounge, tripping over Toby. She didn't even notice her poor dog yelping and limping away. Instead, Aunt Karissa swayed and slurred, 'Well, how was the handsome Ryder? Was he a good kisser?'

The alcohol seemed to have little or no effect on my mum. She stood rigid, like a starched shirt. I grinned. There was nothing new there.

'Really, Karissa, you've had one too many glasses of wine. Leave Amelina alone. I'm sure she'll tell us about Ryder when she's good and ready.' Mum gave me a look that hot-wired to my brain, dissecting and probing my thoughts.

I opened my mouth to speak, but Dad got there first. 'Well, she came home with a nice young man called Kyle, a vast improvement on that other lad, Ryder, if you ask me.' Dad put down his cross-word puzzle on the side table.

I exuded fury. It took everything I had for my brain to not explode. I forced my breath to slow, and I glared at Dad with red-rimmed eyes. *How could he?*

Aunt Karissa pounced like a cat staggering to drag off a recent kill. 'Really? Sounds fascinating! Come on, Amelina, tell us all about it. What happened with Ryder?' My aunt swayed on her feet but stood rooted to the ground awaiting my reply.

I fidgeted and glanced down at my shoes. 'Ryder had to help Emily with some schoolwork. Kyle's just a friend, Aunt Karissa, that's all.'

'What a romantic-sounding name for just a friend—Kyle, you say?' Karissa wavered back and forth with a dreamy expression on her face. She paused, her brows wrinkled in deep thought. She turned to Dad. 'Why our parents called me Karissa and you Mark, I'll never know. Although, you're marked by... oh, I'm saying too much. I mustn't ramble on like this.' Aunt Karissa hiccupped and covered her mouth with her hand.

Dad's face turned stony, reminding me of a frightening sculpture I'd seen in an art gallery. He frowned. Without saying another word, he stood up and shuffled off to his computer room.

Mum spun around and growled at my aunt. 'Really, Karissa, now you've upset Mark. You always put your foot in it. I think you're doing it on purpose.'

Karissa adopted a guilty expression as she hung her head. 'Oh, I'm so sorry. I say the first thing that pops into my head. Most unfor-tunate habit, one I must try to change.'

I coughed to hide a smirk behind my hand but knew I'd failed when Mum glared at me with an unpleasant expression. 'Amelina. Don't stand there gawking; go make us a cup of tea.'

Aunt Karissa spoke up. 'No, I should do it. I've been rude

enough for one day.' Staggering to her feet, my aunt climbed up the stairs unsteadily to Dad's office. 'Do you want a cuppa, Mark?'

'I'm OK.' I heard the pain in Dad's voice and sat on the settee. I knew this conversation wasn't over. I closed my eyes to drown out the sounds of my family arguing.

'Oh, dear, I think he's dreadfully cross with me,' whispered Aunt Karissa to Mum as she stumbled back into the lounge.

'Well, that's no surprise.' Mum's voice rose to a shrill decibel like a pneumatic drill that had lost all hope of finding its controller.

'You know I don't mean it.' Aunt Karissa looked sharply at Mum.

'Of course.' Mum turned her back on my aunt and sat down in a chair.

I could tell by the sound of Mum's voice she didn't believe a word that Aunt Karissa had said. I watched my aunt teeter out of the room.

'Well then, I'm off to make the tea.'

'You sure you can manage?' Mum rubbed her eyes in a tired gesture.

'Of course, I will, but I shall have a shot of espresso first, to sober up!'

I sat in silence with Mum while Aunt Karissa disappeared into the kitchen. My aunt was gone for a ridiculous length of time. Finally, she careened her way back into the lounge, clutching two fragrant mugs of Earl Grey. I knew it was her way of giving a peace offering. The women sipped their tea in silence.

After Aunt Karissa's magical concoction had warmed their bones, Mum's attitude changed, and she cheered up. It was a miracle.

Mum smiled at my aunt. 'Thanks for the excellent tea and the superb dinner, Karissa. Much appreciated.'

I nearly gasped in surprise but stopped myself in time. Instead, I sipped my cola to keep my mouth shut.

'My pleasure; we should do it more often.' My aunt gushed. She turned in her chair and smiled at Mum and gulped her tea.

. . .

What did my aunt put in the tea? Magic bergamot leaves, perhaps?

Mum glanced at the clock on the mantel. 'It's getting late.'

Since the change in our fortunes, I couldn't remember a time that Mum hadn't gone to bed at eleven o'clock. The only exception was New Year's Eve when she stayed up to two minutes past twelve.

'Off to bed already, Eleanor? Oh, I hope I can find my book when I trot off to snooze land. I wanted to read tonight,' said Aunt Karissa, frowning.

Mum set her cup down and looked at my aunt. 'Where did you leave it?'

'Next to my reading glasses on the bedside table, but they've vanished too. You must have a residing ghost with impeccable taste that likes to steal them.'

Mum sighed. 'What an unlikely explanation!'

I smiled faintly. Aunt Karissa had a habit of losing things. I was sure they were somewhere around the house.

Mum stood up and gathered her things, ready to begin her night-time ritual. I watched through half-closed eyes as she wished everyone good night. Tired, I followed Mum. When I reached my room, I shut the door, hoping to escape my mother's critical eyes.

But Mum saw the closed door as a flashing neon invitation to come barging in. 'Amelina! Look at your room! How could you leave it in such a state?'

I surveyed the mess. 'I'm sorry, Mum. I was rushing to get ready and didn't have time to tidy up. I'll do it now.' I walked over to my bed and grabbed a dress I had discarded earlier.

'You always say that, but then you never keep your promises. No, I've had enough. This time I'll do it!' Mum grabbed a black refuse bag from the top wardrobe shelf and stuffed my precious things into the bag in a fit of temper.

I backed off and watched Mum have her adult tantrum from the side of the room. All I could think of was that those bergamot leaves had worn off. I watched in horror as she opened my camphor-wood chest and tipped my crystals into an empty box I had been saving for an art project. Next, Mum grabbed my precious dreamcatcher, which I hung up every night above my bed.

What is she thinking of? Hyperventilating, I hopped from foot to foot, doing a very wretched jig as if I was walking on fire. Tears threatened to overflow, and I struggled to control myself. 'Mum, don't touch my crystals and dream catcher, I promise to keep my room tidy. *Please* don't take them.' Mum's face set hard, a statuesque, no chance. She wasn't about to listen. Anger was etched in the lines around her mouth.

'It's too late. It's all too late, I'm confiscating your things to teach you a lesson,' shrieked Mum, as she tied the bag up and walked out of the door.

My mum did scary like no one else I had ever seen. She gave off this strange vibe like she was about to combust into a fireball of uncontrollable anger. That was it! I lost it, and tears streamed down my face. The more I wailed, the more all my pent-up emotions poured out of me. I felt like a volcano erupting in a fury, a hot lava flow of emotions and words. Poor Aunt Karissa stood motionless at the door watching, a silent, motionless, observer.

Still wearing my dress from my date with Ryder, I crawled into bed and sobbed, my heart broken by Mum's cruel attitude. At some point, I fell asleep. Later that night, I awakened and listened to Mum and Aunt Karissa arguing. I could hear my aunt urging Mum to return my things, but if anything, my aunt's pleas made Mum more determined to keep my trinkets hidden.

I slept off and on that night. I would hear a noise and wake up startled, my unhappiness overwhelming me. Mum didn't go to bed for hours, and the sound of her cleaning the house, angrily banging brooms, moving furniture, and scraping the floor, set my nerves on edge. I could swear I heard a droning noise coming from the electricity sockets. It sounded like a hive of bees lived within the walls. Shadow hid under my bed, seeking shelter from the awful atmosphere.

Near dawn, I crept downstairs and ran towards the patio door. Esme watched me open the door and shouted after me. 'Whoa. Where're you going, Amelina?'

'Out.'

'That pretty much sounds like what I want to do, but I can't.'

She peered at me through the glass of the mirror, a wistful expression in her eyes.

'Wish I could take you.'

'Yeah, me too. You're coming back, aren't you? I know we've got the weirdest friendship ever, but if you go, who in the heck will I talk to, apart from my own tragic self?'

I shrugged. At that moment, I felt a shitload of pent-up frustration and anger boil over inside me. It was a cesspit of ugly. I wanted to escape and never come back even if it meant abandoning Esme to her solitary prison and leaving Mum and Dad to their miserable fate.

I stopped and thought for a minute. To give Esme credit, she wasn't one for giving up. As I watched, Esme extended her right arm and leg as if she was ready to run in a sprint. Without hesitation, she raced toward me. Esme's head hit the glass walls of her prison, and she bounced backward into the blackness behind the mirror. I stepped closer to the mirror and peered inside to see if Esme had hurt herself. I could see her hazy silhouette, and she appeared to be okay. I waved. Esme touched her eye and wiped away a tear. A tiny quartz crystal appeared in her palm. This time she got lucky. She kept it. She waved back as I left. I noticed Esme's wave was an uncertain wave and given reluctantly.

I stormed ahead alone, and in my pent-up anger, the pounding of my shoes on the slabs echoed in the cold air. I pulled my cardigan closer and paused to think. How could I bear to be without my crystals? Without them, all the light had gone from my world. Before me, the garden lay cloaked in blackness, full of eerie shadows. Overhead, clouds drifted in the sky as if they couldn't find a peaceful place to rest. I felt like running forever, never turning back, and sprinting until my heart burst with the freedom of it all. But I didn't. I couldn't leave. I couldn't abandon my family, Esme, or my mum and dad.

I sat cross-legged on the lawn, my thoughts racing as they followed the path of the drifting shadows. *Why was my mother such an almighty bitch?* As soon as the word bitch crept into my mind, I regretted it. In my heart, I knew Mum had changed that strange day

Dad had evaporated into thin air. I pushed my guilt away. *If only I could turn back time, perhaps then everything would be as it was.*

Mum and Dad would be happy again, and Dad and Aunt Karissa would get on. There were just the two of them, yet they couldn't bear the sight of each other, which seemed harsh on my aunt's part. The strange thing was, Aunt Karissa knew why my father, her only brother, had changed. Whatever it was, it had driven a wedge between them. I sensed my aunt could never forgive him for whatever hurt he had done.

Raindrops gently fell on my head. The angrier I felt, the harder the rain appeared to fall. In my angry stupor, I realised that the rain felt as if it was washing away my feelings of desperation. I sat in the rain, wondering what my dad could have done to deserve such a life sentence. If only I could figure out the secret, but no one would tell me. Subconsciously I knew that I would never solve the mystery without my precious crystals. I was lost. Useless.

My aunt found me. It must have been a half an hour later. I felt like I'd been out in the garden all night. I was soaked through and shivering. Aunt Karissa extended a comforting hand to me and spoke in a hushed whisper as if she feared that her kind words would be stolen by the wind.

'Come, Amelina, you're drenched through. Poor dear. It's creepy out here in the dark; you never know who may be lurking in the shadows.'

I hesitated for a moment. 'Tell me, Aunt Karissa, why is Dad the way he is?'

Karissa didn't reply. This was a first. Instead, she sighed. I thought she intended remaining silent, but then she spoke.

'He was such a rascal as a boy, always getting into trouble, making friends with the wrong people, and trusting dodgy characters. Sometimes younger sisters get fed up helping their big brothers out of scrapes. This time he went too far. I tried, but I couldn't help him. You see, the curse states that it must be a firstborn child of his blood with pure, uncompromised abilities that will restore him. As a second-born Krystallos, all I can hope to offer is a few magical gifts to help you increase your skills, dear Amelina. You must act before you turn sixteen. A younger sister will no longer do.'

Sixteen? I felt the panic rise in my throat. Oh, my God! No pressure then. It would be my sixteenth birthday in a few months' time. My hand flew to my throat. I was really shivering now.

'Can you tell me what to do, Aunt Karissa?'

'I wish I could, Amelina, but sadly I don't know. However, I sense that you will figure it out, and be the one to save him.'

'How? I'm just an ordinary girl. I have no idea how to do that.'

'You are so much more than you realise; you are no ordinary girl! They say that on the day you were born the stars aligned in a brilliant pattern prophesying that in time you would solve a great mystery and become a receptacle for good magic, able to receive the magic of the crystals.'

Aunt Karissa's words acted upon my uncertainties, driving them away. She wrapped her arms around me. My tears flowed freely and mingled with the rain. I reluctantly allowed myself to be drawn back into the house. Esme greeted me with a relieved smile. She used her hands and made the shape of a heart. Shadow welcomed me with a meow and rubbed his head on my leg. It was quite the homecoming. No tears were spared.

PUZZLE PIECE 26:
THE NIGHTMARE OF LOSS

Nightmares pick your brain,
Like a hungry bird feasting,
On wriggling worms,
You have to puzzle through it,
To pick the fact from fiction.

That night I had a terrible time staying asleep. I tossed and turned for hours, thinking about what Aunt Karissa had told me. I had to help my dad. I didn't understand how to even begin.

Eventually, I fell into a deep but restless sleep punctuated by a series of frightening nightmares... but one particular dream stood out.

The vision began in stages, first with me crawling along the threads of my dream catcher as if I had become a spider caught in a tangled web. My hands and feet felt sticky, and it was difficult to cling to the rope. I had trouble climbing through the many woven levels of the dream catcher. When I arrived at the core, instead of protecting me from bad dreams, an awful nightmare began.

I stood on a deserted beach, looking at the sea. For mere moments it reminded me of a picture postcard of tranquillity. With a furious explosion, tiny stones rose from the ocean bed, skimming the surface of the water and bouncing several times towards the shore. No longer peaceful, the picture postcard scene changed. It was then, from the heart of the malevolent sea, an invisible force spewed stones in my direction. The pebbles piled up in a steady stream, rising from the foaming waves until they reached the sandy shore.

I tried to dodge the stone missiles, diving away, but my every move continued to be thwarted by shells, broken crabs' claws, and stones cutting into my skin. Above, the sky turned black and menacing. The winds howled and battered against my body. I couldn't continue. The strength of the wind grew too strong. The shells cut and slashed at my defenceless skin as I fought the onslaught. I opened my mouth to scream for help, but my mouth flooded with sand. Gasping for breath, I spat until the choking sensation subsided.

An area free of debris formed a protective orb around me. To my surprise, only a few metres away, I spotted Ryder accompanied by Emily. I watched them huddled together on the sand—kissing, locked in a passionate embrace and surrounded by the swirling sand.

At the furthest corner of the beach, I spied Will and Mitch. Those were the strange boys from the river walk the day Ryder had come to my rescue. I observed them taking photos of the sandstorm. The two boys wore tee-shirts. Their upper arms revealed black tattoos which danced on the surface of their skin, and then escaped, twirling into the air, becoming two distinct shadow shapes. Each shadow man kept repeating the same words: 'He kissed me and told me so, he told me so. His beguiling words filled my head. His black tattoo shadows crept in my body. I had no power to shake them off, so I spoke his words. Spoke his words.' I drew back in shock, confused by the strange words the shadow men had spoken. The protective orb disintegrated, and the sand flooded inward, choking me once more. With terrified eyes, I watched as Ryder and Emily's bodies engulfed in sand up to their necks. The couple didn't appear to notice, and they remained locked in a continuous kiss with no pause button. The shadow men circled the couple, picking up pace, dancing faster and faster.

Frightened, I curled into a ball, feeling the blood pounding in my head. I cried out for help, but no one answered. The unrelenting sandstorm swallowed my screams. Cautiously, I lifted my head, hoping for this nightmare to end. It was then a new threat appeared. The lifeless feathers from my woven dream catcher had knitted together to form a criss-cross pattern in the shape of a flock of malicious seagulls.

The largest of the seagulls grew until it was the size of a human-sized bird of prey. The thing transformed before me, and I took in the huge beak and blood-red eyes. Sharp hooked talons dug into the sandy earth. I cowered on the sand, crying and whimpering, fearful for my life. I hoped and prayed the creature would spare me. As it flew towards me, I closed my eyes, prepared to meet my maker. However, instead of killing me, the hideous bird grabbed me and flew off into the stormy sky. Fearing this was the end, I clutched the feathers on the bird's back, afraid I would fall off. On the beach below, I watched Ryder and Emily break from their embrace and glance up and wave as the bird propelled me to an unknown fate. As I flew over the beach, hanging onto the bird for dear life, I saw Will and Mitch. They were no longer possessed by shadow men; they were oblivious to my distress. They recorded the scene like a pair of professional photographers.

My captor flew me towards a large crag of rocks that resembled the outline of a sleeping lion. The enormous bird banked right and dumped me unceremoniously on the ground. I tumbled and rolled in the dirt until I stopped at the centre of the lion shaped crag. There before me rose a towering volcano. The rocks at the front of the crags contained red-hot stones, swirling around in a circular motion.

To the rear of the cliff, the rocks took on the appearance of a lion's haunches. Tiny, multi-faceted, sparkling crystals were strewn amongst the rocks. I couldn't believe my eyes, but those gems looked just like the crystals I'd attached to the bottom of my dream catcher.

At the centre of the volcano, I spied a massive, metallic grasshopper with red eyes sitting next to Ryder. I don't know how Ryder got there, but I could make out his features with little trouble. It was then it hit me. I recognised this monster— the grasshopper of the Corpus Chronophage clock! The strange pair pointed at me and spoke in words I couldn't understand. The mechanical grasshopper creaked and groaned as it popped smouldering crystals into its belly compartment. The grasshopper paused for a moment as if contemplating what to do next. Then he took an ancient key out of his belly compartment and dangled it in the air mysteriously. I heard a pitifully deafening sound that tormented me. I tried to block out the noise by covering my ears. But it made no difference. Thereafter, I heard the unmistakable refrain of an ice-cream van playing a children's tune that disturbed rather than pleased me. A terrible darkness filled my thoughts. My stomach churned with nausea as if I had been on the fastest, most terrible rollercoaster ride.

The sound of a clock ticking increased in decibels until the noise echoed against the walls of the cliff. The volcano bubbled and belched, shooting smoke and rocks into the air. It roared like a lion, finally awakened from its slumber, furious that its precious crystals were being stolen by the mechanical insect.

I couldn't take it anymore. Blood pounded in my head, and I ran in the opposite direction. The earth trembled and splintered, cracking beneath my feet. I sprinted and leaped over chasms to avoid the hot lava as it spread a burning path of terror.

The cracks in the ground deepened, and a gaping hole opened before me. I stopped before the chasm while my heart hammered in my chest. There was nowhere left to run. My legs trembled, and I launched off the ground in one last enormous, death-defying leap. The ground opened beneath me. I fell deep into the open chasm, screaming. Within the volcano's centre, the size of the gap increased and lava ebbed and flowed, sending roaring sparks exploding around me. I continued to free fall; the wind whizzing by my ears from the swift decent. There in front of me loomed the Scottish parliament rising out of the volcanic rock of Arthur's Seat, a building ablaze in a strange glory of colour. It was the most curious thing, but I could hear the loud clamour of politician's voices grumbling and those of the citizens arguing. I wondered if their divisive words were cracking the core of the earth. Such strange thoughts for a Cambridgeshire girl plummeting to her death in a volcano dream.

The heat was intense, and knowing I had reached the end of my rope, I fainted. I drifted in and out of consciousness, swirling in a miasma of fog. Ryder's concerned face appeared in the mist before me. I heard his voice. 'Quick, follow me, the volcano's about to erupt again.'

I reached out my hand towards Ryder as the volcano roared with a fury that shook me to the foundations of my soul.

———

Something dragged me from my disturbed dream and released me from the nightmare with a hellacious rumble. Curious pounding noises reverberated from the walls, vibrating throughout my room. It was hot, and I felt like I was suffocating. I watched as ghostly flickers of burning embers danced and played on my bedroom walls.

Terror crept into my throat. I sat up and spied Shadow. I could see two of him. I rubbed my eyes, trying to remove the double image. When I glanced at the cat once again, the double images of Shadow crouched on the floor, twin faces filled with a curious picture of concern.

Drenched in sweat, my body continued to tremble. Nightmarish screams erupted from the pit of my stomach, and I howled, releasing them into the stillness of the night.

Mum rushed in, her pale ghost-like face mirroring my own, a luminous, disturbing glow in the darkness. 'Oh, my God, Amelina, what are you screaming for? What's the matter?'

From the mirror over my dressing table, Esme woke up, rubbing the sleep from her eyes.

Aunt Karissa nearly tripped over Dad as she rushed into the room in her haste to see what had happened. Dad swayed, righted himself, and approached my bed. Concern etched the lines around his eyes.

I felt disorientated, but somehow I managed to sit up and lean back on my elbows. Fear clawed at my heart. I stared at my covers, bit my lower lip, screwed my eyes shut, and threw the quilt back. I opened each eye in turn, fearful of what I might find. My legs were right where they should be, attached to my hips. I gazed at pure flesh and bone, not a weird apparition of ebbing and flowing brought on by this crazy nightmare. 'My legs, they're okay. Yes! They're normal. I'm okay.'

'Yep, you really are the most entertaining friend ever, Amelina. Who needs TV,' Esme giggled, evidently on one of her highs. I glared at her with a look on my face that told her to shut up. Esme clamped her lips together and moved to the back of the mirror.

'Of course, your legs are normal, Amelina. What else could they be?' said Mum. The expression on her face said it all. She thought I was bonkers.

'You sure you're all right, Amelina? You screamed the house down and woke us all.' Dad's voice faltered, his speech slower and more slurred than usual.

'You scared the living daylights out of me, Amelina,' cried my aunt, raising her hand to her forehead in a pretend swoon.

'I'm sorry. That was the worst nightmare I've ever had. I felt the earth cracking apart, and all hell broke loose. I can't be without my dreamcatcher, Mum. I can't. Please... please, can I have it back?'

'I want one, too, *please,*' said Esme, laughing. Her bottom lip quivered as her laughter faded and she sobbed, 'Because I'm in a living nightmare.' I ignored the tears and gave Esme another *if you can't be quiet, I'll have to work out a way to throttle you* look.

Mum pulled a face but relented. 'Okay, Amelina, that's quite enough ridiculous commotion and theatrics for one night. I'll get your dreamcatcher and your precious crystals before you do a repeat performance and upset the neighbours.'

My heart soared, and I made a hasty promise. 'Thanks, Mum. I promise I'll do my best to keep my room tidy.' In the mirror, Esme couldn't help but stifle a giggle at that one.

Mum raised an eyebrow. 'Promises are meant to be kept.'

'I know.' My voice sounded shrill to my ears.

Mum eyed me suspiciously. 'Amelina, I hope you mean it. Your promises always sound like a hollow ping-pong ball, quick to fire off but with little substance fulfilled on their return.'

'I promise.' I looked Mum right in the eye. Esme wagged her finger at me. She gave me a glare which had an uncanny resemblance to Mum's. Esme placed her hands on her hips and laughed so hard that seconds later she was crying. Poor Esme, her emotions were all over the place.

Mum pulled the covers over me and said, 'Straight to sleep, Amelina. You have your art exam tomorrow.'

'Thanks, Mum.'

Mum shook her head in puzzlement and left without saying another word. Aunt Karissa leaned down and gave me a peck on the cheek. 'Sweet dreams and good luck.' She smoothed my hair away from my face. She turned toward the door and blew another kiss.

Dad stooped down to deposit a gentle kiss on my forehead. But his skin was so rough it felt like I'd cut myself with an abrasive razor. I winced.

'Sorry, Amelina, I forgot,' said Dad sadly. He shuffled out of the room with his slow gait.

Mum crept back into my room with my dream catcher and crystals in her hands. She stood by the bed and hung the dream catcher back on the hook. She paused for a minute, and then placed my crystals on my bedside table before she said, 'Goodnight.'

As soon as she had shut the door, I turned on Esme. 'Well, that was quite a show you put on; one minute you were laughing, the next minute you were crying.'

'Come on, it gets so annoying around here. I have zero fun… all I get to do is hear you fighting with your mum. My moods are up and down like a demented Yo-Yo. One minute I'm sliding into despair, the next I'm on a high like I've been sniffing some hot glass!'

'Keep off the hot glass, and shove over on your mirrored bed. Try to get some sleep before I unfriend you forever.'

'You can't do that. I've no social media.' Esme's bottom lip curled in disgust.

I shook my head. 'That sucks. Truly it does. But you know what I mean. Now, behave yourself!'

'Humph, that's harsh! Nightie-night social media junkie!' Esme yawned.

'Yeah, sweet dreams, social-media nada girl. And no more crying,' I said.

Esme nodded. Seconds later, I could see she was fast asleep. Lucky girl. She always went to sleep so fast, and right then I assumed her continual seesawing emotions must exhaust her.

There didn't seem to be any sign of Mum returning, so I cleaned and polished my precious crystal collection until they gleamed.

I laid back on my bed and relaxed a little, but not too much, as I had my art exam to think about. The house sighed with great rumbling groans while Shadow purred from under the bed. The rest of the night was tranquil, apart from Esme's loud breathing.

The unexpected jangle of my mobile ringing launched me out of bed. I answered the call and found Ryder at the other end of the line. He had phoned to wish me luck in taking my art exam and suggested that we meet up afterward.

As soon as I put down my mobile, it dawned on me that I hadn't told him about my exam. I scratched my head. How had he known? Normally I would have been pleased to hear from him, but the disturbing dream catcher nightmare had caused me to consider a lot of unanswered questions. Ryder's strange ability to read my thoughts had left me with more than a touch of impending anxiety.

PUZZLE PIECE 27:

THE ART EXAM

Exam nerves try this,
Watercolour life exists,
Anxiety shot,
It's puzzling, can't be real,
But shocked silence says it is.

I overslept. Of all the days, this had to be the worst. I scrambled from my bed and threw on my dressing gown.

'Good luck in your exam, Amelina.' Esme grinned and gave me an enthusiastic thumbs-up sign.

'Thanks. I think I'll need it.' I smirked, trying my best to grin.

The after-effects of the nightmare had left my limbs feeling heavy and my mind slow to react. I walked about the house in a stupor, my face pale and ghost-like. My footsteps thudded about as if I carried lead weights on my ankles. By the time I'd slipped into my school uniform, packed my school bag and art materials, there was no time for breakfast. I placed my art folder by the front door, and in my haste, I forgot to take it or to say goodbye to Mum.

She caught me as I was about to leave. 'Amelina, your art folder! Last night and now this!'

'Sorry, Mum.' I picked up the folder and made for the door.

Mum's eyes narrowed, and her lips tightened. 'Why can't you remember it? You are hopeless. You have your exam today!'

'I've got it, stop stressing me!'

'Have you had your breakfast?' Mum glared at me.

'Yes,' I lied, making a dash for it before she found out the truth.

I heard her final two words, 'Good luck.'

My mood didn't improve as I walked down the path. The ten-minute walk to the bus stop allowed ample time for the exam nerves to whisk a stir in my bubbly tummy. To add to my already spiralling levels of anxiety, I realised I'd forgotten my chalk pastels. I couldn't believe my stupidity.

As soon as I found a seat on the bus, I rummaged through my art folder. The unique paint set that Aunt Karissa had asked me not to use at school caught my eye hidden in a corner amongst folded scraps of paper. I didn't understand how it had gotten there. What choice did I have? It was just as well it was there, or else I wouldn't have been able to take part in the exam.

My thoughts returned to the last time I'd used the paints, and that weird creature had arrived on my doorstep. That was the last thing I needed. I only hoped that monster wouldn't jump out of my canvas in the middle of my exam!

My art teacher, Miss Crowther, always came to class dressed in vibrant colours with coordinating accessories. Today she'd completed her stylish ensemble with an elaborate silky scarf and bright red lipstick.

I hadn't dressed to impress. I'd left without brushing my wavy hair or applying any makeup. It was so bad I'd even forgotten to brush my teeth. My polo shirt bunched up, and I had a snag in my tights. I looked a sight!

Miss Crowther rushed about the class, her bubbling personality bursting forth, trying to motivate us. Soon the dreaded examiner arrived, a short, balding man with a quiet, stern face.

I took out my equipment and waited for the examiner to ask us to proceed. The canvas I'd brought appeared large, almost too big to fill. My hands trembled as I contemplated the bare whiteness staring back at me.

I picked up the brush and started painting. Soon, it became laden with crystal paint, its fibres tingling and glowing. With every stroke of the brush, an inexplicable surge of energy pulsated through the nerve endings in my fingertips straight into my pounding heart. My nails turned the brown hue of the brushes, though fainter, much less noticeable than before. This time the brushes were silent as if they knew an exam was in progress.

The phenomenal rush I felt from using the paints again made me feel superhuman. I worried that if my heart pounded any louder, it would jump out of my chest and land in my clammy hands!

An overwhelming desire forced me to paint intricate leaves, debris, and mud, in an elaborate jigsaw puzzle of art. I painted trees and ferns, leaves and grass, rocks, and horses. In the centre of the canvas, I painted a lone person standing and looking lost. Her expressionless face stared at me as if she was in a trance. The girl could have just stepped out of bed, dressed in her pyjamas but ready to go for a walk in the woods.

I carried on painting like a demon possessed. My brush strokes increased and became more deliberate. The ticking sound of the clock above the teacher's desk magnified and echoed. Trickles of perspiration formed on my forehead. I wiped the sweat on my shirt and glanced at the clock once again. It was already twelve o'clock. Time was running out. I'd almost finished the piece, and my hands were shaking. One last stroke and I'd be finished. Done.

A tiny whisper sounded in my ear. I knew it was the brushes congratulating me for a job well done. The pots released a gentle note, an almost flat coca cola fizz pop, expressing their delighted opinion. I smiled in relief and closed the lids. The silence was welcome.

At lunch, I felt exhausted but exhilarated. Jade was the first to mention my manic painting. 'Amelina, what'd you do, that was crazy. I've never seen you paint like that before. You're drenched with sweat. No offence, but you look like you need a shower.' Jade stepped back as if my unpleasant fragrance made her gag.

'Thanks. A shower would be good. I can't stop sweating.' I mopped my forehead with a sodden tissue. 'I don't know what's happening.'

'What d'you mean?' asked Ilaria.

'It's weird, and I don't know for sure. The brushes, and paints, that, um… my aunt gave me are so peculiar. They give me this jolt of energy. It was strange, but I ended up painting a jigsaw puzzle. How weird! A jigsaw of art, but the pieces make little sense to me.'

'Couldn't agree more,' said Ilaria with a giggle.

'Amelina, what are you on? Oh, my God, your hands are trembling, and your eyes are as wide as oversized teacups.' Joselyn grabbed my hands, trying to still them.

'Too much of this,' I replied, picking up my energy drink and taking a long drink from the can.

'Yeah, I can see that. You're totally charged. Are you sure you're okay?' added Joselyn, her concerned eyes searching for a clue to my current state.

'I think so,' I said, feeling anything but.

The class returned to finish the exam. I wasn't sure what to do. I fiddled around, pretending I was adding final touches. But it was all an act. At the end of the test, everybody huddled around my painting, looking to see what I had created. Nobody said a word. Perhaps the jigsaw painting had stolen their unspoken words and slotted them away.

PUZZLE PIECE 28:
LEANNE'S WARNING

Time to understand,
Leanne's elaborate words,
Whilst in the middle,
Of life's thunderous pathway,
Guard those precious wizard stones.

After the stress of the exam, I knew the perfect antidote to my adrenalin-charged day had to be the Crystal Cottage. So I returned home for a shower and a quick change of clothes.

I rushed out of the house, and as I walked down the river pathway, a sense of calm enveloped me. I struggled to contain my excitement at visiting the cottage once again. Just as before, the cottage rose out of the ground with an enormous roar. The welcome mat shone, free from dust, and the cottage windows gleamed, anticipating my long overdue arrival.

I knocked and waited to enter. The door creaked open. I took that as my invitation to slip through the opening and breezed inside. As before, my eyes searched out the sparkling crystals, and for a moment I almost forgot why I'd come. I stood motionless, in awe of the surrounding beauty.

In the corner, I spotted Leanne unpacking new stones that must have recently arrived. As I watched Leanne at work, the crystals freed themselves from her protective hands. They flew across the room, whizzing, creating a trailing rainbow of spectacular light and sound. In no time at all, they found their allotted places, embedding themselves with ease in the walls.

At last, I drew my eyes away from this amazing sight. I turned to face Leanne. 'I need to speak to you.'

'What can I help you with?' replied Leanne in a dream-like voice.

'Recently things have been happening that are beyond my usual level of acceptable peculiarity. I wondered if you could help.'

Leanne's eyes widened, and she nodded her head. I explained about how my new paint set seemed to have a mind and purpose all of its own. I described the strange events that had happened since I used my aunt's gift. She listened but made no comment.

I stomped my foot and thought I would burst with frustration at her lack of response. 'Leanne, what shall I do?'

'Embrace these events.' Cupping her hands together, fingertips touching, Leanne rocked on her heels. She turned back to her unpacking duties.

'Whatever do you mean?' I wailed, shocked at her response.

'This is happening for a reason. You must not be fearful, Amelina. Welcome all that's happening, and the truth of who you are will dawn on you.'

The room was quiet except for the rustling of paper as Leanne unwrapped the remaining crystals. I listened but was unsure what to do next. I walked over to the wall of gems, ensnared once again in the magical beauty they exuded. Three crystals twinkled more brightly than the rest and caught my eye. I carefully removed *the Black Obsidian, the Bloodstone, and the Merlinite* and weighed each gem in the palm of my hand. An aura of light burst from the stones and encircled me. Each crystal's field of energy exploded in a kaleido-scope of colour and joined together, forming a solid beam of brilliant intensity. I felt an invisible energy force rush through me, shooting all the way into my fingers. I glanced down, and my fingertips were glowing the brightest pink I had ever seen.

I had never felt such raw power. I could tell something beyond my comprehension was taking place. I staggered back, filled with wonder, and my mouth dropped open. The experience made me feel complete, as if something elemental had been missing from my life all this time, until now. I had no doubt these crystals were the perfect choice to give me the answers I sought.

I stumbled over to Leanne, who winced from the brightness of my aura. I gently handed her the gems. She inclined her head and pondered over my selection. 'Interesting... such a choice of crystals, Amelina. I'm sure these gems will set you on the right path towards discovery.'

The patter of rain punctuated by rumbles of thunder interrupted my thoughts. The cottage darkened, highlighted only by flashes of lightning. The crystals lining the cottage walls shrank into their protective spaces, their colours dull, seeming to hide from the suddenly approaching storm.

Leanne's face darkened, mirroring the impending storm. She paused under the boom of thunder. 'You must take extra care with these stones, for all three hold immense power. Guard the Wizard Stones, the Black Obsidian, and the Merlinite. Keep them safe, and remember, the power they may unleash could overwhelm you.'

The luminosity surrounding me swirled and intensified. I swallowed and asked my question carefully. 'How?'

Leanne peered at me from the darkness. 'These are Wizard Stones. She pointed to the gems still cupped in my hand. Used without care they can drive you mad, make you hallucinate, or even provoke seizures.' Her forehead creased and her eyes blinked as the lightning flashed through the windows. 'You must protect them from damage, taking particular care to avoid scratches, blows, harsh chemicals and extreme temperature. Don't forget to cleanse the Bloodstone if it comes in contact with anyone else.'

'What happens if I don't follow your instructions?'

Leanne leaned in close to my face and whispered, 'The crystals will become impure, open to evil manipulations, wielded by darkness and used by black-hearted, devious souls.'

I whispered back a scared, 'I promise.'

'A promise is more than words spoken,' replied Leanne, a serious expression shadowing her gentle face. Her anxious eyes darted around, searching every nook and cranny of the cottage. I felt a chill in the air and wondered what she was searching for. 'In the Middle Ages, the Bloodstone's special powers were legendary. The stone is a powerful cleanser, a binding force in family love, and a powerful tool in weather magic,' she whispered.

I blinked. 'A binding force in family love. A cleanser. Does that mean I should use it to heal my dad from the curse?'

'Perhaps. However, only you can discover whether that will be the case.'

After her last words, the fury of the storm subsided, and rays of sunlight trickled through the windows. The crystals relaxed their tight grip on the walls and resumed their natural appearance stuck to the walls.

Leanne stood rooted to the spot. She stared at me with eyes focused on something far away as if she was unaware of the change in the atmosphere. Drawing breath, she continued. 'The Merlinite is a conjurer's stone; a spiritual stone that allows one to journey into past lives. Placed under your pillow at night, it can transport you to Arthurian times.'

My heart thudded in my chest and my breath caught in my throat. 'Arthurian times? You're kidding, aren't you? Next thing you'll be telling me the crystals can turn into a Tardis.'

'A time machine? Hmmm, that would be interesting. Unheard of, but with magic, nothing is impossible. I never jest, dear Amelina. You will see. I only speak the truth. Believe in the crystal's power, and they will take you places you have never imagined.'

Leanne continued to stare straight ahead, her gaze transfixed and unwavering on a spot in the distance. Her words tumbled out. 'The Black Obsidian hails from volcanic rock and is a source of a different power. It is a Wizard's Stone, a traveller's stone by night and is also called the Stone of Truth. When you gaze into the gem, our true nature cannot be hidden. Due to its extreme powers, the crystal must be used with extreme caution and respect.'

Leanne swayed. The effort of surrendering so much information had visibly drained her face of all colour. I moved to help her. Her trembling hand pointed towards a pocket on her long skirt. I reached inside and found a sugar pastille. I ripped off the wrapping and passed it to her. The sugar revived her in seconds. I let out the breath I had been holding, worrying about the elderly woman's mental status.

Leanne's hands shook as she returned the crystals to my outstretched hands. The aura had ceased, and the gems were back to their natural state. 'Amelina, beware the river pathway, as many shadowed souls pass by the area.' The old woman walked away and returned to her unpacking.

My time with Leanne had come to an end. Clutching the crystals close to my heart, I left the Cottage with a heavy heart. I knew I would have the wisdom to use them wisely. I had no other choice. I had listened to each of Leanne's wise words, spoken in great detail. I had to find the strength to become the rightful guardian of these powerful crystals. As usual, my body felt heavy, and my movements were weighed down by the overwhelming responsibility that fell on my shoulders. Would I remember each detail of Leanne's instructions?

My next problem was that today happened to be the day Ryder had asked to get together with me, but I had the crystals in my possession. I didn't know what to do, and I had to figure out a plan, fast.

PUZZLE PIECE 29:

RYDER'S SHADOW IS ANGRY

I hoped for a kiss,
Have a bad feeling, somehow,
I'm a known psychic,
Anxiety's bubbling up,
Making it all seem much worse.

R yder didn't sound pleased when I called to tell him I'd be late. I had rushed home the long way avoiding the Riverwalk like Leanne had suggested. I wanted to lock the crystals away. By the time I arrived at the riverbank, I was a good half an hour late. Ryder's grim face matched his fiery, unapproachable eyes. The sunny day had turned, and long shadows lingered everywhere I looked.

'Sorry I'm late, Ryder, I had something important I had to take care of.'

'I'm sure you did,' answered Ryder with a stony expression. I lowered my eyes and wondered why he was overreacting. I was only half an hour late, and I had apologised.

I kicked a pebble on the path with my foot. 'I'm sorry. Shall we take a walk down the river?'

'Yeah, right. If you have the time,' said Ryder, taking long strides, marching in the other direction. His shadow stretched behind him, taut like an elastic band, struggling to catch up with him.

'I can't keep up, Ryder, you're walking too fast,' I said, breathing hard like I was power walking in an enforced military drill.

'Sorry.' Ryder slowed down and in no time, I reached his side. We walked together, stepping in time to some strange dance.

At last, he broke the silence and asked, 'How did your exam go?'

'It was stressful,' I confessed, still panting. *Not as stressful as you, though.*

'Oh. What did you paint?' Ryder relaxed and slowed down even more, which gave me the chance to catch my breath.

'I painted a weird scene. It wasn't what I had planned at all.'

'Sometimes it's better that way.'

Today, Ryder's vibrant eyes were dull and empty. His words sounded forced, and apart from asking about my exam, he spoke little. For the rest of our time together, he sulked. We stopped at the country park for an ice-cream, and we ate in silence. As the afternoon wore on, long shadows cast on the ground by the filtered sunlight hid behind the trees. The light and dark shaded lines reminded me of uncertainty, and I shrank from their appearance.

To my great surprise, Ryder turned and said, 'Amelina, give us a kiss.'

No boy had ever asked before. Usually, boys grabbed me and stole a kiss. But this was different, and because of his asking, it made me more anxious. Ryder was taller, so after a moment of thinking, I stood on tiptoe and kissed him on the lips. He clutched the small of my back, carving his body into mine, as he pressed his lips hard against my mouth. The kiss left me breathless. My knees went weak, and I felt giddy. There was a fierceness about this kiss, and it frightened me. I couldn't explain why, but it felt like an angry kiss stolen for the wrong reason.

I gasped for air and we parted. Ryder remained silent, but I saw a cruel curl to his lip that I'd never noticed before. I sensed there was something dangerous about Ryder, undiscovered and unexplained. I shivered, and a jolt of excitement surged through me. I had to admit that against my better judgment, I found Ryder to be exciting.

I blamed myself for this whole mess. It was true that I'd managed to get Ryder all to myself, and then I'd spoiled it. I should have gone to the Crystal Cottage on another day. I should have known better than to mix the two together in one day only hours apart. Right now, I despised myself.

Yes, it was true that I'd had my kiss, but instead of a passionate embrace, it had felt like a slap in the face. I closed my eyes as I felt that kiss tingle beyond my lips. A haunting sensation remained, urging me to plead for it to never leave me.

PUZZLE PIECE 30:
THE DEVILISH EMBRACE

I wanted a kiss,
Sometimes you should be careful,
About cute wishes,
Crazy tattoos invading,
Isn't really what you need.

The outing in the country park with Ryder had been a disaster, and apart from the strange aftermath of the kiss and the sensations that followed, nothing good had resulted from our tryst. Yet, I tried to rationalise it. The kiss had expressed his hidden anger, so it wasn't surprising that apprehension gnawed at my heart when Ryder turned up at my door the very next day.

The clamour from the bell startled me, and I peered out of the window from the top floor landing. No invitation, yet there was Ryder, standing and looking at the door. I didn't answer straight away. He rang the bell again. I wasn't sure I wanted to see him again, so I continued to ignore him. At this slight, the knocking began. I listened for a few more minutes, and the thought crossed my mind that perhaps he intended to apologise for his behaviour.

I sighed and traipsed downstairs to see what his story would be. As I passed the hall mirror, I caught sight of Esme peering out at me with curiosity shining in her eyes. I opened the door, and Ryder's warm smile greeted me. Shadow brushed past my legs and sat down between the two of us. His black tail curled around his body. Ryder's face fell at the sight of the cat.

From inside the house, I heard Esme gasp. I ignored her, and with a flip of my hair, I sized Ryder up. 'What's up?' I asked, trying to act cool. Esme's antics were making me nervous.

'I came to see you, Amelina. Felt I've neglected you. Besides, I've been an idiot.' Ryder had the decency to glance down at his guilty feet before looking up.

Anger churned in my gut, and I gazed at Ryder's face. 'I can't figure you, Ryder. You keep on playing with my emotions and then flirting with Jade or disappearing to do homework with Emily. How do you expect me to feel?'

'Jade and Emily are gorgeous, but they're not *you*, Amelina.' He reached over and brushed a loose hair away from my face. His fingertip traced a line down my cheek to my chin and neck. It was almost imperceptible, the gentlest of caresses, yet it lingered there long after his hand had left my face. My heart thumped, and I feared he could hear my rapid heartbeat. Shadow circled around my feet determined to provide a protective barrier between Ryder and me.

'Forgive me for being an idiot. I'm sorry I behaved in such a miserable way the last time I saw you. I behaved badly. I'm a wretch.'

'You said it.' I stood my ground, and Ryder sensed my anger. I could see it on his face.

'C'mon, show me around your house. I haven't seen it all before.' Ryder's voice lulled me with caressing syllables. He stepped closer, and his eyes locked onto me with a magnetic pull.

'It's true. You haven't seen the rest of the house before.' I motioned for him to enter. Ryder walked down the hall toward the stairs. I willingly followed him. He climbed the staircase and arrived on the landing at the top of the stairs next to my room. He opened my bedroom door and peeked inside. Hesitantly, he walked inside, and I followed. Ryder closed the door and pushed Shadow out of the way. The cat was left on the other side of the door, meowing and clawing at it.

As soon as the door closed, Ryder moved without warning. He grabbed me and pulled me towards him. His mysterious eyes bore into me, one a single black coal fire raging, and the other eye, green and penetrating. The muscles in his upper arm were taut and rippled as he encircled me in his grip. My breath caught in my throat, and I felt trapped, unable to move. He gripped me so tightly I could hardly breathe. I felt like a delicate butterfly waiting to be crushed between his nimble fingers.

There were no romance or gentle caresses. Instead, Ryder's lips pressed down on mine, crushing me with his bruising strength. I felt sick. His mouth tasted like ash, like burned, decaying rubbish. Worse, Ryder reeked of death. Nothing made sense, and I pushed against his chest, but he was too strong. I remained ensnared, wrapped in Ryder's cruel embrace.

My panicked breaths encouraged him to pull me even closer. His body moulded against the length of me. Locked within his arms, I felt his skin become leathery. Black-inked tattoos appeared on his bare skin. He saw my inclination to stare and released me a fraction. Mesmerised, I watched those symbols undulating on his arms. The tattoos slithered from his body onto mine, carving their way into my skin. The pain was unbearable. I cried out as the sensation of needles continued to pierce my skin. The pain withdrew, then pierced again, black shadows invading, forcing their way inside, tattooing black patterns under my flesh. My mind crawled towards the precipice and bleakness overwhelmed me.

My energy drained, like a battery stripped of its charge, and my skin became cold, my lips icy. My body collapsed, and I felt as if I was a dead weight flooded with blackness. In my stupor, I was drowning, and Ryder pushed my head deeper into icy water covered with a slick of black ink. The black water filled my lungs, tattooing my heart and turning it black. The water pulled me deeper, and I realised I was sinking. I struggled and kicked to break the surface of the water. I would break through and gasp for air, but Ryder would push me down again. I plunged deeper into the depths.

When my limbs couldn't struggle anymore, I hung suspended within this strange liquid. It was almost poetic and tranquil. Black velvet waves caressed my skin, and I drifted in the abyss. From out of my watery grave, a firm hand disturbed my tranquillity. Something lifted me up, wrenching me, kicking and screaming, from death's grasp. I pushed my way back to consciousness through a cruel, unforgiving vapour that threatened to consume my body, feasting on my flesh like a hungry demon. A burning sensation scorched behind my eyes, almost as if a lit ember inflamed my thoughts.

I struggled to break through, to breathe, and to survive. With one final gasp, I coughed and released the intrusive miasma, which vanished into thin air. Semi-conscious, I sensed I was lying on my side. I turned my head and glanced up. I found myself on Ryder's lap, and he was caressing my forehead.

'Are you okay, Amelina?'

His words barely registered. I couldn't comprehend what had just happened, but I knew I had to get away. Ryder was charming when he wanted to be, but underneath, he exuded something else—something ugly. I felt trapped. Trapped and terrified. I could barely focus, let alone string two coherent words together. My brain took several minutes to disentangle my thoughts and reply to his last question. 'I don't know if I'm all right or not.'

'Hmmm. One minute we were enjoying each other's company, and the next moment, you threw up. You fainted on me.' Ryder stopped caressing my forehead and gazed into my eyes.

'I, I can't have.' Something was wrong here, and I knew it. For the first time, I glimpsed Ryder in a new light. I saw two of him—a double dose of Ryder, one good, the other bad.

'I'm afraid you did, Amelina.'

I rubbed my eyes with two clenched fists. 'I can't seem to

remember. My mind's all muddled.' I pushed off Ryder's lap and tried to stand up, but my legs struggled to support me.

'I'll get you a glass of water.' Ryder stood up and lifted me into his arms. He gently placed me on my bed. I recoiled from his touch and rolled to the other side. Ryder opened the door, and Shadow launched into the room. The cat lunged and landed in Ryder's arms. He held Shadow's raging, taut body at arm's length. The cat hissed and spit, and a blood-curdling howl escaped his lips.

Ryder scowled at him. 'Hey, what's got into you, Shadow? You… wretched animal, you scratched my arm.' Shadow hissed, and Ryder released the cat. Shadow jumped on the bed and licked his paw while keeping a steady eye on his every move.

I glanced around my room and noticed it seemed different. A pallor clung to the atmosphere, and it seemed darker and colder than usual. My head throbbed, and my body ached. I moaned in the darkness.

My thoughts raced. What had Ryder been doing while I was out cold? Had he touched me, undressed me, or worse? Or had he rummaged through my stuff searching for something? What was he up to?

Ryder hurried back into my room with the glass of water. I noticed how attentive and caring he looked, but I wasn't buying his act. Not anymore. Something had happened, and I wasn't sure what had transpired. Alone with him, in my bedroom, I felt vulnerable and afraid. I gulped as another wave of nausea hit me.

'You seem a bit queasy again. Shall I call an ambulance?' Ryder's question had a sharp edge to it.

I just wanted him out of here, and I chose my words carefully. 'No, I'm better; the water's helping. Maybe I need to get some rest.'

'Oh, right, I'll leave you in peace.'

Ryder stood up to leave, and I tried my legs. They were still wobbly. He put out a hand to steady me. I managed to walk with help towards the door. I caught sight of my reflection in the mirror. How had that happened? What had Ryder done? I pressed my fingers to my bruised lips. They were black. Tattoo black.

'Sorry, Amelina, I seem to have left quite a lasting impression on your lips.' Ryder smirked. He made no effort to hide the triumph on his face. He appeared to be proud of what he had done.

I glared at him. 'You've bruised them so badly it looks like my lips have been tattooed with black bruises, Ryder.'

'Shit, sorry… It was just a friendly kiss, Amelina.' Ryder shrugged his shoulders.

'If that's a friendly kiss, I hate to think what a passionate one is like! I look like I've been attacked. What'd you do?' I rubbed my lips with a finger, trying to change the colour.

'Nothing. All I did was kiss you. I could give you a demonstration if you'd like,' said Ryder, leaning in towards me, puckering his lips.

The aroma of a cesspit hit me. I drew back and stiffened. 'Don't go there, Ryder. I don't remember our kiss, and I certainly don't want to repeat it.'

Ryder blew out a breath. He leaned against the doorjamb. 'I remember enough for both of us. It was nice, but perhaps I was a little rough.'

'Ugh,' I said, gulping down his words like a bitter pill. 'I have no intention of repeating it, ever. I'd be insane to do so—have you forgotten something? Your obsession with Jade?'

'Y'know, I'm just friends with her.'

'Come on, stop lying! I've seen the two of you together, you're always staring at her, and she's just the same, making eyes at you.' Anger rang in my voice. My eyes blazed with a dark fury.

'Right, yeah, I have that effect on the opposite sex.' Ryder shrugged.

By now, I couldn't tell what it was about him that had ever appealed. What was that disgusting smell? Had he started smoking and abandoning his deodorant too? I fought the urge to throw up again.

'Stop it. I don't want to hear any more about your effect on the opposite sex. Jade's my friend. Stay away from her.' I covered my mouth with my hand and swayed from the exertion of sharing my thoughts out loud.

'I think our little kiss was a big mistake, and I don't do bossy girl-friends,' said Ryder, pointing a finger in my face.

'Yeah, and I don't do creepy boyfriends. In fact, the thought of *our little kiss* makes me puke!' I pulled a face.

Ryder grabbed my arm. 'That's harsh; you didn't complain.'

'I couldn't complain. I was being invaded by... blackness. Fricking heck, I can't even remember what happened. If you expect me to keep silent about what a creep you are, then you're mistaken.' I faced him with blazing eyes.

Ryder's face darkened. 'You're mistaken if you think you can cross me. Just forget our friendly little kiss. It never happened.' His eyes gripped mine in a devilish embrace, and his hypnotic words swam through my mind.

Ryder stomped down the stairs and slammed the door as he ran out of my house. Hopefully, forever.

PUZZLE PIECE 31:
THE SLEEPOVER BEGINS

Take a photograph,
At a sleepover party,
It may disappear,
If you shoot a time monster,
Gobbling time—then watch out!

At last, the party weekend had arrived. We'd finished our exams. I should have been excited, but ever since Ryder's visit, doubts had plagued me. I couldn't remember anything apart from a peculiar, frightening sensation of drowning and falling. In my heart, I sensed he had done something wrong, or he'd been up to something, but there was no way for me to prove it. Perhaps he'd rifled through my things. I spent time wondering whether he posed a serious threat to the safety of my crystals. However, it seemed unlikely. Nothing had gone missing, and my crystal collection appeared untouched.

Although that didn't apply to my lips. My bruised lips suggested that Ryder had kissed me and been rough, just like the time before.

What bothered me most was that I didn't remember the kiss. Warning bells clanged loud and clear in my head. I didn't want to draw attention to the bruising, so I covered it up with heavy makeup. I hoped that no one would notice. I had some pretty nosy friends.

I didn't feel like going to the sleepover because the experience with Ryder had left me drained, but I had no choice. I'd upset Joselyn if I didn't come, so out of a sense of friendship, I packed my stuff for the night ahead. I had all the necessities, my makeup bag, pyjamas, and a change of clothes. I squeezed in a few DVDs, some sweets, and my dream catcher. I put my crystals into a zipped bag and tucked them inside my overnight bag, too. They were precious. I had to safeguard them.

I wrapped up Joselyn's surprise, a camera. I had saved for months to buy her this gift. I was sure Joselyn would be excited when she found out what I had chosen for her.

We met at Mitcham's Corner, a popular area of Cambridge, just north of the River Cam, home to numerous shops and pubs. Ilaria and I were the first to arrive. We chatted and waited for Jade and Joselyn to join us. A few minutes later, I spotted the girls and waved. Jade waved back, walking towards us in her usual hurried fashion. Joselyn followed Jade, dragging her heels, looking sheepish. She wore a loud floral top, and her body language shouted embarrassment, spelled with a capital E.

'New top, Joselyn?' I clicked my tongue sympathetically.

'Yeah. My mum got it for my birthday and wearing it makes me want to scream. I didn't have the heart to tell her it's just not me.' Joselyn smoothed the shirt with nervous hands.

'Hmmm… It looks more like Ilaria!' Jade grinned and hugged her friend.

'Yep. It's just my style. Can I borrow it?' replied Ilaria, her eyes lighting up.

Joselyn managed a slight smile. 'Anytime Ilaria! Please.' That got a chuckle out of the foursome.

We linked arms and walked down the river path, which led past the punts to the centre of town. It was a dazzling sunny day to walk along the slatted wooden quayside walkway by Magdalene Bridge. As we approached the sidewalk, a few young men carrying placards tried to interest us in a day of punting. Not in the mood for boating, we politely said no. We didn't have the cash for that; we needed our pennies for cakes, sweets, and shopping.

It was a typical day in the city, and there were plenty of shoppers out and about, and the restaurants were full. Intrigued by history, I stopped and stared at the mediaeval Round Church, built by the Knights Templar. I knew many of the mysterious legends associated with the Templars. The Relics and the Holy Grail were attributed to them. Today, I imagined the knights wearing their white surcoat, with the Red Cross stretched across their tunic. I pondered their fates, wondering if martyrdom had assured them a place in heaven. For a moment, I was transported back in time, away from my troubles. I lagged behind the rest of the girls and forgot where I was and who I was with.

Ilaria cupped her hands around her mouth and shouted back at me. 'C'mon, hurry up, Amelina. Stop daydreaming. We've got more important things to do than to stare at old churches. We've got some serious shopping to do!'

I shook myself out of my reverie and realised I lagged several paces behind. I rushed to catch up. A crowd of hungry people stood outside *Patisserie Valerie*. I watched them staring at the window display of delicious cakes. I smiled and remembered the last time we had been together in the city. We girls had ordered one huge slice of Gateaux between us to share. The waitress had given us a disapproving look. Today, the four of us went straight in and ordered large slices of Black Forest Gateaux, Strawberry Gateaux, Chocolate Ganache and Chocolate éclairs. The desserts were divine and smelled heavenly.

After eating every crumb, we packed up our belongings and left. It was only a short walk past the Round Church to the Grand Arcade Centre, where the actual shopping would begin. Out of necessity, we chose the long way around by taking the tourist vantage point past Hardy's sweet shop. We passed by St. John's and

King's Colleges. I had a certain destination in mind, and I steered the girls toward my goal.

It wasn't a popular decision, but I wanted to take a photo of the Corpus Chronophage Clock with the enormous grasshopper perched on top. The popular tourist attraction was created by the inventor, Dr John C Taylor, OBE. Sightseers bunched in a tight circle around the clock. I squeezed through the throng of people and greedily snapped the photo.

Ilaria stopped and stared at the clock. 'Whoa. Check out those spiky pincer teeth. Look! Geez, they're filed into needle-points. Oh, I wouldn't want to mess with that monster.'

'Me neither,' replied Jade. She stepped back after inspecting the insect close-up.

'It scares the heck out of me,' said Joselyn, pulling a typical freaked out pose. When her face rearranged itself back to semi-normality, she continued, 'Why are you taking so many fricking photos?'

'I don't know why. It's the weirdest thing ever. Every time I pass by, I always hear this weird sound, a moaning coming from far away and yet the sensations seem to travel right through my skin.'

'I can't feel or hear anything, Amelina, but that gruesome bug gives me the creeps,' said Joselyn.

'Me too. I can't help but stop and stare. I'm taking my inquiry to a new level. I wanted to capture the clock in a photograph. Y'know, like kids who keep specimen bugs in a jar.' I smiled and shrugged.

'Well, hurry up then, and snap your photos before that creature buzzes away or does a disappearing act!' replied Ilaria, laughing.

'Yeah, speed up; stop being so bug obsessed,' said Jade.

I gazed at the clock one last time and added, 'Time to buzz off ourselves, we've got some shopping to do.' I smiled as we walked away but couldn't help turning back for one last glance. The grasshopper didn't appear impressed. No doubt shopping held no interest for a time-keeping bug.

It was a short walk to the bustling Grand Arcade, which jostled with a multitude of shoppers, going this way and that. We had agreed beforehand that this would be the perfect opportunity to shop for prom. We stopped in a few shops and tried on some fabulous gowns. What fun we had prancing about in dresses we wouldn't have had the courage to try on by ourselves. Some of the ball gowns looked downright ridiculous and had us in fits of laughter. Each of us managed to find accessories, make-up, and jewellery, but none of us bought a prom dress. Not yet—there was still oodles of time.

As our shopping trip wound down, we made our way to Ilaria's house. She lived in a large old house with a rambling garden. I loved visiting because her home always had a friendly, lived-in aspect to it. There were always masses of books, magazines, bags, and clothes everywhere. It made me feel comfortable.

Ilaria's mother, Pam, greeted us in her typical garden attire, sweatshirt, jeans, welly boots, and muddy trousers. 'Hello, girls, lovely to see you. I haven't seen you all in ages. Happy birthday, Joselyn!'

'Happy birthday, Joselyn,' we all chorused. Joselyn smiled and blushed at all the attention.

'Wipe your feet before you go in, girls, or you'll bring muddy footprints into the house,' said Pam. Ilaria made a show of cleaning her shoes by scraping them on the doormat. We all followed her example and checked our soles to make sure our shoes were clean.

For tea, we had home-made pizza and Pam's fabulous home-made ice-cream. Later, we ate a tonne of sweets from Hardy's Sweet Shop that we had smuggled in and some popcorn too! After feeding our bellies, we camped in the lounge. Things had settled down enough that I thought I'd take a look at the photos I'd taken of the Corpus Chronophage Clock. I switched on my digital camera and started to search.

'Hey, what the heck… my clock grasshopper photos are gone.'

'No!' said Ilaria.

'They can't be,' said Jade. She tried to grab the camera to take a peek. I was annoyed that she didn't ask, so I yanked it back. I gave her a look that would have wilted daisies.

'Let's see,' said Joselyn, leaning towards me.

Because she asked, I passed Joselyn the camera. Ilaria glanced at her phone, more interested in catching up on social media.

'You're right. There's no sign of any photos of the clock,' said Joselyn, frowning. She shook her head, and a puzzled expression spread across her face.

'Not one, and I took at least a dozen photos. They've all fricking vanished. Every fricking one!' I scowled and brushed the hair out of my eyes.

'Oh, yeah right… Give it to me. You two must have missed them,' said Jade, rolling her eyes like she didn't believe me. She searched my camera but found nothing. Not a single shot of the Corpus Chronophage Clock. Frowning, she shrugged her shoulders. 'That's pretty much the weirdest grasshopper ever. It obviously doesn't like its photo being taken.'

'I don't blame it,' said Ilaria, lifting her head from her phone for a moment. 'I'd be sick to death of tourists taking my photo all the time too.'

'Creepy or what,' said Jade, passing the camera back to me. She shivered and wrapped her arms around her body, seeking warmth.

'I don't understand it. Maybe my camera's broken?' I said, flipping through the rest of my digital collection.

'Maybe,' said Joselyn, but she didn't sound like she meant it. 'That grasshopper on top of that clock sends shivers down my spine, Amelina.'

'Oh, Joselyn! You and your shivers. Okay, let's forget it. It's your birthday, and here I am spoiling the celebration vibe. Come on, let's get back to partying. I promise to stay away from Mr Bug Clock for now! Happy Birthday, Joselyn,' I said, passing her present to her.

Joselyn's face lit up with excitement as she ripped the wrapping paper off in one tear. 'Oh, this is incredible. I couldn't have asked for a better present.' She gave me a huge hug, a real squeeze that took my breath away. Joselyn's reaction pleased me even though I wasn't big on hugs. Still, it was a special occasion, so the hug was understandable.

Joselyn was so excited by the camera she paid little attention to the necklace from Ilaria or the purse from Jade. She glanced at their gifts and put them aside with a brief, but polite, thank you. Joselyn's attention stayed riveted one hundred percent on the camera. Joselyn danced around the room taking photos.

I watched as Ilaria's face fell. Of course, I was glad that Joselyn liked the camera, but her reaction embarrassed me. I picked up the forgotten necklace to try to draw Joselyn's attention back to it. 'What a lovely present,' I said, hoping to re-balance the situation.

Joselyn blushed. In one swift movement, she put the camera down. She placed the delicate necklace around her neck. 'Oh, Ilaria, I'm so sorry I got carried away with the camera. Amelina, you've cast a spell on me! The necklace is lovely, Ilaria. Thanks so much.' She reached over and encircled Ilaria in a much-needed hug.

Jade looked upset at this exchange. Joselyn noticed and scooped up the purse. She turned the purse clasp and reached inside. A pair of heart-shaped silver stud earrings caught the light. Joselyn blushed an even deeper shade of red.

'Oh, Jade, they're stunning,' she exclaimed as she put them on. Joselyn bent forward and gave Jade a hug too.

The present crisis over, Jade edged forward in her seat, no doubt judging the moment. Then, like a sprinter about to take off in a running competition, she went for it. 'How was your date, Amelina?'

Joselyn chewed her bottom lip. 'How was it, was it fun?'

'Y'know it must have been more than OK,' answered Jade.

'Hey, don't leave out any juicy details,' said Ilaria, raising an expectant eyebrow.

'Sorry to disappoint but he didn't seem in a good mood yesterday. Although Aphrodite's was fantastic.'

The room grew quiet, and the girls exchanged glances. 'Oh. Maybe he's stressed with exams,' suggested Jade.

'I doubt it. Not much seems to stress Ryder.' I lowered my eyes, not wanting to share too many of my secrets.

'I've never heard of Aphrodite's. Where's that?' asked Jade.

'Oh, it's an amazing seafood restaurant, with a lifelike statue of Aphrodite.' I smiled a small smile remembering that night and

Ryder's kisses. I pushed those thoughts away, remembering what had happened yesterday.

'Cool. I didn't know you liked seafood, Amelina?' asked Joselyn, looking puzzled.

'I don't, but somehow this tasted different. The food was beyond good.'

'Must have been his company. With the likes of him, anything would taste good! I bet he's got a six-pack that you could eat food off!' smirked Jade.

'Jade! You're disgusting and forgetting he's my boyfriend. Or I should say *was*. His company, six-pack or not, was in short supply since his attention was only with his friends who showed up at the last minute.'

'*Was* your boyfriend, Amelina? So it's over between you and Ryder?' asked Jade. She couldn't keep the excitement out of her voice.

I glared at her. 'Yeah, it's over, though it hardly started.'

'You seem a bit down, Amelina, are you okay? What happened?' asked Joselyn.

'I'm fine, Joselyn, but I don't want to talk about it.' I gazed out of the window, hoping someone would change the subject.

'Really? You sure, Amelina?' replied Joselyn, raising an eyebrow of concern.

'One hundred percent,' I answered.

Ilaria glanced around the room at her friend's faces. 'Moving on. Well, if Ryder is no longer your cute boyfriend, does that mean we don't get to meet his cute friends?'

'I'm not sure, Ilaria. Let's see, I suppose it would be a shame if we didn't get to hang out with Kyle. He's really nice and good-looking too.' I grinned at the girls.

Jade's eyes widened. 'What's his fit profile like?'

'Oh, my God! He's fair-haired, medium height, and has brilliant green eyes,' I replied, grateful for the chance to change the topic of conversation away from Ryder who I would rather forget.

'Sounds interesting,' they all chorused, laughing at the same time. Except for me; I smiled half-heartedly.

'So, what happened between you and Ryder?' asked Jade, who was unable to let her curiosity rest.

'Jade, I said I didn't want to talk about it.' My voice rose in irritation.

Jade gave me that look I knew so well. In Jade-speak, that meant she would get to the bottom of it, no matter what.

Jade held my gaze, and I caved. 'The other day didn't go well. I was late to meet Ryder, and he went all dark and gloomy on me. And the next day, he showed up at my house, but it's all a bit hazy.'

'I didn't know you were meeting up yesterday,' said Jade. She raised her eyebrows and pointedly stared at me.

'It was a… last-minute thing.'

'Oh, so something must have happened! What was it, Amelina? Did he kiss you, or did he do something you weren't expecting?' Ilaria rolled her eyes, and her question hung in the air.

Jade waited for my response, and I said nothing. I fidgeted. I didn't want to talk about it—at all.

'C'mon, Amelina, tell us what happened,' coaxed Ilaria, her expression as curious as the cat who swallowed the canary.

'Shit, sorry. I don't know, I can't remember.'

'What do you mean you can't remember?' asked Joselyn, her forehead creasing with worry.

'Just that, I can't remember,' I replied. Anxiety dripped from my voice.

'I knew it. Ryder's a sod, isn't he? Maybe he slipped you a date drug. You sure nothing happened?' Joselyn's eyes bugged out with worry.

'Hey, I never said anything bad happened, Joselyn. I can't remember. I had a weird episode.'

'A weird episode?' asked Jade.

'Yeah, I fainted and can't remember a damn thing.'

'Mmmm. Don't you think that's worrying considering you were alone in the house with him?' asked Joselyn.

'Yeah, I admit it's creepy, especially as Shadow reacted like a crazed feline on the verge of gouging his eyes out. It was all so strange.' I rubbed my forehead with my hand. A headache was coming, I could feel it.

Joselyn squinted and shook her head in anger. 'I'm not surprised. Shadow and I seem to share that opinion. I'd keep arm's length away from him if I were you.'

Jade interrupted. 'Hey, that's a bit harsh. Maybe Ryder came to Amelina's rescue again, like before down the river pathway. Who says he did anything to harm her? She fainted, and he was there to help.'

The girls broke their gaze and looked anywhere but at me. The room felt close and hot. I touched my lips, remembering. I knew Jade would take that view. But no one else came to Ryder's rescue.

PUZZLE PIECE 32:

THE SLEEPOVER – MAKE UP

Make up YouTubers,
Internet everywhere,
How many of these,
Feature smeared makeup parties,
Not one single daring one.

B efore we said another word about what Ryder had or hadn't done, Ilaria's little sister, Emma, peeked into the doorway. She crept into the room, hoping to hide and succeed in staying. Not a chance. Ilaria tried to shoo her away, but she wouldn't budge.

After the interruption we moved on, leaving Ryder as a topic for later discussion. The next party activity was a make-up session in the dark, a fun way to banish my worry blues. Shrieks of laughter erupted, and when we'd finished, we switched the lights back on to see what the end results were.

'You look like you've fallen into a make-up bag!' said Emma, tittering. 'It's my turn. Do me next, do me next!' Emma bounced up and down until I thought she would drive us all crazy. Unable to contain ourselves any longer, we burst into a fit of giggles. Emma waited next in line. Once we'd finished with her makeover, I couldn't recognise anyone, not even Emma.

Emma's painted face grew animated. 'Y'know I'm going to see Justin Bieber in concert.'

'Oh, are you?' we all chorused, unimpressed with her announcement.

Joselyn smiled. 'Have you got good tickets?'

'What'd you mean?' asked Emma as she turned to Joselyn, her mascaraed eyes round in wonder.

'Oh, you know. What kind of tickets do you have? Are you by the stage, on the balcony, or are you standing?'

'Or are you sitting?' asked Jade, her eyes shining with unexploded mirth.

'Or are you flying?' Ilaria added, dissolving into hysterical laughter. She stood up and hopped around the room flapping her arms like a crazy loon. Encouraged by further giggles, Ilaria couldn't resist asking one more question. 'Or are you abseiling? You know, rock climbing in reverse down into the show?'

Fits of hysterics followed, and Emma joined in too. It was one of those moments where the laughter commandeered our thoughts until our stomachs ached, and tears dripped down everyone's faces, all except for me. I stared out the window into the darkness, lost in my own thoughts.

The girls' laughter evolved into hysterics, and they were in grave danger of making themselves sick. Of course, the sweets and popcorn the girls had consumed didn't help. Between the giggling and the occasional raucous burp, the girls continued laughing until long streaks of black mascara smeared with lines of multi-coloured make-up all down their faces. I chuckled at the spectacle while I pushed thoughts of scary circus clowns out of my head.

Emma hopped from foot to foot with urgency apparent to us all. 'You all right, Emma?' I asked.

'Just need the toilet,' she replied, standing up awkwardly.

'You better go!'

Emma rushed out of the door, a blur of patchy makeup and desperation.

'Hey, guys, it's nearly Emma's bedtime. Shall we have a séance after she goes to bed?' asked Jade.

'Yeah, what a great idea,' said Ilaria.

Joselyn shook her head at such news. 'I don't think we should.'

'Stop being such a kill-joy, Joselyn. It'll be fun.' Ilaria nodded her head and grabbed Joselyn's hand, showing comfort where it was needed most.

'Besides, we have our resident séance expert, Amelina, with us,' added Jade. Her almond-shaped eyes glowed with a passionate intensity.

'Me? You've got to be kidding!' I replied.

'You're always wired up to your psychic shit, Amelina,' said Jade. 'Why, not?'

'True. I suppose.'

'Decided?' asked Jade, wide-eyed with excitement.

Joselyn nodded in agreement. Despite her acceptance of the situation, she didn't appear pleased, and her face looked grim.

'Okay, as soon as Emma hits the pillow we'll give it a go...' I replied.

Once Emma returned from her trip to the loo, we resumed chatting and laughing at the "Bieber."

Ilaria's mum, Pam, hurried into the lounge, wondering what all the noise was about. 'What a sight! Look at your black face! Well, I can see you're all having a whale of a time, but I'm afraid to say it's time for Emma to go to bed. Your face will need a good scrub, young lady!'

'Oh, Mum, can't I stay a bit longer?' said Emma, pouting, her lipstick forming a little pink rosebud of disappointment.

'No, you can't, Emma, it's already past your bedtime.'

We all stifled our laughter as Emma sauntered off muttering a sulky and forced 'goodnight.' I popped off to the toilet to clean my face with some face wipes. As I pressed the wipes against my lips, I experienced a burning sensation on my swollen lips. It appeared like I'd had a severe allergic reaction, and to complete the look my bulging lips revealed black tattoo marks. I wiped and wiped, but the swelling wouldn't go down. What would the girls say when I returned to join them? I searched in my makeup bag for some concealer and extra lipstick to hide my grotesque lips. As I glanced in the mirror, about to do what I could to hide the problem, I saw that my lips had returned to their normal size with not even a hint of a tattoo.

PUZZLE PIECE 33:
THE SLEEPOVER – GHOST STORIES

Sleepover bundle,
Ghost stories, giggles, fuelled by,
Curiosity,
Popcorn, confectionary,
Dead rock stars, and air guitar.

After the disturbing lips episode, my nerves were on edge, but I had no intention of sharing what had just happened with anybody. After Emma and Pam had left the room, I sensed an atmospheric change and kicked off the second half of the party with an announcement. 'Hey, now that Emma's gone to bed, let's have that séance? See if we can contact the dead.' I wiggled my eyebrows, trying for a spooky effect, but my hands trembled knowing I'd just had the spookiest moment only minutes ago.

'Yeah, great idea, Amelina. I thought Emma would never leave,' said Jade, screwing up her face with excitement.

'Now we can have some real fun,' agreed Ilaria. 'First, let's wash this gook off of our faces. I'm itching. Amelina's fine, she's already done her face.'

'Yeah, feel much better now, good luck with the gook gunk.' The girls ran down the hall to the loo and took turns washing the makeup from their faces. Once finished, I heard them slink down the hall to the lounge. They didn't want to wake Emma.

Jade couldn't contain her excitement. 'A séance it is. Shall we get started?'

Joselyn shifted in her seat. 'I'm still not sure. A séance sounds too sinister.' Joselyn stared at me with an intensity that creeped me out.

'Sounds creepy, but it'll be fun. We tell ghost stories, anyway, so what's the difference? Come on. It will be a laugh,' said Jade, gurgling with amusement.

'I love ghost stories. Perhaps that's the way to get the spirits in the mood. A gentle warm up. It's just the distraction that I need,' I said to Joselyn, hoping to win her over. I nudged her arm and flashed a smile in her direction.

'Okay,' whispered Joselyn, her voice tiny and filled with uncertainty. A shiver ran up my spine. Joselyn had sounded like her own particular brand of phantom.

Ilaria took that ghostly whisper as a prompt to gush with excitement. 'Yeah, let's move on from Ryder and take a tour of the scariest and creepiest stories instead! Let's start with some ghostly deeds. Did you hear about the Chinese restaurant at Caxton Gibbet? It burnt to a cinder. And what's even stranger is that the original inn, on the same site, also burnt down in the 1920s.' Ilaria bobbed her head, glad to share her news with the group.

'The George Inn, yeah, that's a weird, *spooky* coincidence, isn't it?' agreed Jade, her voice rising with excitement.

'The place's cursed. I heard they hung the landlord on a gibbet for murdering his guests as they slept. The room where they met their deaths was always intensely cold,' I said, joining in the ghoulish fun, hoping to banish Ryder from my thoughts.

'God, that's creepy. Talk about gruesome,' said Joselyn, looking less than happy. 'Thanks. I'll not sleep a wink tonight. Now I have a cold shiver running down my spine.' Joselyn shuddered and grabbed a blanket to spread around her shoulders.

'I didn't expect to sleep a wink, anyway. Maybe while we're wide awake, some dead guy will return from his eternal slumber for a chat. Hopefully, we will be blessed with the likes of a famous rock or pop star,' joked Ilaria.

'Now that would be cool,' I said. 'One night, I had a dream where the rock stars leaped out of the posters hanging in my room. The next thing I knew, we had a crazy party in my house. It was a bit freaky as some of them were long dead. They were rocking out until the wee hours,' I added. I stood up and struck my favourite rock hero pose. The room was silent. Joselyn, Jade, and Ilaria gazed at me with wide-eyed astonishment.

'God, you're crazy, Amelina. You know, I never know whether to believe the things you say or do. Great air guitar poses, by the way,' said Jade with a smirk.

At that moment, I had this strange urge to open the bag containing my crystals. When I arrived at Ilaria's house, I'd popped them into my jeans pocket. The heat from the crystals burned with an intensity so hot that my leg felt like it was on fire. Trying not to draw too much attention to myself, I pulled the bag out of my pocket and poured the gems into my hand. So much for trying to be inconspicuous. Jade caught me.

She stared at the stones, her eyes widening. 'They're alluring crystals, Amelina. They glow with such a mesmerising bright light. Where did you get them?'

I realised my stupid mistake and poured the crystals back into the pouch.

'Hey, I didn't get a chance to hold them,' said Jade.

'Me either,' said Joselyn, jockeying Jade aside to see what I had been doing.

Ilaria had been standing off to the side, copying my air guitar pose, but by now even she was staring at me with curious eyes.

My reluctance to talk about the crystals or to let anyone else near them bubbled up inside of me. I felt protective of the gems but knew my friends wouldn't leave it at that. To keep the peace, I offered them a tiny snippet of information. 'I got them from an older lady who lives in a charming house down by the river.'

Jade looked puzzled. 'I've never heard of or seen any charming houses by the Riverwalk. Are you sure, Amelina? I often ride my horse by the river. How could I have missed a house with that description?'

I knew I had to improvise, so I fibbed. 'It's not a house. It's more like a private club you have to join.'

'A private club?' asked Joselyn. That's interesting. She tapped her finger on her cheek.

'Really,' mumbled Jade. Her voice took on a crisp edge. 'How fascinating. Wonder if I could become a member?' She raised her chin in defiance and stared me straight in the eyes.

'I don't think so, Jade. It's by invitation only.' My eyes wavered, and I turned my gaze away first.

That set her off. Jade put her hands on her hips and said, 'That's mean. Why can't I get an invitation? What's wrong with me?' She faced me, pulling a disappointed face.

'We could gate-crash,' suggested Ilaria with a cheeky glint in her eyes.

'Where exactly is it?' asked Jade firmly in a voice that suggested she would not take 'no' for an answer.

'Yeah, tell us where we can find it, Amelina,' coaxed Ilaria.

I didn't want to share my precious secret with the girls. The Crystal Cottage was hush-hush. I had received an invitation to go there whereas my friends had not. I should have kept my big mouth shut. I gauged my reply to be vague.

'Down by the river on the right-hand side.' I absently waved my hand in the air.

'Near the old terraced houses?' Jade probed.

I remained silent. Why did I open the bag of crystals where everyone could see them? I had made a mess of the situation.

'C'mon, Amelina, why won't you tell me where it is?' asked Jade, her voice rising to a high pitch.

I squinted from the force of her words. I thought for a quick moment and said, 'The wacky old lady owner doesn't like unexpected visitors, *at all.*' I emphasised, "at all," and shook my head to affirm my statement.

'Sounds like my mum,' said Joselyn. She threw her hands up into the air and laughed.

'Mine too!' I nodded and laughed, hoping that a touch of humour would direct their minds elsewhere.

'Oh, I understand,' said Ilaria. She's like me on PMS days, irritable and moody.'

'Okay,' Jade interrupted, ignoring our jokes. 'I promise to knock and be very polite. You can bet I'll have a look next time I'm in that area.' Jade caught my eye, and I saw a strange glint, one I had never noticed before.

I knew I'd said too much. A deep unease came over me. I didn't want to encourage Jade, but I left it at that, hoping that she'd forget all about it.

PUZZLE PIECE 34:
THE SLEEPOVER – SÉANCE

Séance has begun,
An uninvited spirit,
Tells us who we are,
Beware tardy gate crasher,
He is to be feared the most.

I clapped my hands to get everyone's attention. 'Now it's time for the séance,' I announced. I had to stop the turn this dangerous talk had taken. Leanne would be furious that I had broken a confidence. Besides, she would not appreciate my friends being in such proximity to the crystals.

My conscience pricked and stabbed at my heart. I'd brought the crystals and now perhaps they could help me in the conjuring of dead rock-star spirits for our séance. Leanne's words rang in my head: '*You must be very careful with these stones, all three are powerful. You must guard the Wizard Stones, the Black Obsidian, and the Merlinite. Keep them safe. Beware. The power they may unleash could overwhelm you.*' I swallowed hard, remembering how much trust Leanne had placed in me.

From within the pouch, the Black Obsidian stone burned against my leg as it had done before. This time the gem made its intention clear. A high humming noise like the sound of a hive filled with bees echoed in the room. The sound intensified, and I realised the crystal summoned me. In response, I pulled the pouch out of my pocket. I reached inside and grabbed the stone. I cried out as the beauty of the stone captured my gaze and held me suspended in time.

My friends rushed forward, wide-eyed with curiosity. Their greedy hands reached out, clamouring to touch the Black Obsidian. I stepped back, clutching the gem to my heart, shielding it from view. My friends edged forward, crowding me. The first person to reach my side was Jade. In my panic that some harm might befall her because of her closeness to the stone, I pushed Jade away, shouting, 'Get back.'

I didn't need to say anymore. In my hand, the Black Obsidian fizzed and spat in an angry retort. The crystal lost its sheen, and a horrible sulphur smell filled the air. My friends pulled back, choking, clutching their throats, and gasping for air. Jade stood nearest to the stone and seemed to experience the ill effects more than the other girls.

With the girls now at a safe distance away from the rock, the Black Obsidian returned to its natural black colouring. Little by little, the gem glistened in the light and dazzled us with its beauty. I held it in the palm of my hand, basking in the luxurious, dark glow emanating from the crystal. Instead of the sulphur smell, an earthy sweetness filled the room.

The gem's powerful aura attracted me, and rather than being put off by its power, I felt sure I could command it. The sulphuric smell had distressed my friends, and yet I could see a growing unhinged desire shining in their eyes. The girls begged me to let them touch it, but I feared that would be dangerous. So, instead, I suggested they join in by lighting candles to encourage the spirits to bless us with their presence. Jade was the hardest to convince, but at last, she agreed.

While the girls were busy lighting candles in the lounge, I followed Leanne's advice regarding the necessary rituals. First, I ran into the kitchen and turned on the tap, running purifying water over the crystal. I tried not to handle the gem more than was needed. I grabbed a towel and dried the stone to a high sheen. Once again in the lounge, I grabbed a velvet cushion from the settee and placed it in the centre of the room. I then arranged the Black Obsidian on the pillow, and to soften its power, I added the Rose Quartz and set it to the right of the Black Obsidian.

I clutched Joselyn's hand and indicated for the other girls to hold hands and sit down in a circle. We dropped to the floor, holding our positions. I reached over to the floor lamp and switched off the light. After our excited chatter, we all quietened down.

I broke the silence first. 'To allow the spirits into the room, we must all concentrate on the Black Obsidian. If this is too disturbing, shift your gaze to the Rose Quartz. Let your emotions flow. If anxious thoughts occur, don't worry, everything will be all right.' Pausing for a moment, I cleared my throat. 'Don't be afraid. Whatever you do, don't forget to relax.'

My friends giggled nervously. I gazed at the magnificent stone and experienced a powerful, immediate emotional bond with the gem. My intuition was high, and yet I sensed that somehow my bond wasn't enough. The Black Obsidian desired more from me, so much more. I stood up, reluctantly releasing Joselyn's hand. I heard a little whimper escape from her lips. The girls joined hands, completing the circle without me. I took a deep cleansing breath and gathered my courage. I grasped the stone in my fingers and picked it up. At first, nothing happened. The gem felt warm in my hand. Without warning, a jolt of power hoisted me up into the air, lifting me as if I was weightless. For a second, I hung suspended before I was deposited back onto the floor with an almighty thump. Ilaria gasped. Joselyn's eyes did a triple somersault in their sockets. Jade jumped up, intending to catch me, but seeing I had landed safely on the floor, she sat back down again.

A black ribbon of silky light emerged from the obsidian, flowing around us in snaking wisps of energy.

'Oh, my God!' shouted Ilaria.

'Fricking Nora!' screamed Jade.

Joselyn began to whimper. 'This is freaking me out. Can I go?'

'No way!' I shouted. 'No one's allowed to leave, not now.' I ran to Joselyn's side. I squeezed into the circle again. Jade held one of Joselyn's hands; I held the other.

Spellbound, we watched the eerie light hold together in a single spot, harnessing such power that its brilliance blinded us. This source of the power focused on me, streaming forward like a river, becoming a reservoir filled with terrifying images. The Black Obsidian glowed with a demonic light, creating a rock face of emotions, urging me forward on a steep, treacherous climb, which left me scaling a multitude of buried thoughts.

The gem evoked treacherous emotions within me, and I felt my friend's pain twisting and turning as if it was my suffering. I closed my eyes and felt Joselyn's sadness when her father left her mum. Ilaria's suffering at the hands of bullies replayed in my mind. I cringed at her torment. Tears slipped out of my eyes as I experienced Jade's loss when her much beloved horse had to be put down.

My own poignant sorrow at my father's disappearance overwhelmed me. A sob escaped my lips. In an instant, a new image exploded in my mind. It revealed Ryder, clutching my crystals in his hand, an evil glint shining in his eyes. The image receded, and many thoughts and feelings stirred—memories and hidden personal moments. Everyone sat in shocked silence, transfixed, locked inside our own personal experience, staring at the black, beguiling ribbon of light pouring from the rock.

Our clasped hands shook with fear. I waited, afraid to witness the effect the Black Obsidian would have on my friends and me next. Our eyes met, and we strengthened our hold, clasping our hands tighter. The blackness of the moment grew. A flowing ribbon of dark, velvety light encircled our hands and bound our palms together, sealing our bond.

I knew if we let go of each other's hands, the terrors would invade and become stronger, tearing us apart. Our hands shook with the stress of staying together, our knuckles clenched white. Emotions flowed through each of us, uniting us, at this moment captured in time.

Once again, each vision of individual terror held the appearance of each of our personal sorrows, exaggerated to extremes in our woe. At the centre of the circle played the optical illusion of Joselyn's father's face twisting and contorting with hatred as he left her mum. Then the bullies' ugly faces and voices warped beyond recognition, taunting and yelling at Ilaria. The image of Jade's horse lay barely breathing, its chest rising and falling, unable to lift its grotesquely inflated head. Replacing that were the pained expressions of my mum and dad, and their two hollowed-out living ghosts floated before us, without a place to find peace. The last terror to emerge was Ryder. His face appeared a pasty white colour like a clown's features. His lips twisted into a cruel smile. My lipstick, a red smear on his lips.

The visual terrors continued to float above us, taunting, shouting and screaming, poking fun, and harassing. Joselyn's whimpering raised to a fever pitch. Jade sobbed uncontrollably. Ilaria stammered, her words stuck in her windpipe, unwelcome lodgers with no easy exit. I hid my face in my hands. In contrast to all this noise and commotion, the horse in the vision now lay silent, its dead eyes reproaching. Nevertheless, each of us held steadfast in our bond of friendship. We clung to each other, longing for this self-induced misery to end.

It was then that I sensed the terrors' power began to weaken. They were no longer able to break through our circle of trust. The terrible spirits that were once strong now grew weak and began to fizzle out. One after another, they vanished into thin air. At long last, the chain of negativity that had held us began to break down, and our emotions started to balance out. We loosened our grip on each other and rubbed our cramped hands and knuckles. We peered at the Black Obsidian through red-rimmed eyes. It was apparent that there had been a shift in the energy field of the room, and it had linked us together. Our fingers and hands tingled. A ribbon of effervescent energy travelled from me to the rest of the girls. Nobody spoke, and we remained united in our bond of friendship.

A hazy image materialised into a multitude of glistening sparks, which transformed into a vibrantly glowing object. I heard the pounding hearts from each of us becoming louder and more distinct as we gazed at the object. The sparks coalesced, and no longer separate entities, they'd joined to form a spirit or a ghostly apparition. The spectre sparkled like a million candle lights, speaking to each of us in a wisp of a voice that drifted like the wind.

The spirit addressed me, knowing I possessed the gift to understand the crystals. 'You have called me forth to open your heart to the truth. You must accept who you are and not be afraid. Embrace your true self. Encourage others to do the same. Then you will be a truly magical person, able to rekindle your family's happiness. Beware those who want what you possess.'

The spirit turned and pointed at Joselyn. 'Joselyn, you must move on from your past and accept the challenges of the future. Don't be fearful. Your confidence will grow the more you follow your dreams.'

The phantom floated above us on invisible currents and pointed at Ilaria. 'Ilaria, you have no more to fear from the children who taunted you. Your laughter protects you from their wickedness. Heed my words and use your skill wisely.'

Jade was last, and the spirit hovered near her face. 'Jade, you possess the skill and craft of working with animals. You must cherish and nurture it. Be faithful to your friends, and most of all, beware of those who may lead you astray.'

When the spirit finished speaking, the ghostly form drifted toward the candles and hovered above them. Slowly, the flames were extinguished one after the other, and we found ourselves sitting in total darkness. The phantom had vanished. No one spoke. We were shocked into a stunned silence. Ilaria switched on the light, and with one glance, we all knew things between us would never be the same again. That night signalled the beginning of our own personal voyages toward self-discovery.

Later, I hid the crystals away in their pouch and placed them back in my overnight bag. Nobody could sleep a wink. Instead, we huddled together and whispered about the mysterious appearance of the spirit. 'Hey, that was unbelievable! I think I overdid it with the crystals,' I confessed. 'We better not do that again. That Black Obsidian rock is scary!'

'No kidding,' replied Ilaria. 'That was the weirdest, strangest event that ever happened in my entire life.'

'Yeah, it should've been a regular bit of fun, but it wasn't. Now I know not to mess with those Wizard crystals,' I said, moving from the edge of the bed.

'That sulphur smell at the beginning weirded me out,' said Ilaria, squeezing her nostrils together, pulling a hyper-dramatic face.

'Talk about a smell from hell!' said Jade. 'But joking aside, that rock could be a black-hearted demon when messed with.'

'I knew it would be creepy, but I never imagined it would be that creepy. You know what? I think it happened for a reason. The spirit spoke to each of us,' replied Joselyn, as slight frown lines creased her forehead.

'I know, wasn't that incredible? Do you think the spirit was real or did we imagine it all? Maybe we had too much sugar?' Jade wondered out loud. I glanced at her face and realised she was as high as I'd ever seen her. She gulped down another shot of hot chocolate.

'Yeah, perhaps that sulphur smell had something in it which made us hallucinate. Whatever it was, it was real sweet of that spirit to gate-crash your party, Joselyn,' joked Ilaria, her eyes wide with excitement.

'What a birthday party. It sure was different. Thanks, everyone. You know, I feel supercharged after this experience,' exclaimed Joselyn.

'Me too. Maybe I will be a horse whisperer; you know a person who can communicate with horses,' added Jade.

'Yeah, that would be great. But not as handy as someone who can chat up boys. Now that would be useful. A guy whisperer,' said Ilaria, laughing.

'Yeah, that would be more than useful,' Jade said with a chuckle.

'I wonder what the spirit meant by beware of those that may lead me astray.'

'You're always getting led astray, Jade,' replied Ilaria, as she threw a magazine of the latest boy pin up at Jade.

'Yeah, but I think Amelina's the one to watch. She's magical. No surprise there,' said Jade, catching the magazine and surveying its contents with interest.

'Yeah, I always knew you were a weird one, Amelina! But Jade's the one who's boy mad!' said Ilaria, laughing.

I'd started the conversation, but no one noticed how quiet I had become. My friend's laughter and banter helped me to hide a secret. Even though the conjuring of the crystals had strengthened our friendship in ways we would never have imagined, it had also revealed something. No one else had mentioned they'd seen Ryder in the way I had. His terrifying image hadn't appeared to my friends, but I'd seen him. That knowledge scared me. I perceived that the spirit had sent me a message to be careful around Ryder. My conscious prickled, I decided I had better listen. Deep down in my heart, I knew I mustn't share what I'd seen tonight about Ryder with anyone else.

At least not until I knew what to do next.

PUZZLE PIECE 35:
HORSEBACK RIDING

Horses frighten me,
I can't sit on their saddle,
I'd rather play drums,
Then I'm in my element,
It is all about control.

The sound of my mobile phone ringing startled me from my slumber. The captivating tone of Ryder's voice snapped me awake in an instant, sending a tingle of fear down my spine. He didn't bother making conversation, and there were no apologies for his behaviour from the other day. In fact, he didn't mention our last meeting. Instead, Ryder asked to speak to Jade. I glanced over at her sleeping form and was about to hang up when Jade stirred.

'Who's that?' she mumbled, mouthing the words, her blurry eyes half shut.

'Ryder,' I whispered, wishing I hadn't.

She threw off her covers, jumped out of bed, and grabbed my phone in one swift movement.

Anger bubbled up inside of me. I couldn't believe her. Jade knew I'd just broken up with Ryder, and there she was talking to him like they were long-lost lovers. I shot her a nasty look, but she didn't notice.

Fuming, I tried to listen. It sounded like Ryder phoned to ask Jade out for the day. I thought for a minute about what the spirit had said and made my decision. There was no way I would abandon her to Ryder's strange clutches, so I motioned to Jade that I wanted to come too. I wasn't sure whether I could stomach seeing him again, but I had to find out what or who Ryder was. In my estimation, the only way to do that involved muscling in on his invitation too.

Ilaria and Joselyn had already awakened and were busy getting dressed. Jade put the phone on speaker so I could hear. Kyle was coming too. At least that proposed one positive development amongst a bunch of negatives. Ryder sounded keen about going horseback riding. I felt apprehensive because the last time I'd gone riding, I'd sprained my ankle. A sprained ankle seemed nothing compared to the possible threat from Ryder in his worse form.

The more I thought about the outing, the more I wasn't about to let anything bad happen. For protection I would bring my red jade crystal. Leanne's words flooded my brain: '*It is the most passionate and stimulating of the Jade stones. It will urge you to go beyond your comfort zone, to be courageous.*' The red jade crystal would act as a confidence booster and would help me to get over my fear of horseback riding. I hoped the passion bit wouldn't backfire and apply to Jade and Ryder!

When the conversation was over, I packed my sleepover bag and hugged Ilaria and Joselyn. Jade crept back into bed and didn't look like she was in a hurry to go anywhere. Typical Jade. One moment she talked, the next she slept, and then she woke up leapfrogging to the next potential boyfriend. Whatever she did or didn't do, I had to go home, unpack, and get ready to meet Jade, Kyle, and Ryder. I said my goodbyes and ran all the way home.

In no time I'd washed, changed into jeans, and pulled on my favourite tee-shirt. I even painted my nails with a two-toned black and white mosaic polish. Then it hit me, and I sat there wondering what I was doing. I never wore nail polish. I used the polish to doodle a black tattoo pattern on a piece of white scrap paper. My thoughts jostled around in my brain. Was I acting recklessly? Should I go? Would it be wise? I sighed, already knowing the answers to my questions. I had no choice now. I couldn't leave Jade alone with Ryder.

When I arrived at Jade's house, she greeted me with a fresh face bursting with energy. Knowing Jade, she must have whizzed about like a mad thing to get ready in record time. She wore her burgundy riding pants, which clung to her skin like a spray tan. Her dark hair gleamed, tied up in a high ponytail. In comparison, I felt tired and washed out, and wondered how Jade always managed to perfect perfection. What was her secret? Maybe she wore a mask of skilfully applied make-up to hide her flaws.

Unfortunately, Ryder and Kyle arrived late. It was a little after twelve o'clock before Ryder walked through the door closely followed by Kyle. They both looked flustered. 'Hi, sorry we're late, an unfortunate traffic jam held us up,' apologised Ryder, as if nothing had happened, and everything was just as before.

'Yeah, this old lady blocked the road. She stared at her steering wheel in total confusion like she'd forgotten how to drive her car,' explained Kyle.

'We thought we were going to be stuck there all day. Finally, one of the drivers did an awkward manoeuvre to shove past her. We managed to squeeze through a gap in the traffic and be on our way. Luckily nobody's cars were damaged,' said Ryder, shaking his head.

'I wonder what she could have been thinking of? Perhaps she got old lady brain freeze or something,' said Jade, laughing.

'It was a case of temporary brain freeze. She came out of her confusion and pulled off after everyone overtook her,' said Kyle, his face creasing with amusement.

Ryder nodded. 'We thought we would never get here.'

'Well, I'm glad you made it, Ryder,' replied Jade, glancing flirtatiously as she took a strand of her long, jet black hair, and twisted it through her fingertips.

I choked on my spit. I wanted to smack Jade for acting this way, but that wasn't possible. No such luck! The best I could hope for was to divert her attention elsewhere.

'Jade, this is Ryder's friend, Kyle,' I said, watching her response.

Jade merely glanced at Kyle. She played with her hair and managed a brief, disinterested, 'Hi.'

Jade pointed us toward the field where the horses were grazing but spent most of her time talking to Ryder as if he was the only person in her field of vision. 'C'mon. Let's go, shall we? Come and meet Oscar and the other horses, they're all friendly.'

I gulped. I followed, but my legs weren't in happy horse mode.

'You've ridden before, Ryder?' Jade asked, her voice carrying as they walked ahead of Kyle and me. I kept my ear trained on their conversation.

'Yeah, I used to go bareback riding as a child, although it's been some time since I've been on a horse,' Ryder replied, adding, 'Kyle hasn't been riding before. He's nervous about it.'

Jade turned around and glanced at us as if she'd forgotten that Kyle and I were following behind.

'Sorry, guys. You'll be fine. This way,' she said, with a half-hearted smile. She led us toward a field of green grass and few trees.

Jade whispered to Ryder, but I made out what she said. 'Sounds like Amelina.'

'What sounds like me?' I asked.

'Both you and Kyle are frightened of horses.' I rolled my eyes and peeked under my eyelashes at Kyle.

'No denying that. But I'm sure we'll survive,' answered Kyle shyly, catching my glance.

'Hope you don't fall off again, Amelina, like you did last time,' said Jade as she stifled a giggle.

'No way. I'll be all right if I ride Oscar,' I answered, feeling stressed and irritated by Jade's lack of support. As usual, Jade seemed to be doing her best to make me look like an idiot.

So much for the circle of trust! Why wasn't it working? Had Ryder manipulated its power somehow?

I reached into my pocket, feeling for the red jade crystal. I needed help, some way to anxiety proof myself from the growing fear that blossomed within me about falling off my horse. I observed Jade coyly glancing over at Ryder. Typical, I thought. The passion part was working for Jade and Ryder, and I was the one carrying the stone. This wasn't good news. I noticed how Jade's eyes lingered on Ryder's rippling muscles enclosed in his signature tight black tee-shirt and jeans. My anxiety increased with each step I took towards the field and the horses.

Once there, Ryder made his way straight over to Oscar. His face lit up as he stroked the horse's coat. 'What a horse. He's such a handsome devil. I have to ride him, Jade.'

I knew from experience there was no way to resist his charms when he spoke with such a compelling voice. My heart sank. I knew Jade would give in and sure enough; she buckled. Jade turned toward me with a determined expression on her face. 'Hope you don't mind, Amelina. It would be best if Ryder rode Oscar. You should try Otto.'

I felt my face warming, but it wasn't a mild heat. In fact, my anger exploded into a full-scale irritation. 'You know I prefer to ride Oscar, Jade; I feel more comfortable with him.'

'Change is good, Amelina. Otto's gentle too.'

'Don't you remember that I fell off Otto last time?'

'That's because you didn't handle him right. He's as gentle as can be. Much more considerate than most humans I know.'

I realised from the expression on Jade's face that she wasn't about to change her mind, not without a battle.

Jade adopted a nostalgic expression and said, 'Horses are such majestic animals, so proud and powerful.'

I watched Ryder's look of undisguised admiration for Jade blossom on his face. An unpleasant stirring of fear stabbed at my heart.

'Which horse shall I ride, Jade?' asked Kyle, breaking the tension.

'Share Otto with Amelina, he's a treasure,' said Jade distractedly. She flashed a conspiratorial smile at Ryder.

'How can we share him, Jade? Shall I ride side saddle and Kyle ride behind me?' My irritation continued rising.

'Sounds fun,' said Jade with a giggle.

'We'll take turns. Otto looks quite high-spirited. Are you sure it's a good idea?' asked Kyle, his face paling with anxiety.

'He's a darling, don't worry,' replied Jade unconvincingly, her eyes locked on Ryder.

'We're all going to ride together, aren't we?' I asked, my voice squeaking with a high-pitched anxiety I couldn't hide.

'We'll see,' said Jade. 'It might be better if Ryder and I go off together, as we're more experienced.' Jade smiled a wicked grin, and Ryder smirked, taking in her words and implied meaning.

I didn't want Jade to go off with Ryder alone, but what could I do? Jade wasn't about to believe anything I said. There was no point wasting my words. Instead, I called on the power of the crystal to protect us. But it didn't seem to work as it should. I couldn't feel it glowing as strongly in my pocket. Something dampened down the power of the crystal. I knew it was Ryder's influence.

Jade chose her favourite horse, Maximillian, a black beauty with a gleaming coat. Jade and Ryder saddled up without mishap. Her horse had a dignified air about him, and one glance at him told me all I needed to know. Maximillian only allowed the best riders to grace his saddle. Oscar carried Ryder with a practiced grace all his own.

The pair started off at a canter, but after a short while, Jade set Maximillian at a gallop. Ryder struggled at first but somehow kept up. Kyle and I stood next to Otto chatting, but neither of us made a move to mount him. Soon Jade and Ryder were specks in the distance, and Kyle and Otto were my only company.

We struggled to get Otto to move from his spot in the field. The horse balked and wouldn't budge. Kyle grabbed his harness and pulled, but he kept on objecting to everything we suggested with a sharp neigh of retort. Finally, Kyle saddled him and swung up into the saddle. He coaxed Otto into a short canter, but the horse wanted nothing to do with it. Kyle dismounted gingerly. He brushed off his trousers and said, 'I hope you don't mind me slagging off your friend, but I think Jade should have stayed and helped us.'

'Yeah, she shouldn't have gone off like that,' I said.

'Are you okay, Amelina, you seem on edge?' asked Kyle, looking concerned.

'Ryder makes me nervous,' I answered.

'I heard things didn't go well the last time you met up?' said Kyle.

'No, they didn't; in fact, he, um… spooked me. I'm surprised he told you.'

'Spooked? It's that black, green eye thing. It makes him seem kind of creepy sometimes!' replied Kyle.

'Perhaps,' I replied, not wanting to say any more. 'Horses aren't my favourite way to travel!' I turned and watched Otto grazing in the field.

'I prefer to have my two feet planted on the ground, Amelina. Besides, I don't believe Otto is as gentle as Jade said.'

'No, he's a temperamental beast. I don't think horseback riding's my thing either.' Otto decided to agree with me and pronounced his verdict with a loud whinny.

Kyle laughed. 'See, even Otto agrees we're one horseback riding fail! I'm more into music, and so are you. I've heard your YouTube video and all about your amazing live drumming.'

'Oh, right. Did Ryder say that?'

'Yep.'

I frowned. 'I'm a much better drummer than horseback rider, that's for sure.' We both laughed at the same time.

'It would be amazing to hear you play, Amelina.'

I was touched by Kyle's compliment. 'Great. My drum kit's over in the shed. Let's go.'

'Sounds good. Let's return Otto's gear to the horse shed.'

'Fantastic idea,' I said with a relieved laugh. After unsaddling Otto and returning him to his paddock, I led the way to the shed. Kyle put the gear away, and I set up my drum kit and picked up my drumsticks.

Kyle looked thoughtful. 'What an awesome kit. I wish I'd had the chance to play the drums.'

'Here's your chance! You're more than welcome to have a go after I play *Rock Crystal*.' I perched on the edge of my chair, ready to play. I felt more comfortable than I had around the horses. I warmed up and then I thrashed those drums, taking out my frustration and fear for my friend's wellbeing on my poor, unfortunate, drum kit. After I played *Rock Crystal* the first time, I took a deep breath and played the song once more. The second time, my playing became calmer and not so angst-filled. Finished, I handed the sticks over to Kyle.

'That was crazy, Amelina.' Kyle picked up the sticks but paused, unsure of what to do next.

'Kyle, just let the rhythm flow out of you, uninterrupted. It's easy, much easier than riding a horse!' I grinned a smile of encouragement, knowing once he played he wouldn't want to stop.

Kyle smiled back and followed my advice. As he began to play, a lovely, charismatic smile lit up his face. At that moment, I knew Kyle seemed a perfect choice for a best friend.

I glanced at the clock. It was now a good half an hour since I'd last seen Jade and Ryder. I hoped that they would return soon. With each passing moment, I feared for Jade's wellbeing. I couldn't shake this uneasy feeling, and it plagued me. A queasy anxiety settled in my stomach. My uncertainty grew with each passing moment. The ticking clock grew louder, echoing until I almost didn't hear the sound of their approaching steps.

The door opened, and in walked Jade and Ryder, both of them appearing like two models for the outdoorsy, windswept catalogue. Jade's skin glowed, making her seem even more lovely than usual. Her eyes sparkled, and Ryder's gaze fixed on her in an admiring way. I didn't like this turn of events one bit. Jade was preparing to cross a dangerous line, and she didn't even know it.

'Jade's such a gifted rider. You can see Maximillian adores being ridden by her,' enthused Ryder.

Then as an afterthought, he said, 'Sorry we left you behind. We got carried away. But I'm glad you and Kyle got to know each other better.'

I glanced sharply at Ryder's profile. What a strange remark to make. Once again, I received the clear message that Ryder was pushing me to spend more time with Kyle. Being with Kyle was more preferable to being alone with him. Ryder had moved on to his next unsuspecting female, his next potential conquest, Jade. My fear grew that she would fall under his spell more than I had, and where that would lead, I didn't want to imagine.

'That's okay,' I replied, trying to act casual, shrugging my shoulders like I had not a care in the world. 'Kyle's great company. I've been showing him my drumming skills. He wanted to have a go.'

'That's great. Glad you enjoyed the music,' replied Jade, oblivious to my upset. *She only had eyes for Ryder.*

'Amelina's incredible on the drums,' said Kyle, trying his best to make me feel better.

Ryder didn't respond. Instead, he changed the topic of conversation. 'Hey, you'll never guess what happened. After Jade had dismounted, she tripped over a stone and hurt her leg.'

'Oh, I hardly did a thing, Ryder; it was just a scrape,' said Jade, blushing.

'It was not,' said Ryder, putting his arm around Jade. He pulled her towards him in a protective hug, all the while staring at me. His black eye seemed to grow darker, murkier, and more probing.

I knew then Ryder exalted in playing games. It wasn't nice, and it had evolved into a downright nasty scheme. Jade had only scraped her leg this time, but was it a warning or a threat? My fear escalated that he could do much worse next time. How could Jade be so easily led? Why hadn't she listened to the spirit's warning? It struck me that Joselyn had been right all along. A hint of cruelty lingered in his behaviour below the surface of his perfect good looks.

Later, while the boys were preoccupied having a session on the drums, I confronted her. 'What's going on, Jade?'

'What d'you mean?'

'You and Ryder are cosy.' I stood in front of her so she couldn't get away and would have to answer my questions.

'The two of us get on so well together. I'm sorry, Amelina, I know you liked him, but he just sees you as a friend.'

'Come on Jade, you know I don't like him that way anymore. He's dangerous.'

'Dangerous? It was just an innocent kiss, one that he regrets,' said Jade.

My face buckled under a layer of hurt. I couldn't believe Ryder had spoken to Jade about the kiss. My anger flared. 'Never mind the kiss; why don't you listen, Jade? I've warned you that he isn't to be trusted. When I was alone with him, I felt like I had no control over my body, like he manipulated me.'

'You don't know a thing, and you're making it up. And I know why. Because Ryder likes me and not you.'

'No, I'm not making it up. That's simply not true either, Jade. I'm trying to protect you! Ryder has a side to him that you don't ever want to experience.' I implored her to listen, but I could see from the determined expression on her face that she didn't want to believe what I was telling her.

'He has two sides, Jade, and the nasty side far outweighs the good side.'

'What d'you mean?' said Jade, looking at me sceptically.

'He's toying with us, Jade. He enjoys making me suffer by flirting with you. I can see it in his eyes. His eyes are filled with spite.' I tried to make eye contact with her to make her see the truth, but she glanced away.

'Rubbish. You're just jealous, Amelina,' Jade replied, her voice rising in anger.

'No, I'm not. Please listen to me, Jade,' I pleaded. My note of desperation hung suspended in the air and dispersed with her next two words.

'No thanks,' she replied with an angry shuffle of her feet.

I shut my mouth and stared at Jade. 'You can have him if you want Jade, but you better be careful. Just remember what the spirit said, we're meant to be in a circle of friendship, and good friends should listen to each other.'

'Sorry, Amelina, I can't resist him. I know he isn't my usual type, and you're right, there's something different about him. But I think you're exaggerating his threat. He's not some evil gangster. I've tried hard, but I can't stop thinking about him. Don't let it spoil our friendship, Amelina. We can still be friends.' Jade stood her ground, and I cringed at the look in her eyes.

'Friends? We used to be *best friends*, Jade, or have you forgotten?' I replied angrily.

'Huh. How could you say that? I don't want to be best friends with you anymore, Amelina. I don't even want to be friends.' She turned on her heel and strode away.

I called Mum to come pick me up. I didn't even say goodbye to anyone. I'd had enough fun for one day. On the way home in the car, a wave of silent misery engulfed me. Mum didn't pry. For once she respected my silence. As soon as I walked into the house, I rattled my dad by forgetting to say hello. My emotions had engulfed me.

'Amelina, you could at least say hello when you come in the door.' Dad glared at me from his chair.

'Sorry, Dad. Hi,' I said, managing the barest of responses, and then feeling guilty for it. Dad sighed and walked off in a huff, shuffling down the hall, ignoring my grotty mood.

Mum saw the telltale glint of tears in my eyes and asked, 'Whatever's the matter, Amelina? Did you have another fall?'

'No.'

'Did you enjoy the horseback riding?'

'No,' I said, pushing back my rising tears. I ran upstairs, shut my door, and collapsed on my bed, burying my face in my pillow. At first I cried sobs of anger at Jade's hateful words, but the more I thought about Jade, the more the hurt imploded inside of me until the tears flowed so freely that my pillowcase became a soggy, mutilated mess.

It was all too much. First, the strange behaviour and appearance of my parents, and now losing Jade. How could I have such awful luck? I picked up the pillow and squeezed it like I wanted to wring the life out of it. In exasperation, I threw the pillow across the room in an almighty fit of temper. Not even Esme had the courage to talk to me tonight.

PUZZLE PIECE 36:

A SPIRIT WALKS TO ARTHUR'S SEAT

Ever had a day,
When everything seems so strange?
Ridiculous time,
Nonsensical opposites,
Confuse and play mighty tricks.

That night strange noises disturbed my sleep, and the central heating gurgled like a bubbling cauldron, mirroring my thoughts. Dream-like images floated and played in my mind like an old black and white movie. Each scene involved bright colours and flashes of brilliant light, but there didn't seem to be any real substance to the vivid dreams. Frustrated, I pushed back my covers and climbed out of bed. I took the Merlinite stone out of the pouch I had hidden in my drawer. In my hand, the Merlinite hummed a song celebrating the magic it held within.

Leanne's words flooded my consciousness with an intensity that surprised me. I heard her words spoken in that whispery voice she used, *'The Merlinite is a conjurer's stone; a spiritual stone that allows journeys to past lives. Placed under your pillow, it can transport you to Arthurian times.'*

I paused and wondered if I possessed the courage to proceed. I cradled the stone in my hands, contemplating my next move. I knew in my heart I had to see what would happen, so I placed the gem under my pillow. I climbed back into bed and settled down. At last, I drifted off to sleep, soothed by the sweet song that the Merlinite sang. As I rested, my body underwent a change, and I experienced a unique sensation. I felt my soul lift and rise above my body, watching me. I felt no distress; on the contrary, I experienced a profound feeling of peace and tranquillity.

At this moment, caught between sleep and waking, I sensed the power of the Merlinite stone. My hovering spirit burst into tiny, tumbling jigsaw pieces that broke apart and then reassembled and fused back together. My sleeping body lay below, unaware of the miraculous event. My spirit form consisted of my soul, the essence of who I was. I crept out of the door, a shimmering apparition dressed only in my pyjamas. The house encouraged my progress by emitting a low, cheerful hum that seemed to say, *take the challenge but come back safe.*

Waiting at my front doorstep, I discerned the glowing form of my guiding spirit, who had appeared to my friends and me the night of the sleepover. I recognised the healing energy swirling before me straight away.

This benevolent spirit smiled in encouragement and said, 'Much has happened since the night of the sleepover. I can see disappointments have followed. The Merlinite has brought you here.' The spirit turned and pointed, saying, 'Time to bid farewell to Eruterac, I will take you on your journey.'

Eruterac materialised out of thin air. He was the same creature I had painted and who had appeared at my door days ago. Even though I felt nervous when I saw him, I didn't feel afraid. I watched as he spoke, and specks of black debris cascaded, spluttering from his mouth. I drew in a breath of relief that this time he did not bring the bugs, rats, and worms that infested his body.

'Welcome, Amelina, so glad to see you again. Your spirit guide has asked me to bid you farewell.'

I felt a strange sadness that this would be the last time I would see Eruterac. But he wasn't the kind of guy you would hug, so I kept my words simple, 'Farewell, Eruterac.'

'Farewell, Amelina, your final journey is still to come.'

With each step the creature took, the surrounding ground shook, and small portions of his body flaked off, returning to the waiting earth. I thought of the phrase 'ashes to ashes, dust to dust,' finally grasping the meaning.

I watched in astonishment as the wind swirled around like a cyclone, unravelling the creature's body further, piece by piece, detritus dissolving into the cold, hard earth until nothing remained but one twig, lying where he had once been.

Eruterac's final departure had been so spellbinding that I had almost forgotten about the spirit. I turned my head to see that the spirit glowed with an energy I had never envisioned. Perhaps this energy had burst from the power of the wind itself. Sparkling with luminosity, every aspect of the spirit's being screamed for my attention. Twirling round and round, a million candles of celestial brilliance lit and extinguished one by one, creating a light show of such magnitude that my eyes flickered with excitement, bewitched by the sight.

The wind picked up, the spirit continued to spiral, and the flickering lights grew faster and faster, creating a tornado of swirling light and ethereal magic. Dazzled by this stupendous vision, bright blinding spots appeared before my eyes. I closed my eyes, sealing the overwhelming sensation of magnificent warmth and heightened excitement into my body. Even with my eyes closed, I could see the spirit cast a brilliant light show into the night sky, tiny shooting stars whizzed and vanished into the night. One last star twinkled, and then the spirit disappeared into the darkness.

I didn't dare open my eyes until the wind had subsided. When I did, I found my celestial body floating in an area surrounded by woods that reminded me of the drawing I'd painted for my final art exam. It was a replica brought to life. The trees lifted their green leaves in welcome toward the azure sky. Luscious green ferns, rocks, and boulders framed an open clearing leading toward a crystal blue lake. My eyes sparkled with excitement as I gazed at the lake.

I hovered and wondered if this could be the land that Leanne had told me about. In the distance, I made out the outline of the sleeping volcano. How fascinating and tranquil it was. In the backdrop of this peaceful setting, I caught sight of the crags of Arthur's Seat in Edinburgh and the Scottish Parliament. The rocky formations reminded me of the shape of a sleeping lion with the extinct vents of the volcano forming rocks that resembled the lion's head and haunches.

My mind clicked into overdrive, and I recollected that Arthur's Seat had been cited as one of the possible locations for Camelot. My excitement grew with the understanding that the Merlinite stone had deposited me at the castle of the legendary English warrior-chief, King Arthur. I rubbed my eyes in amazement as the King rode toward me on his magnificent white horse, holding Excalibur, the magic sword, in his hand. I drew back, stunned and dazed by the sight of the topaz lights, diamond sparkles, and blood red gemstones gleaming on the hilt of the sword. An overwhelming desire to touch the precious stones consumed me. However, I was not worthy, and the power of the sword blinded me.

During this moment, King Arthur's face and features changed. Now Ryder stood before me, dressed in King Arthur's finery, clutching the mighty sword Excalibur. I blinked several times and wondered whatever would my crazed mind conjure up next. It was beyond puzzling. This man holding Excalibur had to be the rightful king, yet Ryder's face didn't fit the man.

Out of the clearing rode Guinevere astride her horse. Deep within the queen's eyes, I recognised a passion that existed only for her king. I became drawn to the queen's facial features, and little by little the queen's face altered until the image of Jade took its place. I observed the two imposters, Ryder and Jade, as they dismounted and kissed as if their lives depended on it.

When at last they broke free from their kiss, Ryder stared at me, searching my face for a reaction. It was clear he wished to taunt me, to make me suffer, even while I posed no threat in this spirit form. In anger, I reached for the sword. I lifted the resplendent stone encrusted blade to the skies. A rainbow of colours shimmered before me, each band of colour more intense than the one before. From the centre of the rainbow emerged the figure of a young man. He smiled at me, and I thought he looked familiar, but I couldn't put my finger on who he was.

The young man's figure dissolved within the radiance of the rainbow and then reappeared before me, riding upon a grey-coloured horse with a striking French-braided mane of delicately curled horsehair. He stopped, leaned down, and introduced himself to me. I recognised him immediately. He was handsome Lancelot, Arthur's rival for Guinevere's love, but I didn't draw in a breath of excitement when I saw him, though, I imagined that Esme would have drawn in several. It must have been the spring meadow fresh-ness of his eyes and that familiar twinkling that gave him away. A shy smile lit up his face—it was Kyle. Far off in the distance, I could see Guinevere showed no interest in this grand knight of the Round Table. Guinevere (Jade) was too wrapped up in King Arthur's (Ryder's) kiss. My spirit body was horrified and recoiled from the scene. I had to stop this celestial pantomime, now.

I questioned what these apparitions meant. My mind swirled in confusion. Was Ryder attracted to Jade? Or did he enjoy toying with Jade to upset me? Were Jade and Ryder in some twisted way meant for each other? Was it fate? Could the power of their love be so strong that it would make a mockery of such a legend? And who was Kyle, a knight or a fraud?

In answer to my many questions, a churning mist appeared, obstructing my view. The great magician, Merlin, stepped from the fog. This thin elderly man had a narrow chin covered by a long white pointed beard. His brilliantly coloured robes billowed around him as he strode toward me.

He pointed at me and said, 'You hold the great Excalibur in your hands. The touch from this sword will enhance your many powers, but only if you search your soul to find your soulmate. Make sure you choose wisely.'

Pausing for breath, the great wizard continued. 'Do not be drawn by appearance alone. The most handsome of men can cloud your thoughts and create a cloak of deception. Making a decision about their character can be difficult. Remember, Lancelot brought Guinevere great joy, but this was swiftly followed by intense sadness.'

'But I don't understand, Merlin. Why did Kyle appear as Lancelot? He isn't attracted to Jade.'

'It is opposite day; anything can happen, especially when hypnotism is controlling what we believe. Legends can be overturned, or legends can tease you with nonsense. Only time will tell, but follow your heart, and you will learn the answer.'

As Merlin voiced his final words, I felt a strange sensation like my body drifted, and some invisible force was pulling me back to where I belonged. My spirit soared like a weightless bubble suspended in the air. My celestial body moved with lightning speed, slipping back into the sleeping body lying in my bed.

With an incredible jolt, I came to. I had safely returned to my bedroom. I threw back the covers and gaped at my feet, which were soaking wet and covered in mud and leaves. I shivered, chilled to the bone. Confusion gripped me. My first episode of spirit walking left me weak and speechless.

Flashes from my out-of-body adventure played over in my mind. Whatever did it all mean? And what did Merlin mean when he said I had to search my soul for my soulmate? Had it all been a dream? No, that was impossible. I glanced down at the soles of my feet. They were filthy. It was real, all right. I had gone spirit walking.

I brooded about why Kyle had appeared as Sir Lancelot in my spirit walking episode. Though Kyle was classed as good-looking, he couldn't compete with Ryder's handsomeness. Also, it made little sense why Kyle would ride a horse as if he was an expert horseman when he didn't enjoy horseback riding. How was any of this going to help me find the answers to solving the curse that possessed my parents?

A million unanswered questions hammered through my mind. Merlin was teasing me with this nonsense, but why? Perhaps, it was a deceptive device to throw me off course. Or maybe I needed to focus on the root cause of the curse.

I felt a tiny tremble under my feet. Perhaps the house was ready to share some of its secrets. The time had come to break a few family rules. The attic room had always been out of bounds. But I had a hunch that this was the exact place to search.

PUZZLE PIECE 37:
THE STUDY

It's time for locked rooms,
Mysterious to open,
Beyond a secret,
Echoing with memories,
Musical notes choked by dust.

The next morning, I felt tired and drained after the spirit-walking episode. I stayed in the house where I could do some exploring on my own. With no one to disturb me or to see what I was doing, I hoped to find some answers. My plan was to sneak into Dad's study. I had to do a bit of *hidden curse* detective work. The answers to my father's unnatural ageing must be hidden within this well-guarded room.

My dad's study was at the top of the second storey stairs, a single attic room with a large window that overlooked the conifers in the garden below. For as long as I could remember, the study door had remained locked. My only conclusion was that Dad didn't want me nosing about in there. This only intrigued me more; I had to find a way in.

That morning, I rummaged around in the kitchen drawer to find the key to unlock the study. I grabbed the key ring and flew up the stairs. I tried several of them without any success. On my last attempt, I noticed the slanting attic door next to the study and thought that looked more promising. It was strange, but there didn't seem to be any sign of a lock or a handle on the door. I tried to open it, but it wouldn't budge. A light bulb went off in my head, and I ran down to the kitchen for a butter knife. Impressed with my brilliance, I slid the knife down the side of the door, and at last it popped open with a reluctant groaning sound. The cramped room meant that I had to force my slender body through the opening. Scattered about were old toys, dressing-up clothes, books, and many forgotten things. I knew I was on the right path because I had an uncanny feeling that I would find the key to Dad's study in here.

A shaft of filtered light trickled in through a small window highlighting the far corner of the attic. I moved towards the light, avoiding the many obstacles in my way. Nearly twisting my ankle climbing over boxes and old suitcases, I caught sight of an object dangling from a delicate hook on the wall. There hung a golden key.

I grabbed the key and heard what sounded like a shrill voice recording with a constant feedback hum. In a scratchy sing-song, the voice spoke: 'Put me back, thief. I was enjoying the sunshine streaming in. Don't you know how cold it can be in the attic? Sunshine cheers me up. How would you feel surrounded by unwanted things all day and every day?'

I couldn't believe my ears and stopped dead in my tracks. The key was *talking* to me. I turned the key over in my hand, reasoning that keys didn't speak—ever. I scratched my head and decided I had two choices. One, I could accept I was having a hallucination, or two, I could ignore this ranting voice and continue my search. I chose the latter. Anyway, with all the other strange happenings in this house, a talking key wasn't that far-fetched.

I climbed out of the attic opening and stopped—I couldn't move another inch. I saw appearing out of nowhere a sheer drop descending into another staircase that I'd never noticed before. I held my breath and noticed the tiny ledge to my left. There was just enough room for my foot. I took my time because if I didn't balance perfectly, I would fall down the steep steps below into—what? I peered down into the descending darkness. It appeared to be a long way down.

I paused. The angry voice of the key stopped me in my tracks. 'You'll get me into trouble, you will. I'm the keeper of the keys. Bring them back, thief!'

I slowly edged out, placing my foot on the ledge and balancing like a trapeze artist. Finally, as a last resort, I crouched and leaped to the steps below. I almost toppled down the stairs, but at the last moment, I regained my balance. Then with a triumphant backward glance, I placed the key in the lock and opened the door to the study.

The keeper of the keys sighed deeply. 'You've done it now. There's no turning back.'

The loud click of the front door opening startled me. I knew it had to be Mum. If she found me snooping around in the attic, I would be in deep trouble. Who knew how she might react? I sighed. Reluctantly, I closed and locked the study door and crept back down the stairs to the second level and my bedroom. I slipped the key into my pocket without another thought.

The key sighed. 'Thank heavens.'

I muttered and swore under my breath.

The next morning, I decided to talk to Mum and ask some questions about Dad's disappearance, but she wouldn't tell me anything. Frustrated, I planned to ransack the study again later. The gold key remained silent, tucked inside my jeans pocket. I just hoped that the voice of the key wouldn't start ranting when Mum and Dad were around. That would be a problem that I couldn't begin to explain away.

Time dragged on into eternity, and the waiting seemed to last forever. Shadow followed me around the house as if he didn't want to let me out of his sight. Esme had acted much the same. The two of them were driving me mad. However, Esme's vigil paid off; she spotted the key as it slipped out of my jeans pocket as I undressed for bed.

'What are you up to, Amelina? Where did you get that key?'

'I'm going to search the study at the top of the stairs.'

'I wish I could come with you and help you, but I can't,' she said sadly.

'Why?'

'There are no mirrors up there.' Esme's simple reasoning rattled me for a moment.

'Oh, don't worry Esme, I'll be fine. Shadow can come with me.'

Shadow's ears twitched. The black cat glided over to the mirror on silent feet and stared at his reflection. Esme walked from the shadows at the back of the mirror. She pressed her hands against the glass prison that held her captive. Her palms turned white from the pressure, and I wondered if she was reaching out towards Shadow and me.

'Be careful, Amelina, you don't know what's up there,' she warned. 'Take care of her, Shadow.'

Shadow's eyes blinked once and then gleamed in what I took for "*yes*" in cat-speak.

'I'll take my chances, Esme. I have to. The answers to this curse have to be in Dad's study. There is nowhere else to look.'

She nodded. She bit her lower lip, and a drop of blood splattered on the inside of the mirror, captured for a moment before it left a red trail as it slid down the glass. I shivered and hoped that wasn't a bad omen. I'd had enough bad luck and didn't need anymore.

I stretched out on my bed and waited until Mum and Dad were asleep in bed. I knew it was safe to proceed when I heard the reassuring sound of Dad's gentle snoring. Anxious at what lay ahead, I opened my drawer and searched for my red jade crystal to take with me to protect me from harm.

From the mirror, Esme watched me tiptoe out my bedroom door and head towards the stairs. In a dramatic stage whisper, she said, 'Good luck.'

I gave her an enthusiastic thumbs-up. Shadow knew it was his cue to accompany me, and he followed, meowing softly. 'Shadow, knock it off and be quiet,' I hissed. I placed a finger to my lips in warning.

When it was silent, I climbed the stairs to the attic and Dad's study, being careful not to step on the boards that creaked. At the top of the stairs, I turned on the torch so I could see better and not disturb my sleeping parents on the floor below.

Turning the key in the lock, I crept inside Dad's study. Shadow followed. A reproachful groan erupted from the key. Then all fell silent. I flashed the torch around the room for the first time in years. In a corner against the wall, I spotted my dad's old guitar. I remembered the guitar from happier times, whereas it was now just an abandoned instrument. Without a doubt, it had once been stunning.

Intense sadness flooded over me. I cupped the red jade crystal in the palm of my hand, trying to calm emotions that threatened to overwhelm me. It disturbed me so much to see the neglected guitar covered in layer upon layer of dust. My father hadn't played it for years. If only I could pick up the guitar. I would clean off the dust and play it to my heart's content, hoping it would bring my dad back to the way he used to be. I knew better than to touch the guitar, and besides, Dad would be upset at my snooping. Guilt stabbed at my heart. I knew for certain that Dad would be disappointed if he found out that I'd been in his office at all.

Again, my gaze drifted to the guitar. This time I found myself drawn to it, and I yearned to caress the smoothness of the wood-encased instrument. I battled my desire and jumped when the strings began to play on their own. A melancholy song twanged from the strings and I listened, enthralled. I wept genuine tears of sorrow. My emotions were raw, and a well of grief—long suppressed—released with my sobs. At that moment, it struck me that the guitar played the saddest song I'd ever heard. This song told our story, and I felt it resonate in my soul. This song *was* the story of my family.

Shadow wailed. The cat's cry mixed in a tragic note that blended with the guitar's strumming beats, adding an extra layer of anguish to the song. I patted him, trying to reassure the cat that everything would be all right.

Taking a tissue out of my pocket, I blew my nose and wiped my eyes. I walked over to the guitar and brushed away the layers of dust with my hands. When I had finished, I picked the guitar up and held it close to my chest. I could still feel the vibrations of the instrument resonate against my body even though I hadn't played a single note. The wood came alive, and warmth flooded my hands. An appreciative hum burst from within the very heart of the house, saying, *'Don't stop. Play that guitar!'*

My absorption in playing the instrument was so great that I didn't hear my mother's footsteps as she slipped inside the study. Mum spoke, but I didn't hear her. I continued, possessed by the sound of the guitar's strings playing our heart-wrenching song.

A mournful refrain echoed around the room and words tumbled from the guitar. *Oh, Krystallos girl… Not yet sweet sixteen. To cure the curse, you must find the stone that speaks to your young heart.*

Mum raised her voice several times, but I never heard her. My mind was occupied with the words of advice that had drifted in song out of my father's guitar. In frustration, Mum grabbed me by the shoulders and shouted, 'Are you deaf? Can't you hear me? I've been trying to get your attention, Amelina. Why are you in your dad's study? You know he doesn't like you being here. How did you get in anyway? It's always locked when we're out.'

I ignored Mum's questions and gestured at the guitar. 'Oh, Mum, look at it. It's truly a magical instrument. Did you hear the music? I just can't understand why Dad would neglect such a stunning guitar. It's awful,' I groaned.

Mum spun around and faced me. 'Amelina, I've told you—your dad no longer plays. He's too busy with other things.' I picked up on the frustration in her voice. It was palpable, betraying her emotions. I tore my eyes away from the beauty of the guitar that had me entranced. I couldn't understand what she was talking about. Dad often sat staring out of the window, staring at his precious trees in the garden. He had plenty of spare time now that he worked fewer hours. However, Dad did nothing except read, watch television, or work on his puzzles. Why did he choose to be so dull?

In puzzlement, I contemplated Mum's ghostly face highlighted by the torchlight. 'Why did Dad give it up?'

Mum turned her face away and slipped back into the shadows. 'I don't want to talk about it.'

'Please, Mum. I need to know. It's tearing me apart inside,' I pleaded, gently touching my mother's arm, forcing her to return my gaze.

She remained silent. When she spoke, the words tumbled from her taut lips. 'All right.' She swallowed hard and struggled to continue. When she did, her words were almost inaudible, as if they had weighed on her mind. 'After your dad returned from his long disappearance, he became withdrawn and turned to his guitar for solace. All he could think about was that wretched instrument. He played it until his fingers bled and hardly stopped to eat or drink. The guitar became his only companion, his life.'

Mum stopped for a moment, distressed by what she had just shared with me. She held her back straight, and her face reflected determination. A hint of tears wet her eyes as she fought to hold in the suppressed emotions that threatened to overwhelm her.

I hated to see my mum in such pain. We had our differences, but no matter what, she was still my mum. I moved towards her, and we clung together in a tight hug. Our embrace was such a natural response but not one we had shared for so long. I felt reluctant to draw apart, to release her, in case somehow she would crumble, but I had to. As before, she stood tall, hiding her sadness as best she could, but I noticed a change in her eyes, a gentle acceptance.

Mum gazed off in the distance and started again as if remembering the pain that tore our family apart. 'Your dad was obsessed with that instrument.'

'I remember he kept asking for his guitar.' I wrapped my arms around my body, seeking solace from the memories of my dad fighting his demons.

'Yes, he did. I tried so hard to get him to stop,' Mum answered, her voice welling with anguish. 'But Amelina, he responded like an addict. It was a terrible thing to witness, a horrendous experience to stand by and watch your husband lose his soul.'

'How did you get him to stop?'

Her shoulders gave up the fight and slumped, and the tone of her voice dropped too. Finally, she found a melancholic place, and she continued. 'I tried everything to make your dad stop. I even hid the guitar in this attic. I threatened to leave him, but it didn't matter. His drive to play was all that mattered. Then one day his desire for that miserable instrument stopped. At the time, I had wondered if some sort of enforced punishment had ended. After that, your dad could barely glance at his guitar, let alone play it. Yet he refused to throw it away and locked it in his study.'

'How weird. But Mum, in all that time since the curse descended upon us, I've never heard Dad play, or heard you fight about it.'

'The instrument was cursed, Amelina. He played the guitar faithfully, but no sound or notes came out. The richness of musical sound was stolen from his life,' she replied. Her voice became a whisper filled with sorrow. 'We tried to keep it from you; we couldn't bear dragging you into our misery.' Mum placed her face in her hands as sobs wracked her body. After a moment, she regained her strength and wiped her eyes.

'Oh, Mum. I finally understand what you and Dad have been through. Nothing could be crueller for a musician. He must have felt like he lived in a prison without bars. Poor Dad, he's suffered so much.'

Mum paused for a moment. 'Yes. No one should suffer like that. The night he disappeared, you remember, we'd been playing charades. We were all having so much fun. Then, as you know, everything changed. The game became the most awful, fearful reality. The final card called for him to disappear and to sell his soul. He knew it. He read a threat on that card. He feared for the wellbeing of his family unless he obeyed. At the time, I didn't understand. But somehow I guessed it. Years later he finally confessed what had happened. A wicked creature whom he would not name forced him to ride an enormous mechanical monster that speeds up time. This cruel rollercoaster hides below the earth in a tranquil meadow. A winged creature, a guardian of time, carries the key to unlock a monstrous device, a wicked rollercoaster which it brings forth from the earth. If you are an unfortunate victim, the rollercoaster ages you, stealing the essence of your youth. He wanted to spare us this terrible fate. Whoever created this device possesses the blackest of minds. The refrain of an ice cream van plays accompanying your suffering whilst you ride.'

I reeled back in shock. 'An evil rollercoaster, a sicko refrain— who in their wildest, most warped dreams would ever create such a horrible thing?'

'Someone with no soul. Someone who has no heart. Yes, an ugly, twisted so and so, and that ride and the charades game is his or her idea of a sick joke. Your poor Dad, no wonder he's never been the same person since.'

'His whole appearance changed,' I replied, my voice wavering on the verge of tears, trying to process all that Mum had told me.

The memory made Mum blanch as if she'd seen a ghost. 'Yes. He was so thin when he came back, emaciated, and his eyes looked old and rheumy like he had aged beyond his years.'

'Mum, I felt so guilty at his horrible transformation. I had no idea what he had been through. I couldn't even look Dad in the eyes after he returned. I didn't recognise him, and all I saw was a stranger. I was afraid.' Tears slipped from my eyes, and I wiped them away with my hand.

'Yes,' she replied, pausing for a moment, swallowing hard, unable to continue. Mum struggled to speak and eventually found the words to express the heaviness of her heart. 'I wished your dad dead,' she said with anguish ringing in her voice. 'I know it's a terrible thing to say, but I did. I couldn't bear to see him suffering so much.'

'Don't say that, Mum,' I replied, my voice rising. I stepped closer to her sobbing form and wrapped my arms around her waist. I buried my head in her shoulder. 'There's always a way to make things better. One day he'll be free again. We need to bring him back to who he was.'

'Who he was? Oh, if only,' she replied, her words stumbling as if she'd forgotten how to express her true feelings.

'Don't give up, Mum. *Please*, tell me more,' I pleaded.

What came next surprised me. Mum's words didn't falter as they had before; she released them in one long, emotional speech.

'Whatever it was, the curse of time didn't stop as we thought it would. It stole a huge chunk of his life. It aged him and stole his youth. And that was just the beginning. After he returned home, from God knows where the curse struck again, this time attacking his musical ability. It made his guitar playing addictive and destructive. This tormented him, so in a foolish desperation, he arranged for an exchange, a small chunk of his life measured in time, for an unmatched musical ability. The sweet, gullible man was tricked. The final blow silenced his playing. Your dad possessed a natural musical ability, but no one could hear him play.'

Mum gazed at me with an exhausted smile, as if she'd run a marathon against her emotions and had lost the trophy.

'I see. That's why Aunt Karissa's angry with him. Dad sold his gift of a musical heart and soul to the curse maker,' I said.

'Yes. Your dad tainted his pure Krystallos soul with his vanity and the obsessive desire to be the best and most admired guitarist. The crystals gave him many abilities, but he wanted more.'

'My dad was a Krystallos.' I scratched my head. That meant he'd had the capacity to harness the power of the crystals. I repeated the words once again in my mind. *Dad was a Krystallos.* That explained so much. He didn't use his gift for the good of mankind, and his punishment for making a deal with the curse maker was losing his ability to play the guitar and share his musical soul. The notes had been silenced. I jumped when the realisation hit me. 'Mum, the answer to our troubles must be the curse maker?'

'Your dad refused to tell me who or what the curse maker was. He couldn't bear to talk about it; it was too painful, so eventually, I let the subject rest.' Mum dropped her hands to her sides; the race to be free of her suppressed emotions had got the better of her. I stepped away from Mum's arms and paced back and forth in Dad's study, working all this new information through my mind.

'I'll find out, and I'll make sure the curse maker never harms another person. I promise it will pay for all the evil it's done. Dad mustn't give up, he must play again,' I said as I touched Mum's arm.

My mum's face creased with anxiety, and her words became pincer-sharp as she continued. 'You mustn't interfere, Amelina. You can't imagine what you're getting into.'

Shadow swished his tail in irritation. I had forgotten the cat had been here with us the whole time. He had been so unobtrusive, a silent observer of our misery. Unlike Shadow, I didn't have a tail to make my opinion known, but I didn't intend on following Mum's advice. I had to help my dad. I knew that I would do everything in my power to make him well again.

'You must return the key back to where you found it, Amelina. You mustn't meddle in the events of the past.'

'I haven't got the key, Mum.'

'Of course you have, Amelina. How could you have opened the door without it? It's always locked. Dad keeps his key in a special place.'

'Dad must have forgotten to close and lock the door,' I answered, focussing straight into my mother's eyes.

Shadow leaped onto a cupboard, his ears trained on our words, desperate to hear what happened next.

Mum scowled at my upturned face. 'I doubt that. Don't change the subject. If I find that you're lying, Amelina… You don't even want to go there,' she said, her forehead furrowing into a hard line.

I shook my head. 'I haven't got the key, Mum. I promise.' The lie pricked my conscience as if I'd just been stuck by a rose thorn. I hated lying after Mum had bared her soul to me, but I couldn't help it. Right now, lying was a necessary evil.

Mum shook her head in disgust. She had to guess I was lying, but she gave me the benefit of the doubt. Shadow knew I'd won. He preened himself, his tongue licking his shiny black fur in readiness for the coming battle.

The spirit had given me the courage and determination to accept my abilities and stamp out the curse. I knew I would not let anything stand in my way. I could do this.

PUZZLE PIECE 38:
THE BLOODSTONE

They say that it's true,
Blood is thicker than water,
About to find out,
If wizard stone can pummel,
Dad's curse into submission.

While Mum showered, I crept back upstairs into Dad's study and polished his guitar until it gleamed. It glowed with a warm intensity. I traipsed downstairs and hid the guitar in the cubbyhole at the bottom of the stairs near the front door.

A short time later, I heard Dad making his way down the stairs. Seizing my chance, I pulled the guitar from its hiding place and walked towards him. Today, as always, he looked pale and thin, deprived of sunlight and sustenance. The clothes he wore hung on him as if they were a physical manifestation of his daily suffering.

Dad's eyes alighted upon the guitar. He turned the other way, struggling to get his emotions under control. He sneaked another peek at the object of his desire. The expression on his face said it all, and I imagined a painful furrow slicing into his heart.

Dad tore his eyes away from the guitar, cleared his throat and drew out his trembling voice. 'Amelina, how could you?' A long, drawn-out sigh slipped from his chapped lips. 'My study is off limits to you! What have you done? Put the guitar back, *right now.*' Dad staggered and reached out to grab the wall to balance himself.

'Play it for me, Dad.' I ignored his request to return the guitar to his study. He'd said *guitar* as if he hated the instrument and it didn't belong to him, but it did.

Dad fiddled with his collar like it was a tourniquet tightening around his neck. When his muffled voice spoke, he resigned himself to failure. 'I can't do that, Amelina.'

'Why not, Dad?'

'You wouldn't understand if I told you,' he replied, his face paling.

'Try me.'

'Let's say I have an, um… addictive personality. I find it hard to put it down when I play.' Dad bit his fingernails.

'Take control of your desire, Dad. The guitar is crying for you to play it.' I held the instrument out to him and beckoned for him to follow me.

Dad's shuffling steps followed me into the lounge. I had a plan and had stuck the bag holding my crystals into my jeans pocket earlier, ready to battle Dad's demons. I didn't know which crystal to try first, but I sensed the Wizard Stone was the one. Leanne's advice flooded into my brain, and I heard her whispered voice explaining the properties of the Bloodstone. *It's a powerful cleanser, a binding force in family love, and a powerful tool in weather magic.* I knew to place the Bloodstone crystal on the coffee table, on top of a cushion I had grabbed from the settee to protect the stone.

The gem began to speak in a booming voice that rushed through me like the blood of life. 'A blood child is received and stands before her sixteenth birthday. Rejoice, all will be well.'

My tears flowed freely. The Bloodstone had claimed me as the one it was waiting for. I celebrated the comforting words, knowing deep in my heart I could save my dad.

'This crystal is the stone of courage, Dad. It will help wash your anxieties away. This magical stone will let the guitar be a *part* of our family life once again. It will rid you of the curse.' I pointed to the stone and watched my dad's response.

An intense light of desire glowed in Dad's eyes. He stared at his guitar and licked his lips. His fingers reached out and tentatively touched the wooden frame. Dad blinked, frightened to let the overwhelming emotion in, but he did. His eyes filled with the dancing light of harmonies he'd long forgotten.

Dad grinned a tender, sweet smile. Moving over to the settee, he placed the instrument on his lap. The guitar nestled close to his chest as if it belonged there. The wood shone and warmed to his touch. I could see the expression of desire on his face, and his desperate need to play was apparent by the shaking of his hands. The first chords he strummed were silent. A haunted expression crossed his face. I imagined the ghosts of his past music floating around him, jeering, and goading him to play.

'I have no desire to play the music of the dead,' he said, confirming my thoughts.

'Dad, move closer to the Bloodstone.'

He put down the guitar, and leaving his past ghosts behind, he stood up. He hesitated and picked up the Bloodstone and held it in his hand. I walked over to him, and we held the Bloodstone together, clasped inside our joined hands. The crystal glowed, and the blood-red colour flashed around the room, shining like a pulsing heart. We both felt a tremor of hope wash into the room.

As Dad stood there transfixed by the luminosity of the Bloodstone, I witnessed a change in him. The spooks of his past sorrow dispersed, terrified of the pulsing, blood-red heart that rushed through their cold, broken spirits. An intense power flowed into his soul, rejuvenating him. Dad's shoulders lifted, and his face softened. His fingers moved and came alive.

The notes of the guitar filled the room, yet no one had touched the strings. The sound reverberated as if playing from a distant long forgotten shore. The melody rang out, a tune full of anger, fear, and reproach. By the sound of the melancholy tune, I wondered if the guitar was punishing Dad for deserting it.

Dad began to play, strumming long-forgotten notes. The more he plucked at the strings, the more he wept, tears of frustration cascading down his cheeks. Absorbed by the controlling power of the instrument, a fearsome fight to win began. Dad's fingers flew fast and furious. His chords thrashed until his fingers bled.

When I'd almost given up hope, Dad's body language changed. His eyes fixed on the Bloodstone, and I saw his pleading look as if he was asking for forgiveness. The crystal answered his pleas, and a sense of calm washed over him. His playing slowed, allowing the bleeding to stop.

Dad appeared like a dead man jolted back to life by an immediate life-giving transfusion. Maybe the Bloodstone had filtered his blood. I didn't know for sure what had happened, but I knew a new man sat before me. Dad's hands were no longer driven by a misguided force. Instead, he strummed the guitar with great tenderness and love.

Dad and I shared this moment together, my father playing, me listening. It was a brief respite in time, yet it seemed to last an eternity. After he finished playing, he gently placed the guitar down. When Dad spoke, his voice choked from years of suppressed emotion.

'Amelina, thank you so much, I feel alive once more.'

I hugged my father close for the first time in years. No longer a stranger, my much-loved father had returned. He cried great, wracking sobs, and I did the same. At that exact moment, Mum walked into the room, and her hand flew to her mouth when she spotted us. Her eyes travelled from the Bloodstone to the guitar, then back to Dad and me. Dazed, Mum struggled to comprehend what had just occurred. Nervous, she ran her fingertips over the length of the mantelpiece.

'Immaculate, just as you like it,' she said in a faraway voice as if she was still a child speaking to her mother. Staring at her hands, she addressed her long-dead mother. 'Look at your handiwork; my hands are so rough and dry.' Mum opened her mouth to say something then decided against it. She walked to the table and picked up the Bloodstone and turned it over in her hand. The Bloodstone shone and hummed, radiating joy. A serene expression descended upon her face as she glanced at the Bloodstone. 'See, my hands are fine, no longer rough and dry.'

Dad and I had stopped crying by then. Our mouths gaped at Mum's admissions and her recent transformation. We looked at each other and then back at Mum.

Without another thought, Mum placed the Bloodstone Crystal back in its place on the cushion. She had a smile on her face and skipped over to the magazine rack, where she grabbed a neatly folded newspaper. She struggled for a moment as if she was unsure of what to do next. Suddenly, Mum ripped the paper to shreds and scattered it on the floor. A wild expression settled into her eyes, and she reached for the wastepaper basket. In one swift movement, she tore and threw the contents up into the air. On cue, Shadow sauntered into the room. His whiskers twitched in excitement when he saw the mess. He went amok. The cat played like he was a kitten again, attacking those torn papers and wrappers.

Mum spun around and shifted, rearranging her lounge. I gazed in wonder at the expression on her face. I had forgotten that look—such abandon. Mum and Dad turned and caught each other's eyes. They roared with laughter, and I joined in too. The slumbering house spirits awakened and released a thousand emotions within us all. Our humble abode appeared to share in our happiness, and an abundance of sunlight poured into the lounge from the bay windows, illuminating everyone with a liberating joy.

It was then that I heard the faint sound of clocks ticking. What a wonderful sound it was. Running around the house, I checked each clock in turn. The ticking became louder and echoed throughout the rooms. The clocks were working again and shedding layers of imaginary dust with each passing second. I couldn't believe it. I had just witnessed a perfect moment. I watched my parents in stunned silence. The steady, ticking rhythm of the clocks announced that life as we knew it had been restored.

Both of my parents' faces were bright and flushed. The paleness had now disappeared, replaced with the healthy glow of those among the living. Mum's hands flew to her cheeks, and she rushed to the mirror. A warm glow shone from the centre of the glass casting a brilliant beam of light in her direction. A different reflection stared back. Mum's face appeared smooth again, her lips full, her eyes bright and shining. Dad looked renewed. He dashed to Mum's side and put his arm around her waist. His withered looks restored to a youthfulness that nobody could have ever imagined if they hadn't witnessed it themselves. I smiled. It was the kind of grin that travelled from my lips, up to my eyes, and back again. I joined Mum and Dad at the mirror and knew my smile shone with Krystallos light.

PUZZLE PIECE 39:
EPILOGUE

Even if we're free,
Perhaps we're all prisoners,
This is no ending,
There may never be—who knows?
Patience and time will answer.

I ran upstairs to my bedroom, eager to share the good news with Esme about the curse's demise. Esme remained in her regular spot, stuck behind the glass. She beckoned, and I approached the mirror. Esme glared at me with a worried expression on her face. I waited for her to speak. 'He's playing with you, a cat with his prey. He won't dirty his own hands with stealing your crystals. You wait and see.'

She hesitated for a moment, and then her tiny hand slipped out of the glass. She didn't look too happy, as her hand only extended so far. It dangled like a lost limb.

She swore.

In the far corner of the mirror, I thought I recognised a reflection. At first, it blurred and smeared as if I'd just rubbed my fingers across the glass. Then it became apparent. It was the grasshopper of the Corpus Chronophage clock like I'd never seen him before.

The grasshopper now dominated the full width and height of the mirror, his eyes gleaming red like two devil's torches. He smirked, apparently amused by Esme's inability to free herself. She saw him smirking. Terrified, Esme pressed harder against the glass, creating a pattern of hazy condensation filled fingerprints.

A beam of light shot from Esme's fingertips, releasing a sparking fire that grew within the grasshopper's eyeball. The creature morphed into an enormous whirlwind of red heat, and its eyes exploded into smouldering pupils of smoke-filled shadows. The grasshopper's golden eyed shutters opened and closed with a mechanical clanking sound until with one last motion a crack formed across the mirror.

With a great burst of energy, Esme tumbled out through the opening; a dappled shadow traced its way across her face. One minute she was standing next to me with this anxious smile on her face. The next second, Esme vanished. She had suffered bound to the mirror, saved whilst on the verge of dying from her self-harming wounds, but that was now history. Esme's prophecy regarding Ryder had disturbed me, but I was so glad she had found her freedom. But where had Esme disappeared to? I couldn't believe she'd left before sharing a hug with me or joining in with our family celebration.

Shadow meowed and stared into the mirror. The grasshopper blinked. One smouldering eye opened, revealing the silhouette of the two young men who had frightened me down the river path. Both of the grasshopper's eyelids closed tight, locking Will and Mitch's shadows into the clockwork dungeon of his eyes. When he reopened his eyes, I saw Will and Mitch at a party, in the future, laughing and joking with everyone, as if they were my dear friends who might help me fight against evil. Then the clockwork dungeon opened again, and this time I saw Kyle. The dreadful sight made me gasp in shock, a foreshadowing of some terrible episode still to come. In this foreshadowing, I lay sprawled across the floor, and Kyle tried his utmost to rescue me from a dreadful illness that racked my prone body. I witnessed Kyle imploring Ryder to help me. Kyle's kind green eyes were moist with tears. A scowl drifted across Ryder's face; he ignored Kyle's pleas but answered me with these chilling words: 'I cannot help, nor do I want to. Unlike my friend Kyle, I have a shadowed heart. I am not whole, and I am not kind.'

I blinked and returned to the present. The sound of clocks ticking continued. Shadow stretched and arched his back. The cat didn't make a sound or preen himself. He sat, watching the empty space that Esme had occupied. I glanced away for a second, and when I turned back, the grasshopper had vanished, taking the truth with him, leaving my mirror with a giant crack etched into the glass.

Dear reader,

We hope you enjoyed reading *Bloodstone*. Please take a moment to leave a review, even if it's a short one. Your opinion is important to us.

Discover more books by M.J. Mallon at https://www.nextchapter.pub/authors/mj-mallon

Want to know when one of our books is free or discounted? Join the newsletter at http://eepurl.com/bqqB3H

Best regards,

M.J. Mallon and the Next Chapter Team

ACKNOWLEDGMENTS

First of all, a huge thank you to **Dr John C Taylor, OBE**—the inventor of the **Corpus Chronophage clock** for permission to use his photographic images of his incredible chronophage and grasshopper in my book and blog: http://www.johnctaylor.com/

Cambridge Writers and SCBWI — The Society of Children's Writers and Book Illustrators — have been such a wonderful source of help and support.

The blogging community have been awesome. It has been fantastic to 'meet' so many supportive bloggers both on-line and in person. Particular thanks go to awesome authors Colleen Chesebro and Debby Gies (Author D G Kaye,) Sally Cronin, Ritu Bhathal, Adele Marie Park, Sally Cronin, Richard Dee, Lizzie Chantree, James Cudney, Sarah Northwood plus many more too numerous to mention.

I'd like to say a huge thank you to author Colleen Chesboro who has gone beyond a beta read to a full-scale developmental edit with the original version of the manuscript. I owe her a massive debt of thanks.

A big thank you to my friends and family for your encouragement, love and support. Particular thanks go to my mum and dad for reading my less than perfect early drafts, to my bookish daughter Natasha for her enthusiastic beta reading, and to my youngest daughter Georgina for her fabulous suggestions about character names.

I'd like to mention the kind help of my first draft beta reader, author Graeme Cumming: http://www.graemecumming.co.uk/ A sterling bloke who helped me take my first steps out of my early draft muddle!

Thank you to authors Rachael Ritchey and Jack Eason for their considered and helpful edits following on from reading an early copy: https://rachaelritchey.com/ and Jack Eason's blog: https://havewehadhelp.wordpress.com/

Thank you to artist Carolina Russo for creating wonderful artwork for two of my characters: Esme and Eruterac, the Creature. You can see these and discover more about Carolina on my blog: https://mjmallon.com/2018/09/16/a-huge-welcome-to-artist-carolina-russo-art-music-nature-creativity/

Thank you to my husband David for his generous financial support, and continued hard work funding the family, without which I would not have had the time to devote to this novel. Thanks to my sister-in-law Lorraine Mallon for her advice on artistic aspects and her guidance about developing the mirror girl, Esme, who has since become one of my favourite characters!

SELF-HARM DISCLAIMER AND HELP

Disclaimer: This novel does not encourage or endorse self-harm; on the contrary it hopes to facilitate discussion. Mental Health issues should never be hidden. There is no shame in being depressed, or anxious. Sadly, self-harm is a growing problem in our young:

https://www.selfharm.co.uk/get/facts/self-harm_statistics

https://www.mind.org.uk/information-support/types-of-mental-health-problems/self-harm/

https://www.selfharm.co.uk/

https://www.nspcc.org.uk/preventing-abuse/keeping-children-safe/self-harm/

https://youngminds.org.uk/find-help/feelings-and-symptoms/self-harm/

https://www.helpguide.org/articles/anxiety/cutting-and-self-harm.htm

ABOUT THE AUTHOR

On the 17th of November in Lion City: Singapore I arrived, (a passionate Scorpio, with the Chinese Zodiac sign a lucky rabbit,) second child and only daughter to my proud parents' Paula and Ronald. I grew up in a mountainous court in the Peak District in Hong Kong with my elder brother Donald. My parents dragged me away from my exotic childhood and my much-loved dog Topsy to the frozen wastelands of Scotland. In bonnie Edinburgh I mastered Scottish country dancing, and a whole new Och Aye lingo.

As a teenager I travelled to many far-flung destinations to visit my abacus wielding wayfarer dad. It's rumoured that I now live in the Venice of Cambridge, with my six-foot hunk of a Rock God husband, my two enchanted daughters are making their way, nesting not too far away.

After such an upbringing my author's mind has taken total leave of its senses! When I'm not writing, I eat exotic delicacies while belly dancing, or surf to the far reaches of the moon. To chill out, I practise Tai Chi or Yoga. If the mood takes me, I snorkel with mermaids, or sign up for idyllic holidays with the Chinese Unicorn, whose magnificent voice sings like a thousand wind chimes.

My influences have been many and varied, most of which are not of the human variety, but are spectacular, nonetheless. I must mention the black cat that appeared in my garden many years ago, who I fashioned into the much-loved character of Shadow. Such a stunning fellow, so magical, he inspired me to write *The Curse of Time* series. In fact, he was such an incredible creature that I had to find a cat model to take his place when he upped and disappeared. I found

Lily via my blogging friend Gary Jefferies who put me in touch with Lily's owner: Samantha Murdoch. Lily is stunning, a dead ringer for my black cat character Shadow and her owner Samantha is so lovely. She has a fantastic blog about cats and crystals: http://samanthamurdochblog.wordpress.com.

A few years ago, my old school friend Christine Souter suggested an outing with Helen Roberts to a sculpture park, Juniper Artland https://www.jupiterartland.org/ in Wilkieston, Edinburgh. How fortuitous. It was on that day that I first saw the crystal grotto—The Light Pours Out of Me by Anya Gallaccio—that inflamed my imagination to write this story. To this creative mix of crystals, I added reading, a great love of mine (focusing on Dorian Grey,) and a fascination with art, which triggered my story writing skills further.

This labour of love, my first novel in this series, has developed out of my growth as a person. I know that sounds a bit new-agey, but it is true. I suppose the crystals and my love of alternative therapies represent this part of me. My first crystal purchase was Malachite—a stone of transformation! It did its job! I have discovered a 'new me' that has developed like a slow burning fire. The 'new me' is much more adventurous—she likes to write novels, short stories, poetry, Tanka and haiku, and engages in creative pursuits such as photography.

Dear readers, let me share with you my motto of life, the thought that rocks me, that has kept my heart pounding these past years whilst writing, editing, and rewriting this book:

Always Do What You Love, Stay True To Your Heart's Desires, And Inspire Others To Do So Too, Even If It Appears That The Odds Are Stacked Against You Like Black Hearted Shadows.